James Mackintosh

Vindiciae Gallicae

Defence of the French revolution and its English admirers against the accusations

of the right Hon. Edmund Burke

James Mackintosh

Vindiciae Gallicae
Defence of the French revolution and its English admirers against the accusations of the right Hon. Edmund Burke

ISBN/EAN: 9783337230364

Printed in Europe, USA, Canada, Australia, Japan

Cover: Foto ©Andreas Hilbeck / pixelio.de

More available books at **www.hansebooks.com**

VINDICIÆ GALLICÆ.

DEFENCE

OF THE

FRENCH REVOLUTION

AND ITS

ENGLISH ADMIRERS,

AGAINST THE ACCUSATIONS OF

THE RIGHT HON. EDMUND BURKE;

INCLUDING

SOME STRICTURES ON THE LATE PRODUCTION

OF

MONS. DE CALONNE.

By *JAMES MACKINTOSH,*
OF LINCOLN'S INN, ESQUIRE.

THE FOURTH EDITION, WITH ADDITIONS.

LONDON:

PRINTED FOR G. G. J. AND J. ROBINSON,
PATERNOSTER-ROW.

1792.

ADVERTISEMENT.

HAD I forefeen the fize to which the following volume was to grow, or the obftacles that were to retard its completion, I fhould probably have fhrunk from the undertaking; and perhaps I may now be fuppofed to owe an apology for offering it to the Public, after the able and mafterly Publications to which this controverfy has given occafion.

Many parts of it bear internal marks of having been written fome months ago, by allufions to circumftances which are now changed; but as they did not affect the reafoning, I was not folicitous to alter them.

For the latenefs of its appearance, I find a confolation in the knowledge, that refpectable Works on the fame fubject are ftill expected by the Public; and the number of my fellow-labourers only fuggefts the reflection—that too many minds cannot be employed on a controverfy fo immenfe as to prefent the moft various afpects to different underftandings, and fo important, that the more correct ftatement of one fact, or the more fuccefsful illuftration of one argument, will at leaft refcue a book from the imputation of having been written in vain.

Little Ealing, Middlefex,
April 26, 1791.

ADVERTISEMENT to the THIRD EDITION.

I NOW present the following Work to the Public a third time, rendered, I hope, less unworthy of their favor.——Of Literary Criticism it does not become me to question the justice, but Moral Animadversion I feel it due to myself to notice.

The vulgar clamor which has been raised with such malignant art against the friends of Freedom, as the apostles of turbulence and sedition, has not even spared the obscurity of my name. To strangers I can only vindicate myself by defying the authors of such clamors to discover one passage in this volume not in the highest degree favorable to peace and stable government. Those to whom I am known would, I believe, be slow to impute any sentiments of violence to a temper which the partiality of my friends must confess to be indolent, and the hostility of enemies will not deny to be mild.

I have been accused, by valuable friends, of treating with ungenerous levity the misfortunes of the Royal Family of France. They will not however suppose me capable of deliberately violating the sacredness of misery in a palace or a cottage; and I sincerely lament that I should have been betrayed into expressions which admitted that construction.

Little Ealing, August 28, 1791.

INTRODUCTION.

THE late opinions of Mr. Burke furnished more matter of aſtoniſhment to thoſe who had diſtantly obſerved, than to thoſe who had correctly examined the ſyſtem of his former political life. An abhorrence for abſtract politics, a predilection for ariſtocracy, and a dread of innovation, have ever been among the moſt ſacred articles of his public creed. It was not likely that at his age he ſhould abandon to the invaſion of audacious novelties, opinions which he had received ſo early, and maintained ſo long, which had been fortified by the applauſe of the great, and the aſſent of the wiſe, which he had dictated to ſo many illuſtrious pupils, and ſupported againſt ſo many diſtinguiſhed opponents. Men who early attain eminence, repoſe in their firſt creed.

creed. They neglect the progress of the human mind subsequent to its adoption, and
when, as in the present case, it has burst forth
into action, they regard it as a transient mad-
ness, worthy only of pity or derision. They
mistake it for a mountain torrent that will
pass away with the storm that gave it birth.
They know not that it is the stream of human opinion *in omne volubilis ævum*, which
the accession of every day will swell, which
is destined to sweep into the same oblivion
the resistance of learned sophistry, and of
powerful oppression.

But there still remained ample matter of
astonishment in the Philippic of Mr. Burke.
He might deplore the sanguinary excesses—he
might deride the visionary policy that seemed
to him to tarnish the lustre of the Revolution,
but it was hard to have supposed that he
should have exhausted against it every epithet
of contumely and opprobrium that language

can furnish to indignation ; that the rage of his declamation should not for one moment have been suspended ; that his heart should not betray one faint glow of triumph, at the splendid and glorious delivery of so great a people. All was invective—the authors, and admirers of the Revolution——every man who did not execrate it, even his own most enlightened and accomplished friends, were devoted to odium and ignominy.

This speech did not stoop to argument—the whole was dogmatical and authoritative ; the cause seemed decided without discussion ; the anathema fulminated before trial. But the ground of the opinions of this famous speech, which, if we may believe a foreign journalist, will form an epoch in the history of the eccentricities of the human mind, was impatiently expected in a work soon after announced. The name of the author, the importance of the subject, and the singularity of his opinions,

all

all contributed to inflame the public curiofity, which though it languifhed in a fubfequent delay, has been revived by the appearance, and will be rewarded by the perufal of the work.

It is certainly in every refpect a performance, of which to form a correct eftimate, would prove one of the moft arduous efforts of critical fkill. "We fcarcely can praife it, "or blame it too much." Argument every where dextrous and fpecious, fometimes grave and profound, cloathed in the moft rich and various imagery, and aided by the moft pathetic and picturefque defcription, fpeaks the opulence and the powers of that mind, of which age has neither dimmed the difcernment nor enfeebled the fancy, neither repreffed the ardor, nor narrowed the range. Virulent encomiums on urbanity, and inflammatory harangues againft violence; homilies of moral and religious myfticifm, better adapted to the amusement than to the conviction of an incredulous age, though they may rouse the languor of attention, can never be dignified by the approbation of the understanding.

Of the Senate and people of France, his language is such as might have been expected to a country which his fancy has peopled only with plots, assassinations, and massacres, and all the brood of dire chimeras which are the offspring of a prolific imagination, goaded by an ardent and deluded sensibility. The glimpses of benevolence, which irradiate this gloom of invective, arise only from generous illusion, from misguided and misplaced compassion—his eloquence is not at leisure to deplore the fate of beggared artizans, and famished peasants, the victims of suspended industry, and languishing commerce. The sensibility which seems seared by the homely miseries of the vulgar, is attracted only by the splendid sorrows of royalty, and agonizes at the slen-

derest

dereſt pang that aſſails the heart of ſottiſhneſs or proſtitution, if they are placed by fortune on a throne.

To the Engliſh friends of French freedom, his language is contemptuous, illiberal, and ſcurrilous. In one of the ebbings of his fervor, he is diſpoſed not to diſpute " their good in-" tentions." But he abounds in intemperate ſallies, in ungenerous inſinuations, which wiſdom ought to have checked, as ebullitions of paſſion, which genius ought to have diſdained, as weapons of controverſy.

The arrangement of his work is as ſingular as the matter. Availing himſelf of all the privileges of epiſtolary effuſion, in their utmoſt latitude and laxity, he interrupts, diſmiſſes, and reſumes argument at pleaſure. His ſubject is as extenſive as political ſcience——his alluſions and excurſions reach almoſt every region of human knowledge. It muſt

be confeffed that in this mifcellaneous and de-
fultory warfare, the fuperiority of a man of
genius over common men is infinite. He can
cover the moft ignominious retreat by a brilliant allufion. He can parade his arguments
with mafterly generalfhip, where they are
ftrong. He can efcape from an untenable
pofition into a fplendid declamation. He can
fap the moft impregnable conviction by pathos,
and put to flight a hoft of fyllogyfms with a
fneer. Abfolved from the laws of vulgar method, he can advance a group of magnificent
horrors to make a breach in our hearts, through
which the moft undifciplined rabble of arguments may enter in triumph.

Analyfis and method, like the difcipline and
armour of modern nations, correct in fome
meafure the inequalities of controverfial dexterity, and level on the intellectual field the
giant and the dwarf. Let us then analyfe the
production of Mr. Burke, and difmiffing what

is

is extraneous and ornamental, we shall difcover certain leading queftions, of which the decifion is indifpenfible to the point at iffue.

The natural order of thefe topics will dictate the method of reply. Mr. Burke, availing himfelf of the indefinite and equivocal term, Revolution, has altogether reprobated that tranfaction. The firft queftion, therefore, that arifes, regards the general expediency and neceffity of a Revolution in France.—This is followed by the difcuffion of the compofition and conduct of the National Affembly, of the popular exceffes which attended the Revolution, and the New Conftitution that is to refult from it. The conduct of its Englifh admirers forms the laft topic, though it is with rhetorical inverfion firft treated by Mr. Burke, as if the propriety of approbation fhould be determined before the difcuffion of the merit or demerit of what was approved. In perfuance of this analyfis, the following fections will comprife the fubftance of our refutation.

Sect. I. *The General Expediency and Neceffity of a Revolution in France.*

II. *The Compofition and Character of the National Affembly confidered.*

III. *The Popular Exceffes which attended, or followed the Revolution.*

IV. *The new Conftitution of France.*

V. *The Conduct of its Englifh Admirers juftified.*

With this reply to Mr. Burke will be mingled fome ftrictures on the late publication of M. Calonne. That minifter, who has for fome time exhibited to the eyes of indignant Europe the fpectacle of an exiled robber living

in

in the moſt ſplendid impunity, has, with an effrontery that beggars invective, aſſumed in his work the tone of afflicted patriotiſm, and delivers his polluted Philippics as the oracles of perſecuted virtue.

His work is more methodical than that of his coadjutor, Mr. Burke*. Of his financial calculations it may be remarked, that in a work profeſſedly popular they afford the ſtrongeſt preſumption of fraud. Their extent and intricacy ſeem contrived to extort aſſent from

---

It cannot be denied that the production of M. Calonne is, " eloquent, able," and certainly very " inſtructive" in what regards his own character and deſigns. But it contains one inſtance of hiſtorical ignorance ſo egregious, that I cannot reſiſt quoting it.—In his long diſcuſſion of the pretenſions of the Aſſembly to the title of a National Convention, he deduces the origin of that word from Scotland, where he informs us, p. 328, " On lui donna le nom de Convention l'Aſſiſe, le réſultat de ſes délibérations fut appelle *Convenant*, & ceux qui l'avoient ſouſcrit ou qui y adhérerent *Convenanters!* "

public

public indolence, for men will rather believe than examine them. His inferences are
fo outrageoufly incredible, that moft men of
fenfe will think it more fafe to truft their own
plain conclufions than to enter fuch a laby-
rinth of financial fophiftry.

The only part of his production that here
demands reply, is that which relates to general political queftions. Remarks on what he
has offered concerning them will naturally
find a place under the correfponding fections
of the Reply to Mr. Burke. Its moft important view is neither literary nor argumenta-
tive. It appeals to judgments more decifive
than thofe of criticifm, and aims at wielding
weapons more formidable than thofe of logic.
It is the manifefto of a Counter Revolution,
and its obvious object is to inflame every paffion and intereft, real or fuppofed, that has
received any fhock in the eftablifhment of
freedom. He probes the bleeding wounds of

the

the princes, the nobility, the priesthood, and the great judicial aristocracy. He adjures one body by its dignity degraded, another by its inheritance plundered, and a third by its authority destroyed, to repair to the holy banner of his philanthropic crusade. Confident in the protection of all the monarchs of Europe, whom he alarms for the security of their thrones, and having insured the moderation of a fanatical rabble, by giving out among them the savage *war-whoop* of atheism, he already fancies himself in full march to Paris, not to re-instate the deposed despotism (for he disclaims the purpose, and who would not trust such virtuous disavowals!!) but at the head of this army of priests, mercenaries and fanatics, to dictate, as the tutelar genius of France, the establishment of a just and temperate freedom, obtained without commotion and without carnage, and equally hostile to the interested ambition of demagogues and the lawless authority of kings.

Crusades

Crufades were an effervefcence of chivalry, and the modern St. Francis has a knight for the conduct of thefe crufaders, who will convince Mr. Burke, that the age of chivalry is not paft, nor the glory of Europe gone for ever. The Comte d'Artois*, that feyon worthy of Henry the Great, the rival of the Bayards and Sidneys, the new model of French Knighthood, is to iffue from Turin with ten thoufand cavaliers, to deliver the peerlefs and immaculate Antonietta of Auftria from the durance vile in which fhe has fo long been immured in the Thuilieries, from the fwords of the difcourteous knights of Paris, and the fpells of the fable wizards of democracy.

* *Ce digne rejeton du grand Henri*—Calonne, p. 413. *Le nouveau modèle de la Chevalerie Françoife.* Ibid. p. 114.

VINDICIÆ GALLICÆ.

&c. &c.

SECTION I.

*The General Expediency and Neceſſity of a
Revolution in France.*

IT is aſſerted in many paſſages * of Mr.
Burke's work, though no where with
that preciſion which the importance of the aſſertion demanded, that the *French Revolution*
was not only in its parts reprehenſible, but
in the whole was abſurd, inexpedient, and
unjuſt; yet he has no where exactly informed
us what he underſtands by the term. The
French Revolution, in its moſt popular ſenſe,
perhaps would be underſtood in England to

* Page 187, 200, 243, and many other paſſages.

conſiſt

confift of thofe fplendid events that formed the prominent portion of its exterior, the Parifian revolt, the capture of the Baftile, and the fubmiffion of the King. But thefe memorable events, though they ftrengthened and accelerated, could not conftitute a Political Revolution. It muft have been a change of Government, but even limited to that meaning, it is equivocal and wide.

It is capable of *three* fenfes. The King's recognition of the rights of the States General to a fhare in the legiflation, was a change in the actual government of France, where the whole legiflative and executive power had, without the fhadow of interruption, for nearly two centuries been enjoyed by the Crown; in that fenfe the meeting of the States-General was the Revolution, and the 5th of May was its æra. The union of the three Orders in one affembly was a moft important change in the forms and fpirit of the legiflature. This too may be called the Revolution, and the 23d of June will be its æra. This body, thus united, are forming a new Constitution. This may be also called a Revolution, because it is of all the political changes the most important, and its epoch will be determined by the conclusion of the labours of the National Assembly.

Thus equivocal is the import of Mr. Burke's expressions. To extricate them from this ambiguity, a rapid survey of these events will be necessary. It will prove too the fairest and most forcible confutation of his arguments. It will best demonstrate the necessity and justice of all the successive changes in the State of France, which formed the mixed mass called the Revolution. It will discriminate legislative acts from popular excesses, and distinguish transient confusion from permanent establishment. It will evince the futility and fallacy of attributing to the

B   conspiracy

conspiracy of individuals, or bodies, a Revolution which, whether it be benificial or injurious, was produced only by general causes, where the most conspicuous individual produced little real effect.

The Constitution of France resembled in the earlier stages of its progress the other Gothic governments of Europe. The history of its decline and the causes of its extinction are abundantly known. Its infancy and youth were like those of the English government. The *Champ de Mars*, and the *Wittenagemot*, the tumultuary assemblies of rude conquerors, were in most countries melted down into republican [illegible]. But the downfall of the feudal [illegible] in France before Commerce [illegible] elevated [illegible] other class of citizens [illegible] importance, its power devolved on [illegible]. [illegible] the conclusion of the [illegible] power [illegible] of the States [illegible] assemblies.

The

Their momentary re-appearance under Henry III. and Louis XIII. served only to illustrate their insignificance. Their total disuse speedily succeeded.

The intrusion of any popular voice was not likely to be tolerated in the reign of Louis XIV. a reign which has been so often celebrated as the zenith of warlike and literary splendor, but which has always appeared to me to be the consummation of whatever is afflicting and degrading in the history of the human race. Talent seemed, in that reign, robbed of the conscious elevation, of the erect and manly port, which is its noblest associate and its surest indication. The mild purity of Fenelon*, the lofty spirit of Bossuet, the masculine mind of Boileau, the sublime fervor of Corneille, were confounded by the conta-

* " And Cambray, worthy of a happier doom,
    " The virtuous slave of *Louis* and of ROME."

gion

gion of ignominious and indiscriminate servility. It seemed as if the " representative
" majesty" of the genius and intellect of
man were proftrated before the fhrine of a
fanguinary and diffolute tyrant, who prac-
tifed the corruption of Courts without their
mildnefs, and incurred the guilt of wars without their glory. His higheft praife is to have
fupported the ftage trick of Royalty with
effect; and it is furely difficult to conceive
any character more odious and defpicable,
than that of a puny libertine, who, under the
frown of a ftrumpet, or a monk, iffues the
mandate that is to murder virtuous citizens,
to defolate happy and peaceful hamlets, to
wring agonizing tears from widows and or-
phans. Heroifm has a fplendor that almoft
atones for its exceffes; but what fhall we think
of him, who, from the luxurious and daftardly
fecurity in which he wallows at Verfailles,
iffues with calm and cruel apathy his orders
to butcher the Proteftants of Languedoc, or

to

to lay in afhes the villages of the Palatinate?
On the recollection of fuch fcenes, as a fcholar, I blufh for the proftitution of letters; as
a man, I blufh for the patience of humanity.

But the defpotifm of this reign was preg-
nant with the great events which have figna-
lized our age. It foftered that literature which
was one day deftined to deftroy it. Its profligate conquefts have eventually proved the
acquifitions of humanity; and the ufurpations
of Louis XIV. have ferved only to add a
larger portion to the great body of freemen.
The fpirit of its policy was inherited by the
fucceeding reign. The rage of conqueft, repreffed for a while by the torpid defpotifm of
Fleury, burft forth with renovated violence in
the latter part of the reign of Louis XV.
France, exhaufted alike by the misfortunes of
one war and the victories of another, groaned
under a weight of impoft and debt, which it
was equally difficult to remedy or to endure.

The

The profligate expedients were exhaufted by which fucceffive Minifters had attempted to avert the great crifis, in which the credit and power of the government muft perifh.

The wife and benevolent adminiftration of M. Turgot, though long enough for his glory, was too fhort, and perhaps too *early* for thofe falutary and grand reforms which his genius had conceived, and his virtue would have effected. The afpect of purity and talent fpread a natural alarm among the minions of a Court, and they eafily fucceeded in the expulfion of fuch rare and obnoxious intruders.

The magnificent ambition of M. de Vergennes, the brilliant, profufe and rapacious career of M. de Calonne, the feeble and irrefolute violence of M. Brienne, all contributed their fhare to fwell this financial embarraffment. The *deficit*, or inferiority of the re- to the expenditure, at length rofe to
the

the enormous fum of 115 millions of livres, or about 4,750,000*l.* annually*. This was a difproportion between income and expence with which no government, and no individual, could long continue to exift.

In this exigency there was no expedient left, but to guarantee the ruined credit of bankrupt defpotifm by the fanction of the national voice. The States General were a dangerous mode of collecting it. Recourfe was therefore had to the Affembly of the *Notables*, a mode well known in the hiftory of France, in which the King fummoned a number of individuals, felected, at *his* difcre-

---

* For this we have the authority of M. de Calonne himfelf. See his late publication, page 56. This was the account prefented to the Notables in April, 1787. He, indeed, makes fome deductions on account of part of this *debt* being expirable. But this is of no confequence to our purpofe, which is to view the influence of the *prefent* urgency, the political, not the financial ftate of the queftion.

                              tion,

tion, from the mass, to advise him in great emergencies. They were little better than a popular Privy Council. They were neither recognized nor protected by law. Their precarious and subordinate existence hung on the nod of despotism.

They were called together by M. Calonne, who has now the inconsistent arrogance to boast of the schemes which he laid before them, as the model of the Assembly whom he traduces. He proposed, it is true, the equalization of impost, and the abolition of the pecuniary exemptions of the Nobility and Clergy; and the difference between his system and that of the Assembly, is only in what relates to the distinction in human action—its end. He would have destroyed the privileged Orders, as obstacles to despotism. *They* have destroyed them, as derogations from freedom. The object of *his* plan was to facilitate *royal* oppression. The motive of *theirs* is to fortify general liberty. *They* have levelled all Frenchmen as men—*he* would have levelled them all as flaves.

The Affembly of the Notables, however, foon gave a memorable proof, how dangerous are all public meetings of men, even without legal powers of controul, to the permanence of defpotifm. They had been affembled by M. Calonne to admire the plaufibility and fplendour of his fpeculations, and to veil the extent and atrocity of his rapine. But the fallacy of the one, and the profligacy of the other, were detected with equal eafe. Illuf- trious and accomplifhed orators, who have fince found a nobler fphere for their talents, in a more free and powerful Affembly, ex- pofed this plunderer to the Notables. Detefted by the Nobles and Clergy, of whofe privi- leges he had fuggefted the abolition; under- mined in the favour of the Queen, by his rival, once one of her favourites (*Breteuil*);

expofed

expofed to the fury of the people, and dreading the terrors of judicial profecution, he fpeedily fought refuge in England, without the recollection of one virtue, or the applaufe of one party, to confole his retreat*.

Thus did the Notables deftroy their creator Little appeared to be done to a fuperficia obferver; but to a difcerning eye, ALL was done; for the dethroned authority of Public opinion was reftored. The fucceeding Minifters, uninftructed by the example of their predeceffors, by the deftruction of Public credit, and the fermentation of the popular mind, hazarded meafures of a ftill more prepofterous and perilous defcription. The ufurpation of fome fhare in the fovereignty by the Parliament of Paris had become popular and ufeful, becaufe its tendency was ufeful,

* [illegible], &c. tom. i. p. 18

and its exercise virtuous.—That body had, as it is well known, claimed a right, which, in fact, amounted to a negative on all the acts of the King. They contended, that their registering his Edicts was necessary to give them force. They would, in that case, have possessed the same share of legislation with the King of England.

It is unnecessary to descant on the historical fallacy, and political inexpediency, of doctrines, which should vest in a narrow aristocracy of lawyers, who had bought their places, such extensive powers. It cannot be denied that their resistance had often proved salutary, and was some feeble check on the capricious wantonness of despotic exaction.—But the temerity of the Minister now assigned them a more important part. They refused to register two edicts for the creation of imposts. They averred, that the power of imposing taxes was vested only in the National
Representatives,

Reprefentatives, and they claimed the immediate convocation of the States General of the kingdom. The Minifter banifhed them to Troyes. But he foon found how much the French were changed from that abject and frivolous people, which had fo often endured the exile of its magiftrates. Paris exhibited the tumult and clamour of a London mob.

The cabinet, which could neither advance nor recede with fafety, had recourfe to the expedient of a compulfory regiftration. The Duke of Orleans, and the magiftrates who protefted againft this execrable mockery, were exiled or imprifoned. But all thefe hacknied expedients of defpotifm were in vain. Thefe ftruggles, which merit notice only as they illuftrate the progreffive energy of Public opinion, were followed by events ftill lefs equivocal. *Lettres de Cachet* were iffued againft *M. M. d'Eprefmenil & Goeflard.* They took refuge in the fanctuary of juftice, and the Parliament

liament pronounced them under the fafeguard of the law and the King. A deputation was fent to Verfailles, to intreat his Majefty to liften to fage counfels. Paris expected, with impatient folicitude, the refult of this deputation : when towards midnight, a body of 2000 troops marched to the palace were the Parliament were feated, and their Commander, entering into the Court of Peers, demanded his victims. A loud and unanimous acclamation replied, " We are all *d'Eprefmenil &* " *Goflard!*" Thefe magiftrates furrendered themfelves, and the fatellite of defpotifm led them off in triumph, amid the execrations of an aroufed and indignant people.

Thefe *fpectacles* were not without their effect. The fpirit of refiftance fpread daily over France. The intermediate commiffion of the States of *Bretagne*, the States of Dauphiné, and many other public bodies, began to affume a new and menacing tone. The Cabinet diffolved

folved in its own feeblenefs, and M. Neckar was recalled. That Minifter, probably up-right, and not illiberal, but narrow, pufillani-mous, and entangled by the habits of detail* in which he had been reared, poffeffed not that erect and intrepid fpirit, thofe enlarged and original views, which adapt themfelves to new combinations of circumftances, and fway in the great convulfions of human affairs. Accuftomed to the tranquil accuracy of com-merce, or the elegant amufements of litera-ture, he was, " called on to ride in the whirl-wind, and direct the ftorm." He feemed fu-perior to his privacy while he was limited

* The late celebrated Dr. Adam Smith, always held this opinion of Neckar, whom he had known intimately when a Banker in Paris. He predicted the fall of his fame when his talents fhould be brought to the teft, and always empha-tically faid, " He is but a man of detail." At a time when the commercial abilities of Mr. Eden, the prefent Lord Auckland, were the theme of profufe eulogy, Dr. Smith characterized him in the fame words,

to it, and would have been adjudged by hiſtory equal to his elevation had he never been elevated*. The reputation of few men, it is true, has been expoſed to ſo ſevere a teſt; and a generous obſerver will be diſpoſed to ſcrutinize leſs rigidly the claims of a Stateſman, who has retired with the applauſe of no party, who is deteſted by the ariſtocracy as the inſtrument of their ruin, and deſpiſed by the democratic leaders for puſillanimous and fluctuating policy.

But had the character of M. Neckar poſſeſſed more originality or deciſion, it could have had little influence on the fate of France. The minds of men had received an impulſe. Individual aid and individual oppoſition were equally vain. His views, no doubt, extended only to palliation; but he was involved in a

<hr>

*Major Privato viſus dum privatus fuit & omnium con-
.. pax imperii niſi imperaſſet.—Tac.

ſtream

ftream of opinions and events, of which no force could refift the current, and no wifdom adequately predict the termination. He is reprefented by M. Calonne as the Lord Sunderland of Louis XVI. feducing the King to deftroy his own power. But he had neither genius nor boldnefs for fuch defigns.

To return to our rapid furvey.—The Autumn of 1788 was peculiarly diftinguifhed by the enlightened and difinterefted patriotifm of the States of Dauphiné. They furnifhed, in many refpects, a model for the future Senate of France. Like them they deliberated amidft the terrors of minifterial vengeance and military execution. They annihilated the abfurd and deftructive deftinction of Orders, the three eftates were melted into a Provincial Affembly; and they declared, that the right of impofing taxes refided ultimately in the States General of France. They voted a deputation to the King to folicit the convocation of that Affembly.

Affembly. They were emuloufly imitated by all the provinces that ftill retained the fhadow of Provincial States. The States of Languedoc, of Velay, and Vivarois, the Tiers Etat of Provence, and all the Municipalities of Bretagne, adopted fimilar refolutions. In Provence and Bretagne, where the Nobles and Clergy, trembling for their privileges, and the Parliaments for their jurifdiction, attempted a feeble refiftance, the fermentation was peculiarly ftrong. Some eftimate of the fervor of public fentiment may be formed from the reception of the Count de Mirabeau in his native Province, where the Burgeffes of *Aix* affigned him a body-guard, where the citizens of Marfeilles crowned him in the theatre, and where, under all the terrors of defpotifm, he received as numerous and tumultuous proofs of attachment as ever were beftowed on a favourite by the enthufiafm of the moft free people. M. Caraman, the Governor of Provence, was even reduced to im-

C

plore

plore his interpofition with the populace, to appeafe and prevent their exceffes. The conteft in Bretagne was more violent and fanguinary. It had preferved its independence more than any of thofe Provinces which had been united to the Crown of France. The Nobles and Clergy poffeffed almoft the whole power of the States, and their obftinacy was fo great, that their Deputies did not take their feats in the National Affembly till an advanced period of its proceedings.

The return of M. Neckar, and the recall of the exiled magiftrates, reftored a momentary calm. The perfonal reputation of the Minifter for probity, re-animated the credit of France. But the finances were too irremediably embarraffed for palliatives; and the fafcinating idea of the States General, prefented to the public imagination by the unwary zeal of the Parliament, awakened recollections of ancient freedom, and profpects

of

of future fplendor, which the virtue or popularity of no Minifter could banifh. The
convocation of that body was refolved—but
many difficulties refpecting the mode of
electing and conftituting it remained, which
a fecond Affembly of Notables was fummoned
to decide.

The Third Eftate demanded reprefentatives
equal to thofe of the other two orders jointly.
They required that the number fhould be regulated by the population of the diftricts,
and that the three Orders fhould vote in one
Affembly. All the Committees into which
the Notables were divided, except that of
which Monsieur was Prefident, decided
againft the Third Eftate in every one of thefe
particulars. They were ftrenuoufly fupported
by the Parliament of Paris, who, too late
fenfible of the fuicide into which they had
been betrayed, laboured to render the Affembly impotent, when they were unable to pre-

 vent

vent its meeting. But their efforts were in vain. M. Neckar, whether actuated by refpect for juftice, or ambition of popularity, or yielding to the irrefiftible torrent of public fentiment, advifed the King to adopt the propofitions of the *Third Eflate* in the two firft particulars, and to leave the laft to be decided by the States General themfelves.

Letters patent were accordingly iffued on the 24th of January, 1789, for affembling the States General*, to which were annexed regulations for the detail of their elections. In the conftituent affemblies of the feveral provinces, bailliages, and conftabularies of the kingdom, the progrefs of the public mind became ftill more evident. The Clergy and Nobility ought not to be denied the praife of having emuloufly facrificed their pe-

* Lettre du Roi pour la convocation des Etats Generaux & reglement pour l'execution des lettres de convocation, donné le 24 Janvier, 1789.

cuniary

cuniary privileges. The inſtructions to the Repreſentatives breathed every where a ſpirit of freedom as ardent, though not ſo liberal and enlightened, as that which has ſince pre-ſided in the deliberations of the National Aſ-ſembly. Paris was eminently conſpicuous. The union of talent, the rapid communica-tion of thought, and the frequency of thoſe numerous aſſemblies, where men learn their force, and compare their wrongs *, ever make a great capital the heart that circulates emo-tion and opinion to the extremities of an em-pire. No ſooner had the convocation of the States General been announced, than the batteries of the preſs were opened. Pamphlet ſucceeded pamphlet, ſurpaſſing each other in boldneſs and elevation; and the advance of Paris to light and freedom was greater in three months than it had been in almoſt as many centuries.

Doctrines* were univerfaliy received in May, which in January would have been deemed treafonable, and which in March were derided as the vifions of a few deluded fanatics.

It was amid this rapid diffufion of light, and increafing fervor of public fentiment, that the States General of France affembled at Verfailles on the 5th of May, 1789; a day which will probably be accounted by pofterity one of the moft memorable in the annals of the human race. Any detail of the parade

---

* The principles of freedom had long been underftood, perhaps better than in any country of the world, by the philofophers of France. It was as natural that they fhould have been more diligently cultivated in that kingdom than in England, as that the fcience of medicine fhould be lefs underftood and valued among fimple and vigorous, than among luxurious and enfeebled nations. But the progrefs which we have noticed was among the lefs inftructed part of fociety.

and

and ceremonial of their Affembly would be
totally foreign to our purpofe, which is not
to narrate events, but to feize their fpirit, and
to mark their influence on the political progrefs from which the Revolution was to arife.
The preliminary operation neceffary to conftitute the Affembly gave rife to the firft great
queftion—The mode of authenticating the
commiffions of the Deputies. It was contended by the Clergy and Nobles, that according to ancient ufage, each Order fhould
feparately fcrutinize and authenticate the commiffions of its own Deputies. It was argued
by the Commons, that, on general principles,
all Orders, having an equal intereft in the
purity of the national reprefentative, had an
equal right to take cognizance of the authen-
ticity of the commiffions of all the members
who compofe it, and therefore to fcrutinize
them in common. To the authority of precedent it was anfwered, that it would eftablifh
too much: for in the ancient States, their ex-

amination of powers was fubordinate to the revifion of Royal Commiffaries, a fubjection too degrading and injurious for the free and vigilant fpirit of an enlightened age. This controverfy involved another of more magnitude and importance. If the Orders united in this fcrutiny, they were likely to continue in one Affembly ; the feparate voices of the two firft Orders would be annihilated, and the importance of the Nobility and Clergy reduced to that of their individual fuffrages.

This great Revolution was obvioufly meditated by the leaders of the Commons. They were feconded in the Chamber of the Nobleffe by a minority eminently diftinguifhed for rank, character, and talent. The obfure and ufeful portion of the Clergy were, from their fituation, acceffible to popular fentiment, and naturally coalefced with the Commons. Many who favoured the *divifion* of the Legiflature in the ordinary arrangements of Government,

vernment, were convinced that the grand and radical reforms, which the ſituation of France demanded, could only be affected by its union as one Aſſembly*. So many prejudices were to be vanquiſhed, ſo many difficulties to be ſurmounted, ſuch obſtinate habits to be extirpated, and ſo formidable a power to be re-

* Il n'eſt pas douteux que pour aujourd'hui, que pour
" cette premiere tenue une CHAMBRE UNIQUE n'ait été
" préférable & peut-être *neceſſaire*. Il y avoit tant de diffi-
" cultés à ſurmonter, tant de prejugés à vaincre, tant de
" ſacrifices à faire, de ſi vieilles habitudes à deraciner, une
" puiſſance ſi forte à contenir, en un mot, tant à detruire &
" *preſque tout à creer*."—" Ce nouvel ordre de choſes que
" vous avez fait eclore, tout cela vous en êtes bien ſurs n'a
" jamais pu naitre que de la reunion de toutes les perſonnes,
" de tous le ſentiments, & de tous les cœurs."—*Diſcours
*d. M. Lally Tolendahl à l'Aſſemblée Nationale, 31 Aout,
1789, dans ſes Pieces Juſtificatifs, p.* 105—6.———This paſſage is in more than one reſpect remarkable. It fully evinces the conviction of the Author, that changes were neceſſary great enough to deſerve the name of a REVOLUTION ; and, conſidering the reſpect of Mr. BURKE for his authority, ought to have weight with him.

ſiſted,

fifted, that there was an obvious neceffity to concentrate the force of the reforming body. In a great Revolution, every expedient ought to facilitate change. In an eftablifhed Government, every thing ought to render it difficult. Hence the divifion of a Ligiflature, which in an eftablifhed Government, may give a beneficial ftability to the laws, muft, in a moment of Revolution, be proportionably injurious, by fortifying abufe and unnerving reform. In a Revolution, the enemies of freedom are external, and all powers are therefore to be united. Under an eftablifhment her enemies are internal, and power is therefore to be divided.

But befides this general confideration, the ftate of France furnifhed others of more local and temporary cogency. The States General, acting by feparate Orders, were a body from which no fubftantial reform could be hoped. The two firft Orders were interefted

in the perpetuity of every abuſe that was to
be reformed. Their poſſeſſion of two equal
and independent voices muſt have rendered
the exertions of the Commons impotent and
nugatory, and a colluſion between the Aſſembly and the Crown would probably have
limited its illuſive reforms to ſome ſorry palliatives, the *price* of financial diſembarraſſ-
ment. The ſtate of a nation lulled into com-
placent ſervitude by ſuch petty conceſſions,
is far more hopeleſs than the ſtate of thoſe
who groan under the moſt galling hope of
deſpotiſm, and the condition of France would
have been more irremediable than ever. Such
reaſonings produced an univerſal conviction,
that the queſtion, whether the States General
were to vote individually, or in Orders, was
a queſtion, whether they were or were not to
produce any important benefit. Guided by
theſe views, and animated by public ſupport,
the Commons adhered inflexibly to their principle of incorporating the three Orders. They
adopted

adopted a *provifory* organization, but ftudi-
oufly declined whatever might feem to fuppofe legal exiftence, or to arrogate conftitutional powers. The Nobles, lefs politic or
timid, declared themfelves a legally conftituted Order, and proceeded to difcufs the
great objects of their convocation. The Clergy
affected to preferve a mediatorial character,
and to conciliate the difcordant claims of the
two hoftile Orders. The Commons, faithful
to their fyftem, remained in a wife and mafterly inactivity, which tacitly reproached the
arrogant affumption of the Nobles, while it
left no pretext to calumniate their own conduct; gave time for the encreafe of popular
fervor, and diftreffed the Court by the delay
of financial aid. Several conciliatory plans
were propofed by the Minifter, and rejected
by the haughtinefs of the Nobility and the
policy of the Commons.

Thus

Thus paſſed the period between the 5th of May and the 12th of June, when the popular leaders, animated by public ſupport, and conſcious of the maturity of their ſchemes, aſſumed a more reſolute tone.

The Third Eſtate commenced the ſcrutiny of commiſſions, ſummoned the Nobles and Clergy to repair to the Hall of the States General, and reſolved that the abſence of the Deputies of ſome diſtricts and claſſes of citizens could not preclude them, who formed the repreſentatives of ninety-ſix hundred parts of the nation, from conſtituting themſelves into a National Aſſembly.

Theſe deciſive meaſures betrayed the deſigns of the Court, and fully illuſtrate that bounty and liberality for which Lewis XVI. has been ſo idly celebrated. That feeble Prince, whoſe public character varied with every fluctuation in his Cabinet, the inſtrument

ment alike of the ambition of Vergennes, the prodigality of Calonne, and the oftentatious popularity of Neckar, had hitherto yielded to the embarraffment of the finances, and the clamor of the people. The cabal that retained its afcendant over his mind, permitted conceffions which they hoped to make vain, and flattered themfelves with fruftrating, by the conteft of ftruggling Orders, all idea of fubftantial reform. No fooner did the Affembly betray any fymptom of activity and vigor, than their alarms became confpicuous in the Royal conduct. The Comte d'Artois, and the other Princes of the Blood, publifhed the boldeft manifeftoes againft the Affembly; the credit of M. Neckar at Court declined every day; the Royalifts in the Chamber of the Nobleffe fpoke of nothing lefs than an impeachment of the Commons for high-treafon, and an immediate diffolution of the States; a vaft military force and a tremendous artillery were collected from all parts of the kingdom

towards

towards Verſailles and Paris, and under theſe menacing and inauſpicious circumſtances, the meeting of the States General was prohibited by the King's order till a Royal Seſſion, which was deſtined for the 22d but held on the 23d of June. The Commons, on repairing to their Hall on the 20th, found it inveſted with ſoldiers, and themſelves excluded from it by the point of the bayonet. They were ſummoned by their Preſident to a *Tennis-Court*, where they were reduced to hold their aſſembly, and which they rendered famous as the ſcene of their unanimous and memorable oath, never to ſeparate till they had atchieved the regeneration of France.

The *Royal Seſſion* thus announced, correſponded with the new tone of the Court. Its exterior was marked by the gloomy and ferocious haughtineſs of deſpotiſm. The Royal puppet was now evidently moved by different perſons from thoſe who had prompted its ſpeech

ſpeech at the opening of the States. He probably ſpoke both with the ſame ſpirit and the
ſame heart, and felt as little firmneſs under
the cloak of arrogance, as he had been conſcious of ſenſibility amidſt his profeſſions of
affection. He was probably as feeble in the
one as he had been cold in the other; but his
language is ſome criterion of the ſyſtem of his
prompters.

This ſpeech was diſtinguiſhed by inſulting
condeſcenſion and oſtentatious menace. He
ſpoke not as the Chief of a free nation to its
ſovereign Legiſlature, but as a Sultan to his
Divan. He *annulled* and *preſcribed* deliberations at pleaſure. He affected to repreſent
his will as the rule of their conduct, and his
bounty as the ſource of their freedom. Nor
was the matter of his harangue leſs injurious
than its manner was offenſive. Inſtead of
containing any conceſſion important to public
liberty, it indicated a relapſe into a more lofty

deſpotiſm

defpotifm than had before marked his pretenfions.   Tithes, feudal, and feignorial rights,
he confecrated as the moft inviolable property; and of *Lettres de Cachet* themfelves,
by recommending the regulation, he obvioufly condemned the abolition. The diftinction
of Orders he confidered as effential to the
Conftitution of the kingdom, and their prefent union as only legitimate by his permif-
fion.   He concluded with commanding them
to feparate, and to affemble on the next day
in the Halls of their refpective Orders.

The Commons, however, inflexibly ad-
hering to their principles, and conceiving
themfelves conftituted as a National Affembly, treated thefe threats and injunctions with
equal neglect.   They remained affembled in
the Hall, which the other Orders had quitted,
in obedience to the Royal command; and
when the Marquis de Breze, the King's Mafter of Ceremonies, reminded them of his

D   Majefty's

Majesty's orders, he was answered by *M. Bailli*, with Spartan energy, " The Nation " assembled has no ORDERS to receive."— They proceeded to pass resolutions declaratory of adherence to their former decrees, and of the personal inviolability of the members.— The Royal Session, which the Aristocratic party had expected with such triumph and confidence, proved the severest blow to their cause. Forty-nine members of the Nobility, at the head of whom was M. de Clermont Tonnerre, repaired on the 26th of June to the Assembly*. The popular enthusiasm was inflamed to such a degree, that alarms were either felt or affected, for the safety of the King, if the Union of Orders was delayed. The union was accordingly resolved on, and

* It deserves remark, that in this number were Noblemen who have ever been considered as of the *moderate* party. Of these may be mentioned M. M. Lally, Virieu, and Clermont Tonnerre, none of whom certainly can be accused of democratic enthusiasm.

the

the Duke of Luxemburg, Prefident of the Nobility, was authorized by his Majefty to announce to his Order the requeft and even command of the King, to unite themfelves with the other Orders. He remonftrated with the King on the fatal confequences of this ftep. The Nobility, he remarked, were not fighting their own battles, but thofe of the Crown. The fupport of the Monarchy was infeperably connected with the divifion of the States General. Divided, that body was fubject to the Crown—united, its authority was fovereign, and its force irrefiftible*. The King was not, however, fhaken by thefe confiderations, and on the following day, in an official letter to the Prefidents of the Nobility and Clergy, he notified his pleafure. A gloomy and re-

---

* Thefe remarks of M. de Luxemburg are equivalent to a thoufand defenfes of the Revolutionifts againft Mr. Burke. They unanfwerably prove that the divifion of Orders was fupported *only* as neceffary to palfy the efforts of the Legiflature againft the Defpotifm.

D 2

filcant

luctant obedience was yielded to this mandate, and the union of the National Reprefentatives at length promifed fome hope to
France.

But the general fyftem of the Government
formed a fufpicious and tremendous contraft
with this applauded conceffion. New *hordes*
of foreign mercenaries were fummoned to
the blockade of Paris and Verfailles, from
the remoteft provinces; an immenfe train of
artillery was difpofed in all the avenues of thefe
cities; and feventy thoufand men already invefted the Legiflature and Capital of France,
when the laft blow was hazarded againft the
public hopes, by the ignominious banifhment
of M. Neckar. Events followed the moft
unexampled and memorable in the annals of
mankind, which hiftory will record and im-
mortalize, but, on which, the object of the
political reafoner is only to fpeculate. France
was on the brink of civil war. The Provinces

vinces were ready to march immenſe bodies to the reſcue of their Repreſentatives. The Courtiers and their minions, Princes and Princeſſes, male and female favorites, crowded to the camps with which they had inveſted Verſailles, and ſtimulated the ferocious cruelty of their mercenaries, by careſſes, by largeſſes, and by promiſes. Mean time the people of Paris revolted, the French ſoldiery felt that they were citizens, and the fabric of Deſpotiſm fell to the ground.

Theſe ſoldiers, whom poſterity will celebrate for patriotic heroiſm, are ſtigmatized by Mr. Burke as " baſe hireling deſerters," who ſold their King for an increaſe of pay*.

* Mr. Burke is ſanctioned in this opinion by an authority not the moſt reſpectable, that of his late countryman *Count Dalton*, Commander of the Auſtrian troops in the Netherlands. In *September*, 1789, he addreſſed the *Regiment de Ligne*, at Bruſſels, in theſe terms, " J'eſpere que vous " n'imiterex jamais ces laches François qui ont abandonné " leur Souverain !"

This

This pofition he every where afferts or infinuates; but nothing feems more falfe. Had
the defection been confined to Paris, there
might have been fome fpecioufnefs in the accufation. The Exchequer of a faction might
have been equal to the corruption of the
guards. The activity of intrigue might have
feduced by promife, the troops cantoned in
the neighbourhood of the capital. But what
policy, or fortune, could pervade by their
agents, or donatives, an army of 150,000
men, difperfed over fo great a monarchy as
France. The fpirit of refiftance to *uncivic*
commands broke forth at once in every part
of the empire. The garrifons of the cities
of Rennes, Bourdeaux, Lyons, and Grenoble,
refufed, almoft at the fame moment, to refift
the virtuous infurrection of their fellow citizens. No largeffes could have feduced, no
intrigues could have reached fo vaft and divided a body. Nothing but fympathy with
the national fpirit could have produced their
noble

noble difobedience. The remark of Mr. Hume is here moſt applicable, that what depends on a few may be often attributed to chance (*ſecret circumſtances*) but that the actions of great bodies muſt be ever aſcribed to general cauſes. It was the apprehention of *Montefquieu*, that the ſpirit of increaſing armies would terminate in converting Europe into an immenſe camp, in changing our artizans and cultivators into military ſavages, and reviving the age of Attila and Genghis.—Events are our preceptors, and France has taught us that this evil contains in itſelf its own remedy and limit. A domeſtic army cannot be increaſed without increaſing the number of its ties with the people, and of the channels by which popular fentiment may enter. Every man who is added to the army is a new link that unites it to the nation. If all citizens were compelled to become foldiers, all foldiers muſt of neceſſity adopt the feelings of citizens, and the defpots cannot increaſe their

D 4

army

army without admitting into it a greater
number of men interefted to deftroy them.
A fmall army may have fentiments different
from the great body of the people, and no intereft in common with them, but a numerous
foldiery cannot. This is the barrier which
Nature has oppofed to the increafe of armies.
They cannot be numerous enough to enflave
the people, without becoming the people itfelf. The effects of this truth have been hitherto confpicuous only in the military defection of France, becaufe the enlightened fenfe
of general intereft has been fo much more
diffufed in that nation than in any other defpotic monarchy of Europe. But they muft
be felt by all. An elaborate difcipline may for
a while in Germany debafe and brutalize
foldiers too much to receive any impreffions
from their fellow men—artificial and local inftitutions are, however, too feeble to refift the
energy of natural caufes. The conftitution
of man furvives the tranfient fafhions of defpotifm,

potifm, and the hiftory of the next century will probably evince on how frail and tottering a bafis the military tyrannies of Europe ftand.

The pretended feduction of the French troops by the promife of the increafed pay, is in every view contradicted by facts. This increafe of pay did not originate in the Affembly. It was not therefore any part of their policy—It was prefcribed to them by the inftructions of their conftituents, before the meeting of the States*. It could not therefore be the project of any cabal of demagogues to feduce the army; it was the decifive and unanimous voice of the nation, and if there was any confpiracy, it muft have been that of the people. What had the demagogues

* I appeal to M. Calonne, as an authority beyond fufpicion on this fubject.—See his Summary of the *Cahiers*, or Inftructions. Art 73.—" *L'Augmentation de la Paie du Soldat.*" Calonne, p. 390,

to

to offer. The foldiery knew that the States muſt, in obedience to their inſtructions, increaſe their pay. An increaſe of pay therefore, was no temptation to fell their King, for of that they felt themſelves already ſecure, as the national voice had preſcribed it. It was in fact a neceſſary part of the ſyſtem which was to raiſe the army to a body of reſpectable citizens, from a gang of mendicant ruffians.

It muſt infallibly operate to limit the increaſe of armies in the north. This influence has been already felt in the Netherlands, which fortune ſeems to have reſtored to Leopold, that they might furniſh a ſchool of revolt to German ſoldiers. The Auſtrian troops have there murmured at their comparative indigence, and ſupported their plea for increaſe of pay by the example of France. The ſame example muſt operate on the other armies of Europe. The ſolicitations of armed petitioners muſt be heard. The indigent deſpots

ſpots of Germany and the North will feel a limit to their military rage, in the ſcantineſs of their Exchequer. They will be compelled to reduce the number, and increaſe the pay of their armies, and a new barrier will be oppoſed to the progreſs of that depopulation and barbariſm, which philoſophers had dreaded from the rapid increaſe of military force. Theſe remarks on the ſpirit which actuated the French army in their unexampled, miſconceived, and calumniated conduct, are peculiarly important, as they ſerve to illuſtrate a principle, which cannot too frequently be preſented to view, that in the French Revolution all is to be attributed to general cauſes influencing the whole body of the people, and almoſt nothing to the ſchemes and the aſcendant of individuals.

But to return to our rapid ſketch. It was at the moment of the Pariſian revolt, and of the defection of the army, that the whole

power

power of France devolved on the National Affembly. It is at that moment, therefore, that the difcuffion commences, whether that body ought to have re-eftablifhed and re-formed the Government *which events had fub-verted,* or to have proceeded to the eftablifh-ment of a new Conftitution, on the general principles of reafon and freedom. The arm of the ancient Government had been palfied, and its power reduced to formality, by events over which the Affembly poffeffed no con-troul. It was theirs to decide, not whether the monarchy was to be fubverted, for that had been already effected, but whether, from its ruins, fragments were to be collected for the re-conftruction of the political edifice.

They had been affembled as an ordinary Legiflature under exifting laws. They were transformed by thefe events into a NATIONAL CONVENTION, and vefted with powers to organize a Government. It is in vain that

their

their adverfaries conteft this affertion, by ap-
pealing to the deficiency of forms*. It is in
vain to demand the legal inftrument that
changed their Conftitution, and extended
their powers. Accurate forms in the convey-
ance of power are prefcribed by the wifdom
of law, in the regular adminiftration of
States. But great Revolutions are too immenfe for technical formality. All the fanction that can be hoped for in fuch events, is
the voice of the people, however informally
and irregularly expreffed. This cannot be

---

* This circumftance is fhortly ftated by Mr. Burke.
" I can never confider this Affembly as any thing elfe than
" a voluntary affociation of men, who have availed them-
" felves of circumftances to feize upon the power of the
" State. They do not hold the authority they exercife un-
" der any Conftitutional law of the State. They have de-
" parted from the inftructions of the people that fent them,
" &c." Burke, p. 242—3. The fame argument is treated
by M. Calonne, in an expanded memorial of 44 pages,
againft the pretenfions of the Affembly to be a convention,
with much unavailing ingenuity and labour.—See his Work
from p. 314 to 358.

pretended to have been wanting in France. Every other fpecies of authority was annihilated by popular acts, but that of the States General. On them, therefore, devolved the duty of exercifing their *unlimited** truft, ac--

* A diftinction made by Mr. Burke between the *abftract* and *moral* competency of a Legiflature (p. 27) has been much extolled by his admirers. To me it feems only a novel and objectionable mode of diftinguifhing between a *right* and the *expediency* of ufing it. But the mode of illuftrating the diftinction is far more pernicious than a mere novelty of phrafe. This moral competence is fubject, fays our author, to " faith, juftice, and fixed fundamental po- " licy." Thus illuftrated, the diftinction appears liable to a double objection. It is falfe that the *abftract* competence of a Legiflature extends to the violation of faith and juftice. It is falfe that its *moral* competence does not extend to the moft fundamental policy, and thus to confound fundamental policy with faith and juftice, for the fake of ftigmatizing innovators, is to ftab the vitals of morality. There is only one maxim of policy truly fundamental—*the good of the go-verned*—and the ftability of that maxim, rightly underftood, demonftrates the mutability of all policy that is fubordinate to it.

cording to their beſt views of general intereſt. Their enemies have, even in their invectives, confeſſed the *ſubſequent adherence* of the people, for they have inveighed againſt it as the infatuation of a dire fanaticiſm. The authority of the Aſſembly was then firſt conferred on it by public confidence, and its acts have been ſince ratified by public approbation. Nothing can betray a diſpoſition to puny and technical ſophiſtry more ſtrongly, than to obſerve with M. Calonne, that this ratification, to be valid, ought to have been made by France, not in her new organization of municipalities, but in her ancient diviſion of bailliages and provinces. The ſame *individuals* act in both forms. The approbation of the *men* legitimates the Government. It is of no importance, whether they are aſſembled as bailliages, or as municipalities. If this latitude of informality, this ſubjection of laws to their principle, and of Government to its ſource, are not permitted in Revolutions,

how

how are we to juftify the affumed authority of the Englifh Convention of 1688? " They " did not hold the authority they exercifed " under any conftitutional law of the State." They were not even *legally* elected, as, it muft be confeffed, was the cafe with the French Af-fembly. An evident though irregular ratifi-cation by the people, alone legitimated their acts. Yet they poffeffed, by the confeffion of Mr. Burke, an authority only limited by pru-dence and virtue. Had the people of Eng-land given *inftructions* to the Members of that Convention, its ultimate meafures would pro-bably have departed as much from them as the French Affembly have deviated from thofe of their conftituents, and the public acquiefcence in the deviation would, in all likelihood, have been the fame.

It will be confeffed by any man who has confidered the public temper of England at the landing of William, that the majority of thofe inftructions would not have proceeded

to

to the depofition of James. The firft afpect of thefe great changes perplexes and intimidates men too much for juft views and bold refolutions. It is by the progrefs of events that their hopes are emboldened, and their views enlarged.

This influence was felt in France. The people, in an advanced period of the Revolution, virtually recalled the inftructions by which the feeblenefs of their political infancy had limited the power of their Reprefentatives; for they fanctioned acts by which thofe inftructions were contradicted. The formality of inftructions was indeed wanting in England, but the change of public fentiment, from the opening of the Convention to its ultimate decifion, was as remarkable as the contraft which has been fo oftentationfly difplayed by M. Calonne, between the decrees of the National Affembly and the firft inftructions of their conftituents.

E This

Thus feeble are the objections againſt the authority of the Aſſembly.

We now reſume the conſideration of its exerciſe, and proceed to enquire, whether they ought to have reformed, or deſtroyed their Government? The general queſtion of innovation is an exhauſted common-place, to which the genius of Mr. Burke has been able to add nothing but ſplendor of eloquence and felicity of illuſtration. It has long been ſo notoriouſly of this nature, that it is placed by Lord Bacon among the ſportive conteſts which are to exerciſe rhetorical ſkill. No man will ſupport the extreme on either ſide. Perpetual change and immutable eſtabliſhment are equally indefenſible. To deſcend therefore from theſe barren generalities to a more near view of the queſtion, let us ſtate it more preciſely. *Was the Civil Order in France* corrigible, *or was it neceſſary to* deſtroy *it?* Not to mention the extirpation of the feudal ſyſtem,

and

and the abrogation of the civil and criminal code, we have firſt to conſider the deſtruction of the three great corporations, of the Nobility, the Church, and the Parliaments. Theſe three Ariſtocracies were the pillars which in fact formed the Government of France. The queſtion then of *forming* or *deſtroying* theſe bodies is fundamental. There is one general principle applicable to them all adopted by the French Legiſlators—*that the exiſtence of Orders is repugnant to the principles of the ſocial union.* An Order is a *legal* rank, a body of men combined and endowed with privileges by law. —There are two kinds of inequality, the one perſonal—that of talent and virtue, the ſource of whatever is excellent and admirable in ſociety—the other that of fortune, which muſt exiſt, becauſe *property* alone can ſtimulate to labour; and labour, if it were not neceſſary to the exiſtence, would be indiſpenſible to the happineſs of man. But though it be neceſſary, yet, in its exceſs it is the great malady

of

of civil fociety. The accumulation of that power which is conferred by wealth in the hands of the few, is the perpetual fource of oppreffion and neglect to the mafs of mankind. The power of the wealthy is farther concentrated by their tendency to *combination,* from which, number, difperfion, indigence and ignorance equally preclude the poor. The wealthy are formed into bodies by their profeffions, their different degrees of opulence (called *ranks,)* their knowledge, and their fmall number.—They neceffarily in all countries adminifter government, for they alone have fkill and leifure for its functions. Thus circumftanced, nothing can be more evident than their inevitable preponderance in the political fcale. The preference of partial to general interefts is however the greateft of all public evils. It fhould therefore have been the object of all laws to reprefs this malady, but it has been their perpetual tendency to aggravate it. Not content with the inevit-

able

able inequality of fortune, they have fuperadded to it honorary and political diftinctions. Not content with the inevitable tendency of the wealthy to combine, they have embodied them in claffes. They have fortified thofe confpiracies againft the general intereft, which they ought to have refifted, though they could not difarm. Laws, it is faid, cannot equalize men. No. But ought they for that reafon to aggravate the inequality which they cannot cure? Laws cannot infpire unmixed Patriotifm—But ought they for that reafon to foment that *corporation fpirit* which is its moft fatal enemy? All profeffional combinations, faid Mr. Burke, in one of his late fpeeches in Parliament, are dangerous in a free State. Arguing on the fame principle, the National Affembly has proceeded farther. They have conceived that the laws ought to *create* no inequality of combination, to recognize all only in their capacity of citizens, and

to

to offer no affiftance to the natural preponderance of partial over general intereft.

But befides the general fource of hoftility
to Orders, the particular circumftances of
France prefented other objections, which it
is neceffary to confider more in detail.

It is in the firft place to be remarked, that
all the bodies and inftitutions of the kingdom
participated the fpirit of the ancient Government, and in that view were incapable of alliance with a free Conftitution. They were
tainted by the defpotifm of which they were
members or inftruments. Abfolute monarchies, like every other confiftent and permanent government, affimilate every thing with
which they are connected to their own genius. The Nobility, the Priefthood, the Judicial Ariftocracy, were unfit to be members of a
free government, becaufe their *corporate* character had been formed under arbitrary eftablifhments.

lifhments.   To have preferved thefe great
corporations, would be to have retained the
feeds of reviving defpotifm in the bofom of
freedom.   This remark may merit the attention of Mr. Burke, as illuftrating an important
difference between the French and Englifh
Revolutions.   The Clergy, the Peerage, and
Judicatures of England, had in fome degree
the fentiments infpired by a Government in
which freedom had been eclipfed, but not extinguifhed—They were therefore qualified to
partake of a more ftable and improved liberty.
But the cafe of France was different.   Thefe
bodies had there imbibed every fentiment,
and adopted every habit under arbitrary power.
Their prefervation in England, and their deftruction in France, may in this view be juftified on fimilar grounds.   It is abfurd to regard the Orders as remnants of that free conftitution which France, in common with the
other Gothic nations of Europe, once enjoyed.
Nothing remained of thefe ancient Orders

E 4

but

but the name. The Nobility were no longer
thofe haughty and powerful Barons, who en-
flaved the people and dictated to the King.
The Ecclefiaftics were no longer that Priefthood, before whom, in a benighted and fuperftitious age, all civil power was impotent
and mute. They have both dwindled into dependents on the crown. Still lefs do the opulent and enlightened Commons of France refemble its fervile and beggared populace in the
fixteenth century. Two hundred years of un-
interrupted exercife had legitimated abfolute
authority as much as prefcription can confe-
crate ufurpation. The ancient French Conftitution was therefore no farther a model than
that of any *foreign* nation, which was to be
judged of alone by its utility, and poffeffed in
no refpect the authority of eftablifhment. It
had been fucceeded by *another* Government,
and if France were to recur to a period antecedent to her fervitude for legiflative models,
fhe might as well afcend to the æra of Clovis

or Charlemagne, as be regulated by the precedents of Henry III. or Mary of Medicis. All thefe forms of government exifted only *hiftorically*.

Thefe obfervations include all the Orders. Let us confider each of them fucceffively. The devotion of the Nobility of France **to** the Monarch was infpired equally by **their** fentiments, their interefts, and their habits. " The feudal and chivalrous fpirit of fealty," fo long the prevailing paffion of Europe, was ftill nourifhed in their bofoms by the military fentiments from which it firft arofe. The majority of them had ftill no profeffion but war, no hope but in Royal favor. The youthful and indigent filled the camps; the more opulent and mature partook the fplendor and bounty of the Court: But they were equally dependents on the Crown. To the plentitude of the Royal power were attached thofe immenfe and magnificent privileges, which divided

vided France into diftinct nations ; which exhibited a Nobility monopolizing the rewards
and offices of the State, and a people degraded
to political *helotifm**. Men do not cordially
refign fuch privileges, nor quickly difmifs the
fentiments which they have infpired. The
oftentatious facrifice of pecuniary exemptions
in a moment of general fermentation is a
wretched criterion of their genuine feelings.
They affected to beftow as a gift, what they
would have been fpeedily compelled to abandon as an ufurpation, and they hoped by the
facrifice of a part to purchafe fecurity for the
reft. They have been moft juftly ftated to be
a band of political *janizaries*,† far more valuable to a Sultan than mercenaries, becaufe attached to him by unchangeable intereft and in-
deliable fentiment. Whether any reform could
have extracted from this body a portion which

---

* I fay *political* in contradiftinction to *civil*, for in the latter
fenfe the affertion would have been untrue.

† See Mr. Rous's excellent " Thoughts on Government."

might

might have entered into the new conftitution is a queftion which we fhall confider when that political fyftem comes under our review. Their exiftence, as a member of the Legifla- ture, is a queftion diftinct from their prefer- vation as a feparate Order, or great corpora- tion, in the State. A fenate of Nobles might have been eftablifhed, though the Order of the Nobility had been deftroyed, and England would then have been exactly copied.—But it is of the Order that we now fpeak, for we are now confidering the deftruction of the old not the formation of the new Government.— The fuppreffion of Nobility has been in Eng- land moft abfurdly confounded with the pro- hibition of titles. The union of the Orders in one Affembly was the firft ftep towards the deftruction of a legiflative Nobility. The abolition of their feudal rights, in the memo- rable feffion of the 4th of Auguft, 1789, may be regarded as the fecond. They retained after thefe meafures no diftinction but what was purely nominal, and it remained to be determined what place they were to occupy in the new Conftitution. That queftion was decided by the decree of the 22d of December, in the fame year, which enacted, that the Electoral Affemblies were to be compofed without any regard to rank, and that citizens of all Orders were to vote in them indifcriminately. The diftinction of Orders was deftroyed by this decree, the Nobility were to form no part of the new Conftitution, and they were ftripped of all that they had enjoyed under the old Government, but their titles.

Hitherto all had paffed unnoticed, but no fooner did the Affembly, faithful to their principles, proceed to extirpate the external figns of ranks, which they no longer tolerated, then all Europe refounded with clamours againft their Utopian and levelling madnefs. The *incredible** decree of the 19th of June,

<hr>

So called by M. Calonne.

1790, for the fuppreffion of titles, is the object of all thefe invectives, yet without that meafure the Affembly would certainly have been guilty of the groffeft inconfiftency and abfurdity. An *untitled* Nobility forming a member of the State, had been exemplified in fome Commonwealths of antiquity. Such were the Patricians in Rome. But a titled Nobility, without legal privileges, or political exiftence, would have been a monfter new in the annals of legiflative abfurdity. The power was poffeffed without the bauble by the Roman Ariftocracy. The bauble would have been reverenced, while the power was trampled on, if titles had been fpared in France. A titled Nobility, is the moft undifputed progeny of feudal barbarifm. Titles had in all nations *denoted offices*, it was referved for Gothic Europe to attach them to *ranks*, yet this conduct of our remote anceftors admits explanation, for with them offices were hereditary, and hence the titles denoting them became

became hereditary too. But we, who have rejected hereditary office, retain an ufage to which it gave rife, and which it alone could juftify.

So egregioufly is this recent origin of titled Nobility mifconceived, that it has been even pretended to be neceffary to the order and exiftence of fociety: A narrow and arrogant bigotry, which would limit all political remark to the Gothic States of Europe, or eftablifh general principles on events that occupy fo fhort a period of hiftory, and manners that have been adopted by fo flender a portion of the human race. A titled Nobility, was equally unknown to the fplendid Monarchies of Afia, and to the manly fimplicity of the ancient Commonwealths*. It arofe from

* Ariftocratic bodies did indeed exift in the ancient world, but *titles* were unknown. Though they poffeffed political privileges, yet as they did not affect the *manners*, they had not the fame inevitable tendency to taint the public character

the peculiar circumstances of modern Europe, and yet its necessity is now erected on the basis of universal experience, as if these other renowned and polished States were effaced from the records of history, and banished from the society of nations. " Nobility is the Corinthian capital of polished states." The august fabric of society is deformed and encumbered by such Gothic ornaments. The massy Doric that sustains it is Labour, and the splendid variety of arts and talents that solace and embellish life, form the decorations of its Corinthian and Ionic capitals.

Other motives besides the extirpation of feudality, disposed the French Legislature to the suppression of titles. To give stability

racter as titular distinctions. These bodies too being in general open to *property*, or *office*, they are in no respect to be compared to the Nobles of Europe. They might affect the *forms* of free Government as much, but they did not in the same proportion injure the *Spirit* of Freedom.

to a popular Government, a democratic character muſt be formed, and democratic ſentiments inſpired. The ſentiment of equality which titular diſtinctions have, perhaps, more than any other cauſe, extinguiſhed in Europe, and without which democratic forms are impotent and ſhort-lived, was to be revived: a free Government was to be eſtabliſhed, by carrying the ſpirit of equality and freedom into the feelings, the manners, the moſt familiar intercourſe of men. The badges of inequality, which were perpetually inſpiring ſentiments adverſe to the ſpirit of the Government, were therefore deſtroyed: Diſtinctions which only ſerved to unfit the Nobility for obedience, and the people for freedom; to keep alive the diſcontent of the one, and to perpetuate the ſervility of the other; to deprive the one of the moderation that ſinks them into citizens, and to rob the other of the ſpirit that exalts them into free men. A ſingle example can alone diſpel inveterate pre-

judices.

judices. Thus thought our anceſtors at the Revolution, when they deviated from the ſucceſſion, to deſtroy the prejudice of its ſanctity. Thus alſo did the Legiſlators of France feel, when by the abolition of titles, they gave a mortal blow to the ſlaviſh prejudices which unfitted their country for freedom. It was a practical aſſertion of that equality which had been conſecrated in the Declaration of Rights, but which no abſtract aſſertion could have conveyed into the ſpirits and the hearts of men. It proceeded on the principle that the ſecurity of a revolution of *government* can only ariſe from a revolution of *character*.

To theſe reaſonings it has been oppoſed, that hereditary diſtinctions are the *moral treaſure* of a State, by which it excites and rewards public virtue and public ſervice, which, without national injury or burden, operates with reſiſtleſs force on generous minds. To this I anſwer, that of *perſonal* diſtinctions this de-

F

ſcription

fcription is moſt true, but that this moral treaſury of honour is in fact impoveriſhed by the improvident profuſion that has made them hereditary. The poſſeſſion of honours by that multitude, who have inherited but not acquired them, engroſſes and depreciates theſe incentives and rewards of virtue. Were they purely perſonal, their value would be doubly enhanced, as the poſſeſſors would be fewer while the diſtinction was more honourable. Perſonal diſtinctions then every wiſe State will cheriſh as its ſureſt and nobleſt reſource, but of hereditary title, *at leaſt in the circumſtances of France**, the abolition ſeems to have been juſt and politic.

The fate of the Church, the ſecond great corporation that ſuſtained the French deſpo-

---

* I have been groſſly miſunderſtood by thoſe who have ſuppoſed this *qualification* an aſſumed or affected reſerve. I believe the *principle* only as *qualified* by the *circumſtances* of different nations.

tifm,

tifm, has peculiarly provoked the indignation of Mr. Burke. The diffolution of the Church as a body, the refumption of its territorial revenues, and the new organization of the Priefthood, appear to him to be dictated by the union of robbery and irreligion, to glut the rapacity of Stock-jobbers, and to gratify the hoftility of Atheifts. All the outrages and profcriptions of ancient or mordern tyrants vanifh, in his opinion, in the comparifon with this confifcation of the *property* of the Gallican Church. Principles had, it is true, been on this fubject explored, and reafons had been urged by men of genius, which vulgar men deemed irrefiftible. But with thefe reafons Mr. Burke will not deign to combat. " You do not imagine, Sir," fays he to his correfpondent " that I am going to compliment this *miferable defcription of perfons* with any long difcuffion ? * What immediately follows

---

* The Abbé Maury, who is not lefs remarkable for the fury of eloquent declamation, than for the *inept* parade of hif-

torical

this contemptuous paſſage is ſo outrageouſly offenſive to candor and urbanity, that an honourable adverſary will diſdain to avail himſelf of it. The paſſage itſelf, however, demands a pauſe. It alludes to an opinion of which *I truſt* Mr. Burke did not know the origin. That the church-lands were national property was not firſt aſſerted among the *Jacobins*, or in the *Palais Royal.* The author of that opinion, the maſter of that wretched

torical erudition, attempted in the debate on this ſubject to trace the opinion higher. Baſe lawyers, according to him, had inſinuated it to the Roman Emperors, and againſt it was pointed the maxim of the Civil Law, " *Omnia tenes Cæſar imperio ſed non dominio.*" Louis XIV. and Louis XV. had, if we may believe him, both been aſſailed by this Machiavelian doctrine, and both had repulſed it with magnanimous indignation. The learned Abbé committed only one miſtake. The deſpots of Rome and France had indeed been poiſoned with the idea that they were the immediate proprietors of their ſubjects' eſtates. That opinion is execrable and flagitious, and it is not, as we ſhall ſee, the doctrine of the French Legiſlators.

deſcription

defcription of perfons, whom Mr. Burke dif-
dains to encounter, was one whom he might
have combated with glory, with confidence of
triumph in victory, and without fear or fhame
in defeat. The author of that opinion was
Turgot! a name now too high to be exalted by eulogy, or depreffed by invective.
—That benevolent and philofophic Statefman
delivered it in the article *Fondation* of the
Encyclopedie, as the calm and difinterefted
opinion of a fcholar, at a moment when he
could have no view to palliate rapacity, or
prompt irreligion. It was no doctrine contrived for the occafion by the agents of tyranny; it was a principle difcovered in pure
and harmlefs fpeculation, by one of the beft
and wifeft of men. I adduce the authority of
Turgot, not to oppofe the arguments (if there
had been any) but to counteract the infinuations of Mr. Burke. The authority of his
affertions forms a prejudice, which is thus to
be removed before we can hope for a fair au-

dience

dience at the bar of reafon. If he infinuates the flagitioufnefs of thefe opinions by the fuppofed vilenefs of their origin, it cannot be unfit to pave the way for their reception, by affigning to them a more illuftrious pedigree.

But difmiffing the genealogy of doctrines, let us examine their intrinfic value, and liften to no voice but that of truth. " *Are the lands* " *occupied by the Church the* PROPERTY *of its* " *Members?*" Various confiderations prefent themfelves, which may elucidate the fubject.

I. It has not hitherto been fuppofed that any clafs of Public fervants are proprietors. They are *falaried** by the State for the performance of certain duties. Judges are *paid* for the diftribution of juftice; *Kings* for the execution of the laws; Soldiers, where there

---

* " Ils font ou *falariés*, ou mendians, ou voleurs." *They are either falaried, or beggars, or robbers*—was the expreffion of M. Mirabeau refpecting the Priefthood.

is a mercenary army, for public defence ; and Priefts, where there is an eftablifhed religion, for public inftruction. The mode of their *payment* is indifferent to the queftion. It is generally in rude ages by land, and in culti-vated periods by money. But a *territorial penfion* is no more property than a *pecuniary one.* The right of the State to regulate the falaries of thofe fervants whom it pays in money has not been difputed. But if it has *chofen to provide the revenue of a certain portion of land for the falary of another clafs of fervants,* wherefore is its right more difputable, to re-fume that land, and to eftablifh a new mode of payment ? In the early hiftory of Europe, before fiefs became hereditary, great landed eftates were beftowed by the Sovereign, on condition of military fervice. By a fimilar tenure did the Church hold its lands. No man can prove, that becaufe the State has intrufted its ecclefiaftical fervants with a portion of land, as the fource and fecurity of their *penfions,*

they

they are in any refpect more the *proprietors* of it, than the other fervants of the State are of that portion of the revenue from which they are paid.

II. The lands of the Church poffefs not the moft fimple and indifpenfible requifites of property. They are not even pretended to be held for the *benefit* of thofe who enjoy them. This is the obvious criterion between private property and a penfion for public fervice. The deftination of the firft is avowedly the comfort and happinefs of the *individual* who enjoys it; as he is conceived to be the fole judge of this happinefs, he poffeffes the moft unlimited rights of enjoyment, alienation, and even abufe: But the lands of the Church, deftined for the fupport of public fervants, exhibited none of the characters of property—They were inalienable, becaufe it would have been not lefs abfurd for the Priefthood to have exercifed fuch authority over thefe lands, than it would

be

be for feamen to claim the property of a fleet which they manned, or foldiers that of a fortrefs they garrifoned.

III. It is confeffed that no individual **Prieft** was a proprietor, and it is not denied that his utmoft claim was limited to a poffeffion for life of his ftipend. If all the Priefts, taken *individually*, were not proprietors, the Priefthood, as a *body*, cannot claim any fuch right. For what is a *body*, but an aggregate of individuals, and what new right can be conveyed by a mere change of name ?—Nothing can fo forcibly illuftrate this argument as the cafe of other corporations. They are voluntary affociations of men for their own benefit. Every member of them is an abfolute fharer in their property, it is therefore alienated and inherited. Corporate property is here as facred as individual, becaufe in the ultimate analyfis it is the fame. But the Priefthood is a Corporation, endowed by the country, and deftined for the

benefit

benefit of other men. It is hence that the members have no *feparate*, nor the body any *collective*, right of property. They are only entrufted with the *adminiftration* of the lands from which their *falaries* are paid*.

IV. It is from this laft circumftance that their *legal femblance* of property arifes. In charters, bonds, and all other proceedings of law, they are treated with the fame formalities as real property.—" They are identified," fays Mr. Burke, " with the mafs of private property;" and it muft be confeffed, that if we are to limit our view to form, this language is correct. But the repugnance of thefe formalities to legal truth proceeded from a very obvious caufe. If eftates are vefted in the

---

* This admits a familiar illuftration. If a land-holder chufes to pay his fteward for the collection of his rents, by permitting him to poffefs a farm *gratis*, is he conceived to have refigned his *property* in the farm? The cafe is precifely familiar.

Clergy,

Clergy, to them moft unqueftionably ought to be entrufted the protection of thefe eftates in all contefts at law, and actions for that purpofe can only be maintained with facility, fimplicity, and effect, by the *fiction* of their being proprietors.—Nor is this the only cafe in which the fpirit and the forms of law are at variance refpecting property. Scotland, where lands ftill are held by *feudal* tenures, will afford us a remarkable example. There, if we extend our views no further than legal forms, the *fuperior* is to be regarded as the proprietor, while the real proprietor appears to be only a tenant for life. Such is the language of the charter by which he obtains a legal right to his eftate. In this cafe, the vaffal is *formally* ftript of the property which he in fact enjoys. In the other, the Church is *formally* invefted with a property, to which in reality it had no claim. The argument of *prefcription* will appear to be altogether untenable, *for prefcription implies a certain period during which the*

rights

rights of property had been exercifed, but in the cafe before us they *never* were exercifed, becaufe they never could be fuppofed to exift. It muft be proved that thefe poffeffions were of the nature of property, before it can follow that they are protected by prefcription, and to plead it is to take for granted the queftion in difpute. If they never were property, no length of time can change their nature.*

---

* There are perfons who may not relifh the mode of reafoning here adopted. They contend that property, being the creature of civil fociety, may be refumed by that Public will which created it, and on this principle they juftify the National Affembly of France. But fuch a juftification is adverfe to the principles of that Affembly, for they have confecrated it as one of the firft maxims of their Declaration of Rights, that the State cannot violate property, except in cafes of urgent neceffity, and on condition of previous indemnification. This defence too will not juftify their felection of Church property, in preference of all others, for refumption. It certainly ought in this view to have fallen equally on all citizens. The principle is befides falfe in the extreme to which it is affumed. *Property* is, indeed *in fome fenfe* created by an act of the Public will; but it is by one

V. When the British Islands, the Dutch Republic, the German and Scandinavian States, reformed their ecclesiastical establishments, the howl of sacrilege was the only armour by which the Church attempted to protect its pretended property. The age was too tumultuous and unlettered for discusions of abstract jurisprudence. The clamour of sacrilege seems, however, to have fallen into early contempt. The treaty of Westphalia secularized many of the most opulent be-

of those *fundamental* acts which constitute society. Theory proves it to be essential to the social state. Experience proves that it has, in some degree, existed in every age and nation of the world. But those public acts which form and endow corporations, are subsequent and subordinate.— They are only *ordinary expedients* of legislation. The property of individuals is established on a *general principle*, which seems coeval with civil society itself. But *bodies* are instruments fabricated by the Legislator for a *specific* purpose, which ought to be preserved while they are beneficial, amended when they are impaired, and rejected when they become useless or injurious.

nefices

nefices of Germany, under the mediation and guarantee of the firſt Catholic Powers of Europe. In our own iſland, on the abolition of epiſcopacy in Scotland at the Revolution, the revenues of the Church peaceably devolved on the Sovereign, and he devoted a portion of them to the ſupport of the new eſtabliſhment. When, at a ſtill later period, the Jeſuits were ſuppreſſed in moſt Catholic Monarchies, the wealth of that formidable and opulent body was every where ſeized by the Sovereign. In all theſe memorable examples, no traces are to be diſcovered of the pretended property of the Church.—The ſalaries of a claſs of Public ſervants are, in all theſe caſes, reſumed by the State, when it ceaſes to deem their ſervice, or the mode of it, uſeful. It is in none of them recognized as property. That claim, now ſo forcibly urged by M. Calonne, was probably little reſpected by him, when he lent his agency to the deſtruction of the Jeſuits with ſuch peculiar

liar

liar activity and rancor. The facredness of their property could not ftrongly imprefs him, when he was inftrumental in degrading the members of that renowned and accomplifhed Society, the glory of Catholic Europe, from their fuperb endowments to fcanty and beggarly penfions. In all thefe contefts, the inviolability of Church poffeffions was a principle that never made its appearance. A murmur of facrilege might, indeed, be heard among the fanatical or interefted few : But the religious horror in which the Priefthood had enveloped its robberies, had long been difpelled, and it was referved for Mr. Burke to renew that cry of facrilege, which, in the darknefs of the fixteenth century, had refounded in vain. No man can be expected to oppofe arguments to *epithets*. When a definition of facrilege is given, confiftent with good logic and plain Englifh, it will be time enough to difcufs it. Till that definition *(with the Greek Calends)* comes, I fhould as foon difpute about

the

the meaning of facrilege as about that of herefy or witchraft.

VI. The whole fubject is indeed fo evident, that little diverfity of opinion could have arifen, if the queftion of church property had not been confounded with the claims of the prefent incumbents. The diftinction, though neither ftated by Mr. Burke nor M. Calonne, is extremely fimple. The State is the proprietor of the Church revenues, but its faith, it may be faid, is pledged to thofe who have entered into the Church, for the continuance of thofe incomes, for which they abandoned all other purfuits. The right of the State to arrange at its pleafure the revenues of any future Priefts may be confeffed, while a doubt may be entertained, whether it is competent to change the fortune of thofe to whom it has folemnly promifed a certain income for life. But thefe diftinct fubjects have been confounded, that fympathy with

fuffering

fuffering individuals might influence opinion on a general queftion, that feeling for the degradation of its hierarchy might fupply the place of argument to eftablifh the property of the Church. To confider this fubject diftinctly it cannot be denied, that the mildeft, the moft equitable, and the moft ufual expedient of polifhed States in periods of emergency, *is the reduction of the falaries of their fervants, and the fuppreffion of fuperfluous places.* This and no more has been done regarding the Church of France. Civil, naval, and military fervants of the State are fubject to fuch retrenchments in a moment of difficulty. They often cannot be effected without a wound to individuals* ; neither can the reform of a civil office, nor the reduction of a regiment: But all men who enter into the public fervice muft do fo with the implied condition of fubjecting their emoluments,

---

This is precifely the cafe of " *damnum abfque injuria.*"

G   and

and even their official exiſtence, to the exigencies of the State. The great grievance of
ſuch derangements is the ſhock they give to
family ſentiments. This is precluded by the
compulſory celibacy of the Romiſh Church;
and when the debts of the Clergy are incor-
porated with thoſe of the State, and their ſub-
ſiſtence inſured by moderate incomes, though
ſenſibility may, in the leaſt retrenchment,
find ſomewhat to lament, juſtice will, in the
whole of theſe arrangements, diſcover little
to condemn. To the individual members of
the Church of France, whoſe hopes and enjoyments have been abridged by this reſump-
tion, no virtuous mind will refuſe the tribute of its ſympathy and its regrets. Every
man of humanity muſt wiſh, that public exigencies had permitted the French Legiſlature to ſpare the income of preſent incumbents, and more eſpecially of thoſe whom
they ſtill continued in the diſcharge of active
functions. But theſe ſentiments imply no

forrow

forrow at the downfall of a great Corporation, the determined and implacable enemy of freedom; at the converſion of an immenſe public property to national uſe, nor at the reduction of a ſervile and imperious Prieſthood to humble utility, as the moral and religious inſtructors of mankind. The attainment of theſe great objects conſole us for the portion of evil that was, perhaps, inſeparable from them, and will be juſtly admired by a poſterity too remote to be moved by theſe minute afflictions, or to be afflicted by any thing but their general ſplendor. The enlightened obſerver of an age thus diſtant will contemplate with peculiar aſtoniſhment, the riſe, progreſs, decay, and downfall * of ſpiritual power in Chriſtian Europe. It will attract his atten-

* Did we not dread the ridicule of political prediction, it would not ſeem difficult to aſſign its period.—Church power (unleſs ſome Revolution, auſpicious to Prieſtcraft, ſhould replunge Europe in ignorance) will certainly not ſurvive the nineteenth century.

tion

tion as an appearance which ftands *alone* in hiftory. Its connection in all ftages of its progrefs with the civil power will peculiarly occupy his mind. He will remark the unprefuming humility by which it gradually gained the favour and divided the power of the Magiftrate; the haughty and defpotic tone in which it afterwards gave law to Sovereigns and fubjects; the zeal with which, in the firft defperate moments of decline, it armed the people againft the Magiftrate, and aimed at re-eftablifhing fpiritual defpotifm on the ruins of civil order; and the afylum which it at laft found againft the hoftilities of reafon in the perogatives of temporal defpotifm, of which it had fo long been the implacable foe.

The firft and laft of thefe periods will prove, that the Priefthood are fervilely devoted when they are weak. The fecond and third, that they are dangeroufly ambitious when ftrong. In a ftate of feeblenefs, they are dangerous to liberty;

liberty; poffeffed of power, they are dangerous to civil government itfelf. But the laft
period of their progrefs will appear peculiarly
connected with the ftate. of France. There
was no protection for the opulence and exiftence * of the European Priefthood in an
enlightened period, but the Throne. It
formed the only bulwark againft the inroads
of reafon: for the fuperftition which once
formed their power was gone. Around the
Throne therefore they rallied. To the Monarch they transferred the devotion which
had formerly attached them to the Church, and
the fiercenefs of prieftly † zeal was fucceeded in their bofoms by the more peaceful fentiments of a courtly and polifhed fervility. Such
is, in a greater or lefs degree, the prefent condition of the Church in every nation of Europe;
yet France has been reproached for the diffolu-

* I always underftand their *corporate* exiftence.

† *Odium Theologicum.*

                              tion

tion of such a body. It might as well be maintained, that in her conquests over despotism, she ought to have spared the strongest fortresses and most faithful troops of her adversary. Such in truth, were the corporations of the Nobility and the Church. The National Assembly ensured permanence to their establishments, by dismantling the fortresses, and disbanding the troops of their vanquished foe.

In the few remarks that are here made on the Nobility and Clergy of France, we confine ourselves strictly to their *political* and *collective* character. Mr. Burke, on the contrary, has grounded his eloquent apology purely on their *individual* and *moral character*. This however is totally irrelevant to the question, for we are not discussing what place they ought to occupy in society as individuals, but as a body. We are not considering the demerit of citizens whom it is fit to punish,

but

but the spirit of a body which it is politic to dissolve. We are not contending that the Nobility and Clergy were in their private capacity bad citizens, but that they were members of corporations which could not be preserved with security to public freedom.

The Judicial Aristocracy formed by the Parliaments, seems still less susceptible of union with a free Government. Their spirit and claims were equally incompatible with liberty. They had imbibed a spirit congenial to the authority under which they had acted, and suitable to the arbitrary genius of the laws which they had dispensed. They retained those ambiguous and indefinite claims to a share in the legislation, which the fluctuations of power in the kingdom had in some degree countenanced. The spirit of a *corporation* was from the smallness of their numbers more *concentrated* and vigorous in *them* than in the Nobles and Clergy ; and whatever arif-

tocratic

tocratic zeal is laid to the charge of the Nobility, is imputable with tenfold force to the *ennobled Magiſtrates*, who regarded their recent honors with an enthuſiaſm of vanity, inſpired by that bigotted veneration for rank which is the perpetual character of upſtarts. A free people could not form its tribunals of men who pretended to any controul on the Legiſlature. Courts of Juſtice, in which ſeats were legally purchaſed, had too long been endured: Judges who regarded the right of diſpenſing juſtice as a marketable commodity, could neither be fit organs of equitable laws, nor ſuitable magiſtrates for a free State. It is vain to urge with Mr. Burke the paſt ſervices of theſe judicial bodies. It is not to be denied that Monteſquieu is correct, when he ſtates, that under bad Governments one abuſe often limits another. The uſurped authority of the Parliaments formed, it is true, ſome bulwark againſt the caprice of the Court. But when the abuſe is deſtroyed, why preſerve the

remedial

remedial evil? Superftition certainly alleviates the defpotifm of Turkey; but if a rational Government could be erected in that empire, it might with confidence difclaim the aid of the Koran, and defpife the remonftrances of the Mufti. To fuch eftablifhments, let us pay the tribute of gratitude for paft benefit; but when their utility no longer exifts, let them be canonized by death, that their admirers may be indulged in all the plenitude of pofthumous veneration.

The three Ariftocracies, Military, Sacerdotal, and Judicial, may be confidered as having formed the French Government. They have appeared, fo far as we have confidered them, incorrigible. All attempts to improve them would have been little better than (to ufe the words of Mr. Burke) " mean reparations on mighty ruins." They were not perverted by the accidental depravity of their members. They were not infected by any

tranfient

tranfient paffion, which new circumftances would extirpate. The fault was in the effence of the inftitutions themfelves, which were irreconcileable with a free Government. But it is objected, thefe inftitutions might have been *gradually* reformed*. The fpirit of Freedom would have filently entered. The progreffive wifdom of an enlightened nation would have remedied, in procefs of time, their defects, without convulfion.

To this argument I confidently anfwer, *that thefe inftitutions would have deftroyed* Liberty, *before Liberty had corrected their* Spirit. Power vegetates with more vigour after thefe gentle prunings. A flender reform amufes and lulls the people ; the popular enthufiafm fubfides, and the moment of effectual reform is irretrievably loft. No important political improvement was ever obtained

* See Mr. Burke's Reflexions, p. 248-52.

in a period of tranquillity. The corrupt intereſt of the Governors is ſo ſtrong, and the
cry of the people ſo feeble, that it were vain
to expect it. If the efferveſcence of the popular mind is ſuffered to paſs away without
effect, it would be abſurd to expect from languor what enthuſiaſm has not obtained. If
radical reform is not, at ſuch a moment, pro-
cured, all partial changes are evaded and de-
feated in the tranquility which ſucceeds*.
The gradual reform that ariſes from the pre-
ſiding principle exhibited in the ſpecious theory of Mr. Burke, is belied by the experience
of all ages. Whatever excellence, whatever
freedom is diſcoverable in Governments, has
been infuſed into them by the ſhock of a

* " Ignore-t-on que c'eſt en attaquant, en renverſant tous
les abus à la fois, qu'on peut eſperer de s'en voir delivré ſans
retour—que les reformes lentes & partielles ont toujours fini
par ne rien reformer : enfin que l'abus que l'on conſerve
eſt l'appui & bientot le reſtaurateur de tousceux qu'on
avoir detruits."—*Adreſſe aux François par l'Evêque*
........—11 Février 1790.

revolution,

revolution, and their fubfequent progrefs has been only the accumulation of abufe. It is hence that the moft enlightened politicians have recognized the neceffity of *frequently re-calling Governments to their firft principles* ; a truth equally fuggefted to the penetrating intellect of Machiavel, by his experience of the Florentine democracy, and by his refearch into the hiftory of ancient Commonwealths. —Whatever is good ought to be purfued at the moment it is attainable. The public voice, irrefiftible in a period of convulfion, is contemned with impunity, when dictated by that lethargy into which nations are lulled by the tranquil courfe of their ordinary affairs. The ardor of reform languifhes in unfupported tedioufnefs. It perifhes in an impotent ftruggle with adverfaries, who receive new ftrength from the progrefs of the day. No hope of great political improvement (let us repeat it) is to be entertained from tran-

quility,

quility*, for its natural operation is to ſtrengthen all thoſe who are intereſted in perpetuating abuſe. The National Aſſembly ſeized the moment of eradicating the corruptions and abuſes which afflicted their country. Their reform was total, that it might be commenſurate with the evil, and *no part of it was delayed*, becauſe to ſpare an abuſe at ſuch a period was to conſecrate it ; becauſe the enthuſiaſm which carries nations to ſuch enterprizes is ſhort-lived, and the opportunity of reform, if once neglected, might be irrevocably fled.

But let us aſcend to more general principles, and hazard bolder opinions. Let us grant that the ſtate of France was not ſo

---

* The only apparent exception to this principle is the caſe where Sovereigns make important conceſſions to appeaſe diſcontent, and avert convulſion. This, however, rightly underſtood, is no exception, for it ariſes evidently from the ſame cauſes, acting at a period leſs advanced in the progreſs of popular interpoſition.

deſperately

desperately incorrigible. Let us suppose that changes far more gentle, innovations far less extensive, would have remedied the grosser evils of her Government, and placed it almost on a level with free and celebrated Constitutions. These concessions, though too large for truth, will not convict the Assembly. By what principle of reason, or of justice, were they precluded from aspiring to give France a Government less imperfect, than *accident* had formed in other States ?—Who will be hardy enough to assert, that a better Constitution is not attainable than any which has hitherto appeared ? Is the limit of human wisdom to be estimated in the science of politics alone, by the extent of its present attainments ? Is the most sublime and difficult of all arts, the improvement of the social order, the alleviation of the miseries of the civil condition of man, to be alone stationary, amid the rapid progress of every other art, liberal and vulgar, to perfection ? Where would be the

atrocious

atrocious guilt of a grand experiment, to af-
certain the portion of freedom and happinefs,
that can be created by political inftitutions?

That guilt (if it be guilt) is imputable to
the National Affembly of France. They are
accufed of having rejected the guidance of experience, of having abandoned themfelves to
the illufion of theory, and of having facrificed great and attainable good to the magnificent chimeras of ideal excellence. If this
accufation be juft, if they have indeed abandoned *experience*, the bafis of human knowledge, as well as the guide of human action,
their conduct deferves no longer any ferious
argument; and if (as Mr. Burke more than
once infinuates) their contempt of it is
avowed and oftentatious, it was furely unworthy of him to have expended fo much
genius againft fo prepofterous an infanity.
But the explanation of *terms* will diminifh
our wonder—Experience may, both in the

arts

arts and in the conduct of human life, be regarded in a double view, either as finishing
models, or *principles*. An artist who frames
his machine in exact imitation of his prede-
cessor, is in the *first sense* said to be guided by
experience. In this sense all improvements
of human life, have been *deviations* from experience. The first visionary innovator was
the savage who built a cabin, or covered himself with a rug. If this be experience, man is
degraded to the unimproveable level of the
instinctive animals—But in the second ac-
ceptation, an artist is said to be guided by ex-
experience, when the infpection of a machine
discovers to him principles, which teach him
to improve it, or when the comparison of
many both with respect to their excellencies
and defects, enables him to frame another
more perfect machine, different from any he
had examined. In this latter sense, the National Assembly have perpetually availed
themselves of experience. History is an im-

menfe

menfe collection of experiments on the nature and effect of the various parts of various Governments. Some inflitutions are *experimentally* afcertained to be beneficial; fome to be moft indubitably deftructive. A third clafs, which produces partial good, obvioufly poffefs the capacity of improvement. What, on fuch a furvey, was the dictate of enlightened experience?—Not furely to follow the model of any of thofe Governments, in which thefe inftitutions lay indifcriminately mingled; but, like the mechanic, to compare and generalize; and, guided equally by experience, to imitate and reject. The procefs is in both cafes the fame. The rights and the nature of man are to the Legiflator what the general properties of matter are to the Mechanic, the firft guide, becaufe they are founded on the wideft experience. In the fecond clafs are to be ranked obfervations on the excellencies and defects of thofe Governments which have exifted, that teach the conftruction of a more perfect ma-

H

chine

chine. BUT EXPERIENCE IS THE BASIS OF ALL. Not the puny and trammelled experience of a *Statesman by trade*, who trembles at any change in the *tricks* which he has been taught, or the *routine* in which he has been accustomed to move, but an experience liberal and enlightened, which hears the testimony of ages and nations, and collects from it the general principles which regulate the mechanism of society.

Legislators are under no obligation to retain a constitution, because it has been found " *to-* " *lerably* to answer the common purposes of " Government." It is absurd to *expect*, but it is not absurd to *pursue* perfection. It is absurd to acquiesce in evils, of which the remedy is obvious, because they are less grievous than those which are endured by others. To suppose the social order is not capable of improvement from the progress of the human understanding, is to betray the inconsistent

absurdity

abſurdity of an arrogant confidence in our attainments, and an abject diſtruſt of our powers.
If indeed the ſum of evil produced by political
inſtitutions, even in the leaſt imperfect Governments, were ſmall, there might be ſome
pretence for this dread of innovation, this horror at remedy, which has raiſed ſuch a clamour over Europe : But, on the contrary, in
an eſtimate of the ſources of human miſery,
after granting that one portion is to be attributed to diſeaſe, and another to private vices,
it might perhaps be found that a *third equal*
part aroſe from the oppreſſions and corruptions
of Government, diſguiſed under various forms.
All the Governments that now exiſt in the
world (except the United States of America)
have been fortuitouſly formed. They are the
produce of chance, not the work of art. They
have been altered, impaired, improved and deſtroyed by accidental circumſtances, beyond
the foreſight or controul of wiſdom. Their
parts thrown up againſt preſent emergencies

H 2

formed

formed no fyftematic whole. It was certainly not to have been prefumed, that thefe *fortuitous Governments* fhould have furpaffed the works of intellect, and precluded all nearer approaches to perfection. Their origin without doubt furnifhes a ftrong prefumption of an oppofite nature. It might teach us to expect in them many difcordant principles, many jarring forms, much unmixed evil, and much imperfect good, many inftitutions which had long furvived their motive, and many of which reafon had never been the author, nor utility the object. Experience, *even in the beft of thefe Governments*, accords with fuch expectations.

A Government of *art*, the work of legiflative intellect, reared on the immutable bafis of natural right and general happinefs, which fhould combine the excellencies, and exclude the defects of the various conftitutions which chance had fcattered over the world, inftead

of

of being precluded by the perfection of any of thofe forms, was loudly demanded by the injuftice and abfurdity of them all. It was time that men fhould learn to tolerate nothing ancient that reafon does not refpect, and to fhrink from no novelty to which reafon may conduct. It was time that the human powers, fo long occupied by fubordinate objects, and inferior arts, fhould mark the commencement of a new æra in hiftory, by giving birth to the art of improving government, and increafing the civil happinefs of man. It was time, as it has been wifely and eloquently faid, that Legiflators, inftead of that narrow and daftardly *caution* which never ventures to lofe fight of ufage and precedent, fhould, guided by the *polarity* of reafon, hazard a bolder navigation, and difcover, in unexplored regions, the treafure of public felicity.

The talk of the French Legiflators was, however, lefs hazardous. The Philofophers of

　　　　Europe

Europe had for a century difcuffed all objects of public œconomy. The conviction of a great majority of enlightened men had, after many controverfies, become on moft queftions of general politics, uniform. A degree of certainty, perhaps nearly equal to that which fuch topics will admit, had been attained. The National Affembly were therefore not called on to make difcoveries. It was fuffi-cient if they were not uninfluenced by the opi-nions, nor exempt from the fpirit of their age. They were fortunate enough to live in a period when it was only neceffary to affix the ftamp of laws to what had been prepared by the refearch of philofophy. They will here, however, be attacked by a futile com-mon-place. The moft fpecious *theory*, it will be faid, is often impracticable, and any at-tempt to transfer fpeculative doctrines into the practice of States is chimerical and frantic. If by theory be underftood vague conjecture, the objection is not worth difcuffion; but if

by

by theory be meant inference from the moral nature and political ſtate of man, then I aſfert, that whatever ſuch theory pronounces to be true, muſt be practicable, and that whatever on the ſubject is impracticable, muſt be falſe. To reſume the illuſtration from the mechanical arts—Geometry, it may be juſtly ſaid, bears nearly the ſame relation to mechanics that abſtract reaſoning does to politics*. The *moral forces* which are employed in politics are the paſſions and intereſts of men, of which it is the province of metaphyſics to teach the nature and calculate the ſtrength, as mathematics do thoſe of the mechanical poweis. Now ſuppoſe it had been mathematically proved, that by a certain alteration in

---

* I confeſs my obligation for this parallel to a learned friend, who though ſo juſtly admired in the republic of letters for his excellent writings, is ſtill more ſo by his friends for the rich, original, and maſculine turn of thought that animates his converſation. But the *Continuator* of " the " Hiſtory of Phillip III." little needs my praiſe.

H 4

the

the ſtructure of a machine, its effect would be increaſed *four-fold*, would an inſtructed mechanic heſitate about the change ? Would he be deterred, becauſe he was the *firſt* to diſcover it ? Would he thus ſacrifice his own advantage to the blindneſs of his predeceſſors, and the obſtinacy of his cotemporaries ?—Let us ſuppoſe a whole nation, of which the artizans thus rejected theoretical improvement. Mechanics might there, as a *ſcience*, be moſt profoundly underſtood, while as an *art*, it exhibited nothing but rudeneſs and barbariſm. The principles of Newton and Archimedes might be taught in the ſchools, while the architecture of the people might not have reached beyond the cabins of New Holland, or the ſhip-building of the Eſquimaux. In a ſtate of political ſcience ſomewhat ſimilar has Europe continued for a great part of the eighteenth century *.

---

* Mechanics, becauſe no paſſion or intereſt is concerned in the perpetuity of abuſe, always yield to ſcientific improvement.

All the great queſtions of general politics had, as we have remarked, been nearly decided, and almoſt all the deciſions had been hoſtile to eſtabliſhed inſtitutions—yet theſe inſtitutions ſtill flouriſhed in all their vigour. The ſame man who cultivated liberal ſcience in his cabinet was compelled to adminiſter a barbarous juriſprudence on the bench. The ſame Montesquieu, who at Paris reaſoned as a philoſopher of the eighteenth, was compelled to decide at Bourdeaux as a magiſtrate of the fourteenth century. The apoſtles of toleration and the miniſters of the Inquiſition were cotemporaries. The torture continued to be practiſ-

provement. Politics, for the contrary reaſon, always reſiſt it. It was the remark of Hobbes, that if any intereſt or paſſion were concerned in diſputing the theorems of geometry, different opinions would be maintained regarding them. It has actually happened as if to juſtify the remark of that great man) that under the adminiſtration of Turgot a ſocial reform, grounded on a mathematical demonſtration ... as ſubmoſt worſtoſt So much for the tſoſ preſent of practice to theory.

ed in the age of Beccaria. The Baftile devoured its victims in the country of Turgot. The criminal code, even of nations in which it was the mildeft, was oppreffive and favage. The laws refpecting religious opinion, even where there was a *pretended* toleration, outraged the moft evident deductions of reafon. The true principles of commercial policy, though they had been reduced to demonftration, influenced the councils of no State. Such was the fantaftic fpectacle prefented by the European nations, who, philofophers in theory, and barbarous in practice, exhibited to the obferving eye two oppofite and inconfiftent afpects of manners and opinions. But fuch a State carried in itfelf the feeds of its own deftruction. Men will not long dwell in hovels, with the model of a palace before their eyes.

A State approaching to it in fome meafure exifted indeed in the ancient world. But the

art

art of Printing had not then provided a channel by which the opinions of the learned pafs infenfibly into the popular mind. A bulwark then exifted between the body of mankind and the reflecting few. They were diftinct nations, inhabiting the fame country, and the opinions of the one (I fpeak *comparatively* with modern times) had little influence on the other. But that bulwark is now levelled with the ground.—The convictions of philofophy infinuate themfelves by a flow, but certain progrefs, into popular fentiment. It is vain for the arrogance of learning to condemn the people to ignorance by reprobating fuperficial knowledge—The people cannot be profound, but the truths which regulate the moral and political relations of man, are at no great diftance from the furface. The great works in which difcoveries are contained cannot be read by the people ; but their fubftance paffes through a variety of minute and circuitous channels to the fhop and the hamlet. The

converfion

converfion of thefe works of unproductive fplendor into latent ufe and unobferved activity, refembles the procefs of nature in the external world. The expanfe of a noble lake, the courfe of a majeftic river, impofes on the imagination by every impreffion of dignity and fublimity. But it is the moifture that infenfibly arifes from them, which, gradually mingling with the foil, nourifhes all the luxuriancy of vegetation, fructifies and adorns the furfaee of the earth.

It may then be remarked, that though liberal opinions fo long exifted with abufive eftablifhments, it was not natural that this ftate of things fhould be permanent. The philofophers of antiquity did not, like ARCHIMEDES, want a fpot on which to fix their engines, but they wanted an engine to move the moral world. The prefs is that engine, which has fubjected the powerful to the wife, by governing the opinion of mankind. The difcuffion of great

truths

truths has prepared a body of laws for the National Assembly. The diffusion of political knowledge has *almost* prepared a people to receive them, and good men are at length permitted to indulge the *hope*, that the miseries of the human race are about to be alleviated; that hope may be illusive, for the grounds of its enemies are strong, the folly and villainy of men. Yet they who entertain it will feel no shame in defeat, and no envy of the triumphant prediction of their adversaries. *Mehercule malim cum Platone errare.* Whatever be the ultimate fate of the French Revolutionists, the friends of freedom must ever consider them as the authors of the greatest *attempt* that has hitherto been made in the cause of man. They never can cease to rejoice, that in the long catalogue of calamities and crimes which blacken human annals, the year 1789 presents one spot on which the eye of humanity may with complacence dwell.

SECTION

SECTION II.

Of the Composition and Character of the
NATIONAL ASSEMBLY.

EVENTS are rarely feparated by the Hiftorian from the character of thofe who are confpicuous in conducting them. From it alone they often receive the tinge which determines their moral colour.———— What is admired as noble pride in SULLY, would be execrated as intolerable arrogance in RICHLIEU. But the degree of this influence varies with the importance of the events. —In the ordinary affairs of State it is great, becaufe in fact they are only of importance to pofterity, as they illuftrate the characters of thofe who have acted diftinguifhed parts on the

theatre

theatre of the world. But in events, which themselves are of immenfe magnitude, the character of thofe who conduct them becomes of far lefs relative importance. No ignominy is at the prefent day reflected on the Revolution of 1688 from the ingratitude of CHURCHILL, or the treachery of Sunderland. The purity of Somers, and the profligacy of Spencer are equally loft in the fplendor of that great tranfaction, in the fenfe of its benefits, and the admiration of its juftice. No moral impreffion remains on our mind, but that whatever voice fpeaks truth, whatever hand eftablifhes freedom, delivers the oracles and difpenfes the gifts of God.

If this be true of the depofition of James II. it is for more fo of the French Revolution. Among many circumftances which diftinguifhed that event, as unexampled in hiftory, it was none of the leaft extraordinary, that it might truly be faid to have been a

REVOLUTION

REVOLUTION *without Leaders.* It was the effect of general caufes operating on the people. It was the revolt of a nation enlightened from a common fource. Hence it has derived its peculiar character, and hence the merits of the moft confpicuous individuals have had little influence on its progrefs.— The character of the National Affembly is of fecondary importance indeed. But as Mr. Burke has expended fo much invective againft that body, a few ftrictures on his account of it will not be improper.

The reprefentation of the third eftate was, as he juftly ftates, compofed of Lawyers, Phyficians, Merchants, Men of Letters, Tradefmen and Farmers. The choice was indeed limited by neceffity, for except men of thefe ranks and profeffions, the *people* had no objects of election, the Army and the Church being engroffed by the Nobility.——" No veftige of the landed intereft of the country appeared

" in this reprefentation."—For an obvious reafon—Becaufe the *Nobility* of France, like the Gentry of England, formed almoft exclufively the landed intereft of the kingdom.—Thefe profeffions then could only furnifh Reprefentatives for the *Tiers Etat.*—They form the majority of that middle rank among whom almoft all the fenfe and virtue of fociety refide. Their pretended incapacity for political affairs is an arrogant fiction of Statefmen which the hiftory of Revolutions has ever belied. Thefe emergencies have never failed to create politicians. The fubtle counfellors of Philip II. were baffled by the Burgomafters of Amfterdam and Leyden. The oppreffion of England fummoned into exiftence a race of Statefmen in her Colonies. The lawyers of Bofton, and the planters of Virginia, were transformed into minifters and negociators, who proved themfelves inferior neither in wifdom as legiflators, nor in dexterity as politicians. Thefe facts evince that the powers

of

of mankind have been unjuftly depreciated, the difficulty of Political affairs artfully mag- nified, and that there exifts a quantity of ta- lent *latent* among men, which ever rifes to the level of the great occafions that call it forth.

But the predominance of the profeffion of the law, that profeffion which teaches men " to augur mif-government at a diftance, and " fnuff the approach of tyranny in every " tainted breeze,"* was the fatal fource from which, if we may believe Mr. Burke, have arifen the calamities of France. The majo- rity of the Third Eftate was indeed compofed of lawyers. Their talents of public fpeaking, and their profeffional habits of examining queftions analogous to thofe of politics, ren- dered them the moft probable objects of popu- lar choice, efpecially in a *defpotic* country, where political fpeculation was no natural

* Mr. Burke's Speech on American Affairs, 1775.

amufement

amufement for the leifure of opulence. But it does not appear that the majority of them confifted of the unlearned, mechanical members of the profeffion*. From the lift of the States General, it fhould feem that the majority were *provincial advocates*, a name of very different import from *country attorneys*, and whofe importance is not to be eftimated by purely *Englifh* ideas.

All *forenfic* talent and eminence is *here* concentered in the capital. But in France, the inftitution of circuits did not exift. The provinces were imperfectly united, their laws various, their judicatures diftinct, and almoft independent. Twelve or thirteen Parliaments formed as many circles of advocates, who nearly emulated in learning and eloquence the Parifian Bar. This difperfion of talent was in

---

* See an accurate lift of them in the Supplement to the *Journal de Paris*, 31ft of May, 1789.

fome

some respect also the necessary effect of the immensity of the kingdom. No liberal man will in England bestow on the Irish and Scottish bar the epithet *provincial* with a view of degradation. The Parliaments of many Provinces in France, presented as wide a field for talent as the Supreme Courts of Ireland and Scotland. The Parliament of Rennes, for example, dispensed justice to a Province which contained two million three hundred thousand inhabitants* ; a population equal to that of some respectable kingdoms of Europe. The Cities of Bordeaux, Lyons, and Marseilles, surpass in wealth and population Copenhagen, Stockholm, Petersburg, and Berlin. Such were the theatres on which the Provincial Advocates of France pursued professional fame. A general Convention of the British empire would yield perhaps as distinguished a place to

---

* See a Report of the Population of France to the National Assembly, by M. Biron de la Tour, Engineer and Geographer to the King, 1790.

CURRAN

CURRAN and ERSKINE, and the other emi-
nent and accomplished barristers of Dublin and
Edinburgh, as to those of the capital. And
on the same principles have the *Thourets* and
Chapeliers of *Rouen*, and *Rennes*, acquired as
great an ascendant in the National Assembly
as the *Targets* and *Camus*'s of the Parisian bar.

The proof that this " *faculty*" influence, as
Mr. Burke chuses to phrase it, was not injuri-
ously predominant, is to be found in the decrees of the Assembly respecting the judicial
Order. It must on his system have been their
object to have established what he calls " a
" litigious Constitution." The contrary has
so notoriously been the case, all their decrees
have so obviously tended to lessen the importance of lawyers, by facilitating arbitrations,
by the adoption of juries, by diminishing the
expence and tediousness of suits, by the destruction of an intricate and barbarous jurisprudence, and by the simplicity introduced

into

into all judicial proceedings, that their fyftem has been accufed of a direct tendency to extinguifh the profeffion of the law. A fyftem which may be condemned as leading to vifionary excefs, but which cannot be pretended to bear very ftrong marks of the fuppofed afcendant of " *chicane.*"

To the lawyers, befides the parochial clergy, whom Mr. Burke contemptuoufly ftiles " *Country Curates**," were added, thofe Noblemen whom he fo feverely ftigmatizes as deferters from their Order. Yet the deputation of the Nobility who firft joined the Commons, and to whom therefore that title beft belongs, was not compofed of men whom defperate fortunes and profligate ambition prepare for civil confufion. In that number were found the heads of the moft ancient and opulent families in France, the Rochefoucaults, the

---

* It is hardly neceffary to remark that *Curé* means *Rector.*

Richlieus,

Richlieus, the Montmorencies, the Noailles.
Among them was M. Lally, who has received fuch liberal praife from Mr. Burke, and it
will be difficult to difcover in one individual
of that body any intereft adverfe to the prefervation of order, the fecurity of rank and wealth.

Having thus followed Mr. Burke in a very
fhort fketch of the claffes of men who compofe the Affembly, let us proceed to confider
his reprefentation of the fpirit and general
rules which have guided it, and which, according to him, have prefided in all the events of
the Revolution. " A cabal of philofophic
" Atheifts had confpired the abolition of Chrif-
" tianity. A monied intereft, who had grown
" into opulence from the calamities of France,
" contemned by the Nobility for their origin,
" and obnoxious to the people by their exac-
" tions, fought the alliance of thefe philofo-
" phers, by whofe influence on public opinion
" they were to avenge themfelves on the No-
" bility,

I 4

" bility, and conciliate the people. The Athe-
" ills were to be gratified with the extirpation
" of religion, and the Stock-jobbers with the
" fpoils of the Nobles and the Church.   The
" prominent features of the Revolution bear
" evidence of this league of impiety and ra-
" pine.   The degraded eftablifhment of the
" Church is preparatory to the abolition of
" Chriftianity, and all the financial operations
" are defigned to fill the coffers of the monied
" *capitalifts* of Paris."   Such is the theory of
Mr. Burke refpecting the fpirit and character
of the French Revolution.   To feparate the
portion of truth that gives plaufibility to his
ftatement from the falfehood that invefts it
with all its horrors, will however neither be
a tedious nor a difficult tafk.

The commercial, or monied intereft, has
in all nations of Europe (taken as a body)
been lefs prejudiced, more liberal, and more
intelligent, than the landed gentry.   Their
views

views are enlarged by a wider intercourse with mankind, and hence the important influence of commerce in liberalizing the modern world. We cannot wonder then that this enlightened clafs of men ever prove the moft ardent in the caufe of freedom, the moft zealous for political reform. It is not wonderful that philofophy fhould find in them more docile pupils; and liberty more active friends, than in a haughty and prejudiced ariftocracy. The Revolution in 1688 produced the fame divifion in England. The monied intereft long formed the ftrength of *Whiggifm*, while a majority of the landed gentlemen long continued zealous *Tories*. It is not unworthy of remark, that the pamphleteers of Toryifm accufed the Whigs of the fame hoftility to religion of which Mr. Burke now fuppofes the exiftence in France. They predicted the deftruction of the Church, and even the downfall of Chriftianity itfelf from the influx of Hereticks, Infidels, and Atheifts, which the new Govern-

ment

ment of England protected. Their pamphlets have perished with the topic which gave them birth, but the talents and fame of SWIFT have preserved his, which furnish abundant proof of this coincidence in clamour between the enemies of the English, and the detractors of the French Revolution.

That the philosophers, the other party in this unwonted alliance between affluence and literature, in this new union of authors and bankers, did prepare the Revolution by their writings, it is the glory of its admirers to avow*.

* Mr. Burke's remark on the English Free-thinkers is unworthy of him. It more resembles the rant by which Priests inflame the languid bigotry of their fanatical adherents, than the calm, ingenuous and manly criticism of a philosopher and a scholar. Had he made extensive enquiries among his learned friends, he must have found many who read and admired COLLINS's incomparable tract on Liberty and Necessity. Had he looked abroad into the world, he would have found many who still read the phi-

losophical

What the speculative opinions of these philosophers were on remote and mysterious questions, is here of no importance. It is not as Atheists, or Theists, but as political reasoners, that they are to be considered in a political Revolution. All their writing, on the subjects of metaphysics and theology, are foreign to the question. If Rousseau has had any influence in promoting the Revolution, it is not by his *Letters from the Mountain*, but by his *Social Contract*. If Voltaire contributed to spread liberality in France, it was not by his *Philosophical Dictionary*, but by his *Defences of Toleration*. The obloquy of their Atheism (if it existed) is personal—it does not belong to the Revolution, for that event could

fophical works of Bolingbroke, not as philosophy, but as eloquent and splendid declamation. What he means by " their successors," I *will* not conjecture. I *will* not suppose that, with Dr. Hurd, he regards David Hume as " a *puny* dialectician from the north ! !"—yet it is hard to understand him in any other sense.

neither

neither have been promoted nor retarded by abstract discussions of theology. The suppofition of their conspiracy for the abolition of Christianity, is one of the most extravagant chimeras that ever entered the human imagination. Let us grant their infidelity in the fulleft extent. Their philofophy must have taught them that the passions, whether rational or irrational, from which religion arifes, could be eradicated by no human power from the heart of man.—Their incredulity muft have made them indifferent what particular mode of religion might prevail. Thefe philofophers were not the Apoftles of any new Revelation that was to fupplant the faith of Chrift. They knew that the heart can on this fubject bear no void, and they had no intereft in fubftituting the Vedam, or the Koran for the Gofpel. They could have no reafonable motives to promote any revolution in the popular faith. Their purpofe was accomplifhed when the Priefthood was difarmed. What

ever

ever might be the freedom of their private
speculations, it was not against religion, but
against the Church, that their *political* hostility was directed.

But, says Mr. Burke, the degraded pen-
sionary establishment, and the elective constitution of the new Clergy of France is sufficient evidence of the design. The Clergy are
to be made contemptible, that the popular reverence for religion may be destroyed, and the
way thus paved for its abolition. It is amus-
ing to examine the different aspects which
the same object presents to various minds.—
Mr. Hume vindicates the policy of an opulent establishment, as a bribe which purchases
the useful inactivity of the Priesthood. They
have no longer, he supposes, any temptation
to court a dangerous dominion over the minds
of the people, because they are independent of
it. Had that philosopher been now alive, he
must on the same principle have remarked, that

an elective Clergy and a scantily endowed Church, had a far greater tendency to produce fanaticism than irreligion. If the priests depend on the people, they can only maintain their influence by cultivating those passions in the popular mind, which gave them an ascendant over it. Their only influence is through the religious passions. To inflame these passions is their obvious ambition. Priests would be in a nation of sceptics contemptible, in a nation of fanatics omnipotent. It has not therefore been more uniformly the habit of a Clergy that depends on a court, to practise servility, than it would evidently be the interest of a Clergy that depends on the people to cultivate religious enthusiasm. Scanty endowments too would still more dispose them to seek a consolation for the absence of worldly enjoyments, in the exercise of a flattering authority over the minds of men.——— Such would have been the view of a philosopher who was *indifferent* to Christianity, on the

new Conftitution of the Gallican Church.
He never would dream of rendering religion
unpopular by devoting her minifters to activity, contemptible by compelling them to purity, or unamiable by divefting her of invidious fplendor. He would have feen in thefe
changes the feeds of enthufiafm and not of
laxity. But he would be confoled by the reflection, that the diffolution of the Church
as a corporation had broken the ftrength of
the priefthood, that religious liberty without
limit would difarm the animofity of fects, and
the diffufion of knowledge reftrain the extra-
vagances of fanaticifm.

I am here only confidering the eftablifhment of the Gallican Church as an evidence
of the fuppofed plan for abolifhing Chriftianity. I am not difcuffing its intrinfic merits.——I therefore perfonate a philofophic
Infidel, and it appears that he muft have dif-
cerned the tendency of this plan to be directly

the

the reverſe of that conceived by Mr. Burke.
* There is a fact, which though little known,
amounts almoſt to a proof of the ſolidity of
theſe ſpeculations. It is in truth rather a *fanatical* than an irreligious ſpirit which dictates
the organization of the Church of France. A
Janſeniſtical party was formed in the Parlia-

* The theory of Mr. Burke on the ſubject of Religious
Eſtabliſhments, I am utterly at a loſs to comprehend. He
will not adopt the impious reaſoning of Mr. Hume, nor
does he ſuppoſe with Warburton any " *alliance* between
" Church and State," for he ſeems to conceive them to be
originally the ſame. When he or his admirers tranſlate his
ſtatements (*Reflections*, p. 145—6) into a ſeries of propo-
ſitions expreſſed in preciſe and unadorned Engliſh, they may
become the proper objects of argument and diſcuſſion. In
their preſent ſtate they irreſiſtibly remind one of the obſer-
vations of Lord Bacon. " Pugnax enim philoſophiæ genus
" & ſophiſticum illaqueat intellectum at illud alterum
" phantaſticum et tumidum et quaſi *poeticum* magis *blanditur*
" intellectui. Ineſt enim homini quædam intellectus am-
" bitio non minor quam voluntatis præſertim in *ingeniis altis*
" et elevatis." Nov. Org. § XLV.

ments

ments of that kingdom by their long hoftilities with the Jefuits and the See of Rome.
Members of this party have in the National
Affembly, by the fupport of the inferior
Clergy, acquired the afcendant in ecclefiaftical affairs. Of this number is M. Camus.
The new conftitution of the Church accords
exactly with their dogmas*. The Clergy
are, according to their principles, to notify to
the Bifhop of Rome their union in doctrine,
but to recognize no fubordination in difcipline. The fpirit of a dormant fect thus revived in a new fhape at fo critical a period,
the unintelligible fubleties of the Bifhop of
Ypres thus influencing the inftitutions of the
eighteenth century, might prefent an ample
field of reflexion to an enlightened obferver
of human affairs. But it is fufficient for our

* See the fpeech of *M. Syeyes* on Religious Liberty,
where he reproaches the Ecclefiaftical Committee with
abufing the Revolution for the revival of *Port Royal*, the
famous *Janfeniftical* Seminary. See alfo M. CONDORCET
fur l'Inftruction Publique.

K

purpofe

purpose to obferve the fact, and to remark the error of attributing to the hoftile defigns of atheifm what in fo great a degree has arifen from the ardour of religious zeal.

The eftablifhment of the Church has not furnifhed any evidence of that to which Mr. Burke has attributed fo much of the fyftem of the National Affembly. Let us examine whether a fhort review of their financial operations will fupply the defect.

* To the gloomy ftatement of French finance offered by M. Calonne, let us oppofe

* It may be remarked, that on the fubject of finance I have declined all details. They were not neceffary to my purpofe, which was to confider the Affembly's arrangements of revenue, more with a view to their SUPPOSED POLITI-CAL PROFLIGACY. than to their financial talents. I confine myfelf, therefore, to general remarks, and this I do with the greater pleafure, becaufe I know the ability with which the fubject will be treated by a gentleman, whom general fagacity and accurate knowledge of France finance, peculiarly qualify for expofing to the public the errors of Mr. Burke.

the report of M. de la Rochefoucault, from the Committee of Finance on the 9th of Dec. 1790, which from premifes that appear indif- putable, infers a confiderable *furplus* revenue in the prefent year. The purity of that dif- tinguifhed perfon has hitherto been arraigned by no party. That underftanding muft be of a fingular conftruction which could hefitate between the Duc de la Rochefoucault and M. Calonne. But without ufing this *argumentum ad verecundiam*, we are to remark, that there are radical faults, which vitiate the whole calculations of that minifter, and the confe- quent reafonings of Mr. Burke. They are taken from a year of confufion, of languifhing and difturbed induftry, and abfurdly applied to the future revenue of peaceful and flou- rifhing periods. They are taken from a year in which much of the old revenue of the State had been deftroyed, and during which the Affembly had fcarcely commenced its fcheme of taxation. It is an error to affert

K 2

that

that the Assembly had destroyed the former oppressive taxes, which formed so important a source of revenue. These taxes perished in the expiring struggle of the ancient Government. No authority remaining in France could have maintained them. Calculations cannot fail of being most grossly illusive, which are formed from a period when so many taxes had failed before they could be replaced by new impost, and when productive industry itself, the source of all revenue, was struck with a momentary palsy*. Mr. Burke discusses the financial merit of the Assembly before it had begun its system of taxation. It is premature to examine their general scheme

* Mr. Burke exults in the deficiency confessed by M. Vernet of 8 millions sterling, in August, 1790. He follows it with an invective against the National Assembly, which one simple reflexion would have repressed. The suppression of the *gabelle* alone accounted for almost a half of that deficiency! Its produce was estimated at 60 millions of livres, or about two millions and a half sterling.

of

of revenue, or to eftablifh general maxims on the furvey of a period which may be confidered as an *interregnum* of finance.

The only financial operation which may be regarded as complete is their emiffion of *affignats*—the eftablifhment of a paper money, the reprefentative of the national property, which, while it facilitated the fale of that property, fhould fupply the abfence of *specie* in ordinary circulation. On this, as well as moft other topics, the predictions of their enemies have been completely falfified. They predicted, that no purchafers would be found hardy enough to truft their property on the tenure of a new and infecure eftablifhment. But the national property has in all parts of France been bought with the greateft avidity. They predicted that the eftimate of its value would prove exaggerated ; but it has fold uniformly for double and treble that eftimate. They have predicted that the depreciation of

the

the *assignats* would in effect heighten the price of the necessaries of life, and fall with the most cruel severity on the most indigent class of mankind: The even has however been, that the *assignats*, supported in their credit by the rapid sale of the property which they represented, have kept almost at *par*, that the price of the necessaries of life has lowered, and the sufferings of the indigent been considerably alleviated. Many millions of *assignats*, already committed to the flames, form the most unanswerable reply to the objections urged against them*.

Many purchasers, not availing themselves of that indulgence for gradual payment, which in so immense a sale was unavoidable, have paid the whole price in advance. This has been peculiarly the case in the Northern Provinces, where opulent farmers have been

---

* At this moment nearly *one-third*.

the

the chief purchasers; a happy circumstance, if it only tended to multiply that most useful and respectable class of men, who are proprietors and cultivators of the ground.

The evils of this emission in the circumstances of France were transient; the beneficial effects permanent. Two great objects were to be obtained by it, one of policy, and another of finance. The first was to attach a great body of Proprietors to the Revolution, on the stability of which depended the security of their fortunes. This is what Mr. Burke terms, making them accomplices in confiscation, though it was precisely the policy adopted by the English Revolutionists, when they favoured the growth of a national debt, to interest a body of creditors in the permanence of their new establishment. To render the attainment of the other great object, the liquidation of the public debt, improbable, M. Calonne has been reduced to so

gross

grofs a mifreprefentation, as to ftate the probable value of the national property at only
two *milliards*, (about 83 millions fterling)
though the beft calculations have rated it at
more than double that fum.   There is every
probability that this immenfe national eftate
will fpeedily difburden France of the greateft
part of her national debt, remove the load of
impoft under which her induftry has groaned,
and open to her that career of profperity for
which fhe was fo evidently deftined by the
bounty of Nature. With thefe great benefits,
with the acquittal of the public debt, and the
ftability of freedom, this operation has, it
muft be confeffed, produced fome evils.   It
cannot be denied to have promoted, in fome
degree, a fpirit of gambling, and it may give
an undue afcendant in the municipal bodies to
the agents of the paper circulation.   But thefe
evils are fugitive. The moment that witneffes
the extinction of *affignats*, by the complete
fale of the national lands, muft terminate

them :

them; and that period, our paft experience renders probable, is not very remote. There was one general view, which to perfons converfant in political economy, would, from the commencement of the operation have appeared decifive. Either the *affignats* were to retain their value, or they were not. If they retained their value, none of the apprehended evils could arife from them. If they were difcredited, every fall in their value was a new motive to their holders to exchange them for national lands. No man would retain depreciated paper who could acquire folid property. If a great portion of them were thus employed, the value of thofe left in circulation muft immediately rife, both becaufe their number was diminifhed, and their fecurity become more obvious. The fall of their value muft have haftened the fale of the lands, and the fale of the lands muft have remedied the fall their value. The failure, as a medium of circulation, muft have improved them as an

instrument

inftrument of fale; and their fuccefs as an inftrument of fale muft in return have reftored their utility as a medium of circulation. *This* action and re-action was inevitable, though the flight depreciation of the *affignats* had not made its effects very confpicuous in France.

So determined is the oppofition of Mr. Burke to the : fures of the Affembly which regard the finances of the Church, that even monaftic inftitutions have in him found an advocate. Let us difcufs the arguments which he urges for the prefervation of thefe monuments of human madnefs. In fupport of an opinion fo fingular, he produces one *moral* and one *commercial* reafon*. " In mo-
" naftic inftitutions," in his opinion, " was
" found a great *power* for the mechanifm
" of politic benevolence."—" To deftroy any

* Burke, p. 232—41.

" *power*

" *power* growing wild from the rank produc-
" tive force of the human mind, is almost
" tantamount, in the moral world, to the
" deftruction of the apparently-active proper-
" ties of bodies in the material." In one
word, the fpirit and the inftitutions of monachifm were an inftrument in the hand of the
Legiflator, which he ought to have converted
to fome public ufe. I confefs myfelf fo far
to fhare the blindnefs of the National Affembly, that I cannot form the moft remote
conjecture concerning the various ufes which
" have fuggefted themfelves to a contriving
" mind." But without expatiating on them,
let us attempt to conftruct an anfwer to his
argument on a broader bafis. The moral
powers by which a Legiflator moves the mind
of man are his paffions; and if the infane fanaticifm which firft peopled the deferts of
Upper Egypt with anchorites, ftill exifted in
Europe, the Legiflator muft attempt the *di-
rection* of a fpirit which humanity forbad him

to

to perfecute, and wifdom to neglect. But monaftic inftitutions have for ages furvived the fpirit which gave them birth. It was not neceffary for any Legiflature to deftroy " that " power growing wild out of the rank pro- " ductive force of the human mind," from which monachifm had arifen. It was like all other furious and unnatural paffions, in its nature tranfient. It languifhed in the difcredit of miracles and the abfence of perfecution, and was gradually melted down in the funfhine of tranquillity and opulence fo long enjoyed by the Church. The foul which actuated monachifm had fled. The fkeleton only remained to load and deface fociety.— The dens of fanaticifm, where they did not become the receffes of fenfuality, were converted into the ftyes of indolence and apathy. The moral power therefore no longer exifted, for the fpirit by which the Legiflator could alone have moved thefe bodies was no more. The product of fanaticifm was therefore not

fit

fit to be the inftrument of wifdom. Nor had any new fpirit fucceeded which might be an inftrument in the hands of legiflative fkill. Thefe fhort-lived phrenzies leave behind them an *inert* product, in the fame manner as, when the fury and fplendor of volcanic eruption is paft for ages, there ftill remains a mafs of *lava* to encumber the foil, and deform the afpect of the earth*.

The

---

* It is urged by Mr. Burke, as a fpecies of incidental defence of monachifm, that there are many modes of induftry, from which benevolence would rather refcue men than from monaftic quiet. This muft be allowed, in one view, to be true. But, though the laws *muft permit* the natural progrefs which produces this fpecies of labour, does it follow, that they ought to create monaftic feclufion? Is the exiftence of one fource of mifery a reafon for opening another! Becaufe noxious drudgery *muft* be tolerated, are we to *fanction* compulfory inutility?—Inftances of fimilar bad reafoning from what fociety *muft* fuffer to what fhe *ought* to enact, occur in other parts of Mr. Burke's production. We in England, he fays, do not think £.10,000 a year

worfe

The fale of the monaftic eftates is alfo queftioned by Mr. Burke on a commercial principle. The fum of his reafoning may be thus
expreffed. The furplus product of the earth
forms the income of the landed proprietor.
That furplus the expenditure of fome one
muft difperfe, and of what import is it to fociety, whether it be circulated by the expence
of one landholder, or of a fociety of monks.
A very fimple ftatement furnifhes an unanfwerable reply to this defence. The wealth
of fociety is its ftock of productive labour.
There muft, it is true, be unproductive confumers, but the fewer their number the greater

worfe in the hands of a Bifhop than in thofe of a Baronet or
a 'Squire. Exceffive inequality is in both cafes an enormous
evil. The laws *muft* permit property to grow as the courfe
of things effect it. But ought they to add a new factitious
evil to this natural and irremediable one? They cannot avoid
inequality in the income of *property*, becaufe they muft permit property to diftribute itfelf. But they can remedy exceffive inequalities in the income of *office*, becaufe the income and the office are their creatures.

(all

(all things else being the same) muft be the opulence of a State. The poffeffion of an eftate by a fociety of monks eftablifhes, let us fuppofe forty, unproductive confumers. The poffeffion of the fame eftate by a fingle landholder only neceffarily produces one. It is therefore evident there is forty times the quantity of labour fubtracted from the public ftock, in the firft cafe, that there is in the fecond. If it be objected that the domeftics of a landholder are unproductive, let it be remarked that a monaftry has its fervants, and that thofe of a *lay* proprietor are not *profeffionally* and perpetually unproductive, as many of them become farmers and artizans, and it is to be obferved above all, that many of them are married.—Nothing then can appear on a plain commercial view of the fubject more evident than the diftinction between lay and monkifh landholders. It is furely unneceffary to appeal to the motives which has every where produced ftatutes of *Mortmain*, the neglected

eftate

eſtate in which the land of ecclefiaſtical corporations is fuffered to remain, and the infinite utility which arifes from changes of property in land. The face of thofe countries
where the transfers have been moſt rapid, will
fufficiently prove their benefit. Purchafers
feldom adventure without fortune, and the
novelty of their acquifition infpires them
with the ardor of improvement.

No doubt can be entertained that the eſtates
poſſeſſed by the Church will encreafe im-
menfely in their value. It is vain to fay that
they will be transferred to Stock-jobbers. Situations, not names, are to be confidered in
human affairs. He that has once taſted the indolence and authority of a land-holder, will
with difficulty return to the comparative fervility and drudgery of a monied capitaliſt.
But fhould the ufurious habits of the immediate purchafer be inveterate, his fon will im-
bibe the fentiments of a landed proprietor from

his

his birth. The heir of the stock-jobbing *Alpheus* may acquire as perfectly the habits of an active improver of his patrimonial estate, as the children of *Cincinnatus*, or *Cato*.

To aid the feeblenefs of thefe arguments, Mr. Burke has brought forward a panegyrical enumeration of the objects on which monastic revenue is expended. On this masterpiece of fafcinating and magnificent eloquence it is impoffible to be lavifh of praife. It would have been quoted by QUINTILIAN as a fplendid model of rhetorical common-place. But criticifm is not our object, and, all that the difplay of fuch powers of oratory can on fuch a fubject fuggeft, is what might perhaps have ferved as a characteriftic motto to Mr. Burke's production.

Addidit invalidæ robur FACUNDIA caufæ.

L   SECT.

SECTION III.

Popular Excesses which attended the Revolution.

THAT no great Revolutions can be accomplished without excesses and miseries at which humanity revolts, is a truth which cannot be denied. This unfortunately is true, in a peculiar manner, of those Revolutions, which, like that of France, are strictly *popular*. Where the people are led by a faction, its leaders find no difficulty in the re-establishment of that order, which must be the object of their wishes, because it is the sole security of their power. But when a general movement of the popular mind levels a despotism with the ground, it is far less easy to

restrain

reftrain excefs. There is more refentment to fatiate and lefs authority to controul. The paffion which produced an effect fo tremendous, is too violent to fubfide in a moment into ferenity and fubmiffion. The fpirit of revolt breaks out with fatal violence after its object is deftroyed, and turns againft the order of freedom thofe arms by which it had fubdued the ftrength of tyranny. The attempt to *punifh* the fpirit that actuates a *people*, if it were juft, would be in vain, and if it were poffible, would be cruel. They are too *many* to be punifhed in a view of juftice, and too *ftrong* to be punifhed in a view of policy. The oftentation of vigor would in fuch a cafe prove the difplay of impotence, and the rigor of juftice conduct to the cruelty of extirpation. No remedy is therefore left but the progrefs of inftruction, the force of perfuafion, the mild authority of opinion. Thefe remedies, though infallible, are of flow operation; and in the interval which elapfes before a

L 2

calm

calm succeeds the boisterous moments of a
Revolution, it is vain to expect that a people,
inured to barbarism by their oppressors, and
which has ages of oppression to avenge, will
be punctiliously generous in their triumph,
nicely discriminative in their vengeance, or
cautiously mild in their mode of retaliation.
" They will break their chains on the heads
" of their oppressors*.

Such was the state of France, and such
were the obvious causes that gave birth to
scenes which the friends of freedom deplore
as tarnishing her triumphs. They *feel* these
evils as men of humanity. But they will not
bestow the name on that womanish and com-
plexional sensibility, towards which, even in
the still intercourse of private life, *indulgence*
is mingled with love. The only humanity

* The eloquent expression of Mr. Curran in the Parliament of Ireland, respecting the Revolution.

which,

which, in the great affairs of men, claims their refpect, is that manly and expanded humanity, which fixes its fteady eye on the object of general happinefs. The fenfibility which fhrinks at a prefent evil, without extending its views to future good, is not a virtue, for it is not a quality beneficial to mankind: It would arreft the arm of a Surgeon in amputating a gangrened limb, or the hand of a Judge in figning the fentence of a parricide. I do not fay, (God forbid!) that a crime may be committed for the profpect of good. Such a doctrine would fhake morals to their center. But the cafe of the French Revolutionifts is totally different. Has any moralift ever pretended, *that we are to decline the purfuit of a good which our duty prefcribed to us, becaufe we forefaw that fome partial and incidental evil would arif from it?* This is the true view of the queftion, and it is only by this principle that we are to eftimate the re-

fponfibility

fponfibility of the leaders of the Revolution
for the exceffes which attended it.

If any of thefe leaders had crimes in contemplation for the attainment of their purpofe,
I abandon them to merited obloquy and execration. The man who would erect freedom
on the ruins of morals, underftands nor loves
neither. But the number againft whom *this*
charge has ever been *infinuated*, is fo fmall,
that fuppofing (what I do not believe) its
truth, it only proves that corrupt and ambitious men will mix with great bodies. The
queftion with refpect to the reft, is reducible
to this—" Whether they were to abftain
" from eftablifhing a free Government, be-
" caufe they forefaw that it could not be ef-
" fected without confufion and temporary di-
" ftrefs—Whether they were to be deterred
" from purfuing that Conftitution which
" they deemed beft for their country, by the
" profpect

" profpect of partial and tranfient evils, or to
" be confoled for thefe calamities by the view
" of that happinefs to which their labours
" were to give ultimate permanence and diffu-
" fion ?"   A Minifter is not conceived to be
guilty of fyftematic immorality, becaufe he
balances the evils of the moft juft war with
that national fecurity that is produced by the
reputation of fpirit and power; nor ought the
Patriot, who balancing the evils of tranfient
anarchy with the ineftimable good of eftablifhed liberty, finds the laft preponderate in the
fcale.

Such, in fact, have ever been the reafonings of the leaders in thofe infurrections which
have preferved the remnant of freedom that
ftill exifts among mankind.   Holland, England, America, muft have reafoned thus, and
the different portions of liberty which they
enjoy, have been purchafed by the endurance
of far greater calamities than have been fuf-

L 4

fered

fered by France. It is unneceffary to appeal to the wars which for almoft a century af-flicted the Low Countries. But it may be neceffary to remind England of the price fhe paid for the eftablifhment at the Revolution. The difputed fucceffion which arofe from that event, produced a deftructive civil war in Ireland, two rebellions in Scotland, the confequent flaughter and banifhment of thoufands of citizens, with the wideft confifcation of their properties ; not to mention the continental connections into which it plunged England, the foreign wars in which it engaged us, and the neceffity thus impofed upon us of maintaining a ftanding army, and accumulating an enormous public debt*.

* Yet this was only the combat of reafon and freedom againft one prejudice, that of hereditary right, whereas the French Revolution is, as has been fublimely faid by the BISHOP OF AUTUN, " Le premier combat qui fe foit jamais " livrée entre TOUS les PRINCIPES et TOUTES les ER-" REURS !—*Addreffe aux François*, 11 *Fev.* 1790.

The

The freedom of America was purchafed by calamities ftill more inevitable. The authors of the Revolution muft have forefeen them, for they were not contingent or remote, but ready in a moment to burft on their heads. Their cafe is moft fimilar to that of France, and beft anfwers one of Mr. Burke's moft triumphant arguments. They enjoyed *fome* liberty, which their oppreffors did not attack. The object of refiftance was conceded in the progrefs of the war.—But like France, after the conceffions of her King, they refufed to acquiefce in an imperfect liberty, when a more perfect one was within their reach. They purfued what Mr. Burke, *whatever were his then fentiments,* on his *prefent* fyftem, muft reprobate as a fpeculative and ideal good. They fought their beloved independence through new calamities, through the prolonged horrors of civil war. ——" Their refiftance," *from that moment,* " was againft conceffion. Their blows were

" aimed

" aimed at a hand holding forth immunity
" and favours."—Events have indeed juftified
that noble refiftance. America has emerged
from her ftruggle into tranquillity and freedom, into affluence and credit.—The authors
of her Conftitution have conftructed a great
permanent *experimental anfwer* to the fo-
phifms and declamations of the detractors of
liberty.

But what proportion did the price fhe paid
for fo great blefling bear to the tranfient
misfortunes which have afflicted France ?—
The extravagance of the comparifon fhocks
every unprejudiced mind. No feries of
events in hiftory have probably been more
widely, malignantly, and fyftematically ex-
aggerated than the French commotions. An
enraged, numerous and opulent body of
exiles, difperfed over Europe, have poffeffed
themfelves of every venal prefs, and filled
the public ear with a perpetual buz of the
crimes

crimes and horrors that were acting in France*. Inſtead of entering on minute ſcrutiny, of which the importance would neither expiate the tedioufnefs, nor reward the toil, let us content ourſelves with oppoſing one general fact to this hoſt of falſehoods. *No commercial houſe of importance has failed in France ſince the Revolution!*—How is this to be reconciled with the tales that have been circulated. As well might the transfers of the *Royal Exchange*, be quietly executed in the ferocious anarchy of *Gondar*,

---

* The *manœuvres* of M. Calonne, in England, are too obvious from the complexion of ſome Engliſh prints. He informs us, that he had it once in contemplation to have inſerted in a note at the end of his work extracts from the public papers in all the nations of Europe, demonſtrating the general horror in which the French Revolution was held. This note would have been the more amuſing, *as probably all theſe paragraphs were compoſed, and tranſmitted to theſe papers by M. Calonne himſelf*:—who would thus be the ſelf-created organ of the voice of Europe.

and

and the peaceful opulence of *Lombard-ftreet*, flourifh amidft *hordes* of *Galla* and *Agows*.— Commerce, which fhrinks from the breath of civil confufion, has refifted this tempeft, and a mighty Revolution has been accomplifhed with lefs commercial derangement than could arife from the bankruptcy of a fecond rate houfe in London, or Amfterdam. The manufacturers of Lyons, the merchants of Bourdeaux and Marfeilles, are filent amidft the lamentations of the Abbé Maury, M. Calonne, and Mr. Burke. Happy is that people whofe commerce flourifhes in *Ledgers*, while it is bewailed in orations, and remains untouched in *calculation*, while it expires in the pictures of eloquence. This unqueftionable fact, is on a fuch a fubject worth a thoufand arguments, and to any mind qualified to judge, muft expofe in their true light thofe execrable fabrications, which have founded fuch a " fenfelefs yell" through Europe.

But

But let us admit for a moment their truth, and take as a specimen of the evils of the Revolution, the number of lives which have been loft in its progrefs. That no poffibility of cavil may remain, let us furpafs in an ex-aggerated eftimate the utmoft audacity of falfehood. Let us make a ftatement, from which the moft frontlefs hireling of *Calonne* would fhrink. Let us for a moment fup-pofe, that in the courfe of the Revolution 20,000 lives have been loft. On the compa-rifon of even this lofs with parallel events in hiftory, is there any thing in it from which a manly and enlightened humanity will recoil? Can it be compared with the flaughter that eftablifhed American freedom, or with the fruits of the Englifh Revolution? But this comparifon is an injuftice to the argument. Compare it with the expenditure of blood by which in ordinary wars fo many perni-cious and ignoble objects are fought.——— Compare it with the blood fpilt by Eng-

land

land in the attempt to fubjugate America, and if fuch be the guilt of the Revolutionifts of France, for having, at the *hazard* of this evil, fought the eftablifhment of freedom, what new name of obloquy fhall be applied to the Minifter of England, who with the *certainty* of a deftruction fo much greater, attempted the eftablifhment of tyranny?

The illufion which prevents the effect of thefe comparifons, is not peculiar to Mr. Burke. The maffacres of war, and the murders committed by the fword of juftice, are difguifed by the folemnities which inveft them. But the wild juftice of the people has a naked and undifguifed horror. Its flighteft exertion awakens all our indignation, while murder and rapine, if arrayed in the gorgeous difguife of acts of State, may with impunity ftalk abroad. Our fentiments are reconciled to them in this form, and we forget that the evils of anarchy muft be fhort-lived,

lived, while thofe of defpotic government are fatally permanent.

Another illufion has particularly in England favored the exaggeration of the exiles. We judge of France by our own fituation. This is to view it through a falfe medium. We ought to judge of it by a comparifon with nations in *fimilar circumftances.* With us " the times may be moderate*, and therefore " ought to be peaceable :" But in France the times were not moderate, and could not be peaceable.

Let us correct that illufion of *moral optics* which makes near objects fo difproportionately large. Let us place the fcene of the French Revolution in a remote age, or in a diftant nation, and then let us calmly afk our own minds, whether the moft reafonable fubject of wonder be not its unexampled mild-

* Junius.

nefs,

nefs, and the fmall number of individuals crufhed in the fall of fo vaft a pile.

Such are the general reflexions fuggefted by the diforders of the French Revolution. Of thefe, the firft in point of time as well as of importance, was the Parifian infurrection and the capture of the Baftile. The mode in which that memorable event is treated by Mr. Burke, is worthy of notice. It occupies no confpicuous place in his work. It is only obfcurely and contemptuoufly hinted at as one of thofe examples of fuccefsful revolt, which have foftered a mutinous fpirit in the foldiery. "They have not forgot the "taking of the KING's CASTLES in Paris "and at Marfeilles. That they murdered "with impunity in both places the Gover- "nors has not efcaped their minds." (Burke, p. 307—8.) Such is the courtly circumlocution by which Mr. Burke defigns the Baftile— *the King's Caftle at Paris.* Such is the igno-

minious

minious language in which he speaks of the summary justice executed on the titled ruffian who was its Governor; and such is the apparent art with which he has thrown into the back ground invective and asperity, which if they had been prominent, would have provoked the indignation of mankind.

" *Je sais*," says Mounier, in the language of that frigid and scanty approbation that is extorted from an enemy, " *qu'il est* " *des circonstances qui legitiment l'insurrection,* " *& je mets dans ce nombre celles qui ont causé* " *le siège de la Bastille."* (*Exposé de Mounier,* p. 24.) But the admiration of Europe and of posterity, is not to be estimated by the penurious applause of M. Mounier, nor repressed by the insiduous hostility of Mr. Burke. It will correspond to the splendor of an insurrection, as much ennobled by heroism as it was justified by necessity, in which the citizens of Paris, the unwarlike inhabitants of a vo-

M

luptuous

luptuous capital, liftening to no voice but that of the danger which menaced their re- prefentatives, their families, and their coun- try, animated, inftead of being awed, by the hofts of difciplined mercenaries that invefted them on every fide, formed themfelves into an army, attacked with a gallantry and fuc- cefs equally incredible, a fortrefs formidable from its ftrength, and tremendous from its deftination; difpelled every hoftile project, and changed the deftiny of France. To pal- liate or excufe fuch a revolt, would be abject treachery to its principles. It was a cafe in which revolt was the dictate of virtue, and the path of duty; and in which fubmiffion would have been the moft daftardly bafenefs, and the fouleft crime. It was an action not to be excufed, but applauded; not to be par- doned, but admired. I fhall not therefore defcend to vindicate acts of heroifm, which hiftory will teach the remoteft pofterity to revere, and of which the recital is deftined to

kindle

kindle in unborn millions the holy enthufiafm of Freedom.

Commotions of another defcription early
followed the Revolution, partly arifing from
the general caufes before ftated, and partly
from others of more limited and local operation. The peafantry of the provinces, buried
for fo many ages in the darknefs of fervitude,
faw, indiftinctly and confufedly, in the firft
dawn of liberty, the boundaries of their duties
and their rights. It was no wonder that they
fhould little underftand that freedom which fo
long had been remote from their views. The
name conveyed to their ear a right to reject
all reftraint, to gratify every refentment, and
to attack all property. Ruffians mingled with
the deluded peafants, with hopes of booty,
and inflamed their ignorance and prejudices,
by forged acts of the King and the Affembly
authorizing their licentioufnefs. From thefe
circumftances arofe many calamities in the

 provinces.

provinces. The country houfes of many gentlemen were burnt, and fome obnoxious perfons were affaffinated. But one may without
exceffive fcepticifm doubt, whether they had
been the *mildeft mafters* whofe *chateaux* had
undergone that fate. Perhaps the peafants
had oppreffions to avenge, thofe filent grind-
ing oppreffions that form almoft the only in-
tercourfe of the rich with the indigent;
which though lefs flagrant than thofe of Government, are perhaps productive of more intolerable and diffufive mifery.

But whatever was the demerit of thefe exceffes, they can by no torture of reafon be
imputable to the National Affembly, or the
leaders of the Revolution. In what manner
were they to reprefs them? If they exerted
againft them their own authority with rigor,
they muft have provoked a civil war. If they
invigorated the police and tribunals of the de-
pofed Government, befides incurring the hazard

zard of the fame calamity, they put arms into the hands of their enemies. Placed in this *dilemma*, they were compelled to expect a flow remedy from the returning ferenity of the public mind, and from the progrefs of the new Government towards confiftence and vigor[*].

A degree of influence exerted by the people, far more than would be tolerated by a firm Government, or could exift in a ftate of tranquillity, muft be expected in the crifis of a

---

[*] If this ftatement be candid and exact, what fhall we think of the language of Mr. BURKE, when he fpeaks of the ASSEMBLY as " *authorizing* treafons, robberies, rapes, " affaffinations, flaughters, and burnings, throughout all " their harraffed land." P. 58. In another place he groupes together the legiflative extinction of the *Order* of Nobles with the popular exceffes committed againft *individual* Noblemen, to load the Affembly with the accumulated obloquy. *See p.* 200. A mode of proceeding more remarkable for controverfial dexterity than for candor.

 Revolution

Revolution which the *people* have made.—
They have too recent experience of their own
ſtrength to abſtain at once from exerting it.
Their political paſſions have been agitated by
too fierce a ſtorm to regain in a moment that
ſerenity which would expeſt with patient
acquieſcence the decrees of their Repreſentatives. From an inflamed multitude, who had
felt themſelves irreſiſtible, and whoſe fancy
annexed to the deciſion of every political queſtion the fate of their freedom, an undue interpoſition in the proceedings of the Legiſlature was to have been expeſted. The paſſions
which prompt it are vehement; the arguments
which prove its impropriety are remote and
refined. Too much, therefore, of this interpoſition was at ſuch a conjunſture inevitable.
It is without doubt a great evil, but it is irremediable. The ſubmiſſion of the people in a
period of tranquillity, degenerates into a liſt-
leſs and torpid negligence of public affairs,
and the fervor which the moment of Revolu-

tion

tion infpires, neceffarily produces the oppofite extreme. That, therefore, the conduct of the populace of Paris fhould not have been the moft decorous and circumfpect refpecting the deliberations of the Affembly, that it fhould be frequently irregular and tumultuous, was, in the nature of things, inevitable. But the horrible picture which Mr. Burke has drawn of that " ftern neceffity" under which this " captive" Affembly votes, is neither juftified by this conceffion, nor by the ftate of facts. It is the overcharged colouring of a fervid imagination. Thofe whom he alludes to, as driven away by affaffins, M. M. Lally and Mounier, might, furely, have remained with perfect fafety in an Affembly in which fuch furious invectives are daily bellowed forth with impunity againft the popular leaders. No man will deny, that that Member of the Minority enjoyed liberty of fpeech in its utmoft plenitude, who called M. Mirabeau " *Le*

" *plus vil de tous les affins.*" " The terrors

" of

" of the lamp-poft and bayonet" have hitherto been vifionary. Popular fury has hitherto
fpared the muft furious declaimers of Ariftocracy, and the only *decree*, fo far as I can difcern, which has even been *pretended* to have
been materially influenced by the populace, is
that refpecting the prerogatives of war and
peace. That tumult has frequently derogated
from the dignity and decorum which ought to
diftinguifh the deliberations of a legiflative
Affembly, is not to be denied. But the only
important queftion regards the *effeci* of thefe
tumults on their decifions. That their debates
have been tumultuous, is of little importance,
if their decifions have been independent.—
Even in the queftion of war and peace, " the
" higheft bidder at the auction of popula-
" rity* " did not fucceed. The fcheme of
M. Mirabeau, with few amendments, pre-
vailed, while the more " fplendidly popular"

* Burke, p. 353.

propofitions,

propofitions, which vefted in the Legiflature alone the prerogative of war and peace were rejected.

We are now conducted by the courfe of thefe ftrictures to the excefies committed at Verfailles on the 5th and 6th of October, 1789. After the moft careful perufal of the voluminous evidence before the *Chatelet*, of the controverfial pamphlets of M. M d'Orleans and Mounier, and of the official report of M. Chabroud to the Affembly, the details of the affair feem to me fo much involved in obfcurity and contradiction, that they afford little on which a candid mind can with confidence pronounce.

They afford, indeed, to frivolous and puerile adverfaries the means of convicting Mr. Burke of fome minute errors. Monf. *Afiomanbre*, the centinel at the Queen's-gate, it is true, furvives, but it is no lefs true, that

he

he was left for dead by his affaffins. On the comparifon of evidence, it feems probable, that the Queen's chamber was not broken into, " *that the afylum of beauty and Majefly was* " *not profaned**. But thefe flight corrections palliate little the atrocity, and alter not, in the leaft, the general complexion of thefe flagitious fcenes.

The moft important queftion which the fubject prefents is, whether the Parifian populace were the inftruments of confpirators, or whether their fatal march to Verfailles was a fpontaneous movement, produced by real or chimerical apprehenfions of plots againft their

* The expreffion of M. Chabroud. Five witneffes affert that the ruffians did not break into the Queen's chamber. Two give the account followed by Mr. Burke, and to give this preponderance its due force, let it be recollected, that the whole proceedings before the *Chatelet* were *ex parte*, See *Procedure Criminelle fait au Chatelet de Paris, &c. deux Parties.* PARIS, 1790.

freedom.

freedom. I confefs that I incline to the latter opinion.—*Natural caufes* feem to me adequate to account for the movement. A fcarcity of provifion is not denied to have exifted in Paris. The dinner of the body-guards might furely have provoked a people more tranquil than thofe of a city fcarce recovered from the fhock of a great Revolution. The maledictions poured forth againft the National Affembly, the infults offered to the patriotic cockade, the obnoxious ardor of *loyalty* difplayed on that occafion, might have awakened even the jealoufy of a people whofe ardor had been fated by the long enjoyment, and whofe alarms had been quieted by the fecure poffeffion of liberty. The efcape of the King would be the infallible fignal of civil war— the expofed fituation of the Royal refidence was therefore a fource of perpetual alarm. Thefe caufes, operating on that credulous jea- loufy which is the malady of the Public mind in times of civil confufion, which fees hoftility

and

and conspiracy on every side, seem sufficient
to have actuated the Parisian populace.

The apprehensions of the people in such a
period torture the most innocent and frivolous
accidents into proofs of sanguinary plots.—
Witness the *war of conspiracies* carried on by
the contending factions in the reign of Charles
the Second. The boldness with which such
charges are then fabricated, and the facility
with which they are credited, form indeed, in
the mind of a wise man, the strongest pre-
sumptions against their truth. It is in peru-
sing the history of such a period, that his scep-
ticism respecting conspiracies is the most vigilant. The research of two centuries has
not, in England, been able to decide disputes
which these accusations have produced. The
participation of Queen Mary in Babington's
Plot against Elizabeth, is still the subject of
controversy. We, at the present day, dispute
about the nature of the connection which sub-

sisted

fifted between Charles the Firſt and the Catholic inſurgents of Ireland. It has occupied the labour of a century to ſeparate truth from falſehood in the *Rye-houſe Plot*, to diſtinguiſh what both the friendſhip and enmity of cotemporaries confounded ; the views of the leaders from the ſchemes of the inferior conſpirators, and to diſcover that Ruſſel and Sydney had, indeed, conſpired a revolt, but that the underlings alone had plotted the aſſaſſination of the King.

It may indeed be ſaid, that ambitious leaders availed themſelves of the inflamed ſtate of Paris, that by falſe rumours, and exaggerated truths, they ſtimulated the revenge, and increaſed the fears of the populace ; that their emiſſaries, mixing with the mob, and concealed by its confuſion, were to execute their flagitious purpoſes ; that conſpiracy was thus joined to popular madneſs, and fanatics, as uſual, were the dupes of hypocritical leaders.

Such

Such is the accufation which has been made againft M. d'Orleans and M. Mirabeau. Their defence is not impofed on the admirers of the French Revolution. The Revolution is not ftigmatized, if its progrefs has not been altogether exempt from the interpofition of profligate ambition, from which who can guard any of the affairs of men ? Their caufe is foreign from that of Revolution, and to become the advocate of *individuals*, were to forget the dignity of a difcuffion that regards the rights and interefts of an emancipated nation. Of their guilt, however, I will be bold to fay, evidence was not collected by the malignant activity of an avowedly hoftile tribunal, which, for a moment, would have fufpended their acquittal by an Engiifh Jury. It will be no mean teftimony to the innocence of M. Mirabeau, that an opponent, not the mildeft in his enmity, nor the moft candid in his judgment, confeffed, that he faw no ferious ground of accufation againft him.——

" *J'avoue,* "

" *J'avoue*," fays the Abbé Maury, " *que je ne*
" *vois aucune imputation grave contre M. de*
" *Mirabeau* *."

One circumftance of repulfive improbability
is on the face of the project attributed to
them, that of intimidating the King into a
flight, that there might be a pretext for ele-
vating the Duke of Orleans to the office of
Regent. But the King could have had no
rational hopes of efcaping †, for he muft have
traverfed 200 miles of a country guarded by
a people in arms, before he could reach the
neareft frontier of the kingdom. The object
of the confpiracy then was too abfurd to be
purfued by confpirators, to whom talent and
fagacity have not been denied by their enemies. That the popular leaders in France

* Difcours de M. l'Abbé Maury dans l'Affemblée Nationale, 1 Octobre, 1790.

† The circumftances of his late attempt fanction this
reafoning.

did,

did, indeed, defire to fix the Royal refidence at Paris, it is impoffible to doubt. The name, the perfon, and the authority of the King, would have been moft formidable weapons in the hands of their adverfaries. The peace of their country, the ftability of their freedom, called on them to ufe every meafure that could prevent their enemies from getting poffeffion of that " Royal Figure." The name of the King would have fanctioned foreign powers in fupporting the ariftocracy. Their interpofi-tion, which *now* would be hoftility againft the King and kingdom, would *then* have been only regarded as aid againft rebellion. The name of the King would fafcinate and inflame the people of the provinces. Againft all thefe dreadful confequences, there feemed only one remedy, the refidence of the King at Paris. Whether that refidence is to be called a capti-vity, or by whatever other harfh name it is to be defigned, I will not hefitate to affirm, that the Parliament of England would have merited

the

the gratitude of their country, and of pofterity, by a fimilar prevention of the efcape of
Charles I. from London. The fame act
would have given ftability to their limitations
of kingly power, prevented the horrors of civil
war, the defpotifm of Cromwell, the relapfe
into fervitude under Charles II. and the calamities that followed the fubfequent Revolution. Fortunate would it have been for England, if the perfon of James II. had been retained while his authority was limited. She
would then have been circumftanced as France
is now; where the odium of perfonal mifconduct would have kept alive a falutary jealoufy
of power, the prejudices of *perfonal right*
would not have been provoked to hoftility
againft the Conftitution, nor the people compelled to entruft their new Sovereign with
exorbitant ftrength to defend *their* freedom
and *his* contefted throne. Such is the general
view which a calm furvey may fuggeft of the
6th October. The march to Verfailles feems

to

to have been the fpontaneous movement of an alarmed populace. Their views, and the fuggeftions of their leaders, were probably bounded by procuring the King to change his refidence to Paris, but the collifion of armed multitudes terminated in unforefeen exceffes and execrable crimes.

In the eye of Mr. Burke, however, thefe crimes and exceffes affume an afpect far more important than can be communicated to them by their own infulated guilt. They form, in his opinion, the crifis of a Revolution, far more important than any change of Government; a Revolution, in which the fentiments and opinions that have formed the manners of the European nations are to perifh. " The " age of chivalry is gone, and the glory of " Europe extinguifhed for ever." He follows this exclamation by an eloquent eulogium on chivalry, and by gloomy predictions of the future ftate of Europe, when the nation that has

been

been fo long accuftomed to give her the tone in arts and manners is thus debafed and corrupted. A caviller might remark that ages, much more near the meridian fervor of chivalry than ours, have witneffed a treatment of Queens as little gallant and generous as that of the Parifian mob. He might remind Mr. Burke, that in the age and country of Sir Philip Sidney, a Queen of France, whom no blindnefs to accomplifhment, no malignity of detraction could reduce to the level of *Maria Antonietta*, was, by " a nation of men " of honour and cavaliers," permitted to languifh in captivity and expire on a fcaffold; and he might add, that the manners of a country are more furely indicated by the fyftematic cruelty of a Sovereign, than by the licentious phrenzy of a mob. He might remark, that the mild fyftem of modern manners which furvived the maffacres with which fanaticifm had for a century defolated, and almoft barbarized Europe, might, perhaps,

refift

refift the fhock of one day's exceffes committed by a delirious populace.   He might thus,
perhaps, oppofe fpecious and popular topics to
the declamation of Mr. Burke.

But the fubject itfelf is, to an enlarged
thinker, fertile in reflexions of a different nature.   That fyftem of manners which arofe
among the Gothic nations of Europe, of which
chivalry was more properly the effufion than
the fource, is without doubt one of the moft
peculiar and interefting appearances in human
affairs.   The moral caufes which formed its
character have not, perhaps, been hitherto
inveftigated with the happieft fuccefs.   But
to confine ourfelves to the fubject before us.
Chivalry was certainly one of the moft prominent features and remarkable effects of this
fyftem of manners.   Candor muft confefs,
that this fingular inftitution is not *alone* admirable as a corrector of the ferocious ages in
which it flourifhed.   It contributed to polifh

and

and foften Europe. It paved the way for that diffufion of knowledge and extenfion of commerce which afterwards, in fome meafure, fupplanted it, and gave a new character to manners. Society is inevitably progreffive.—In Government, commerce has overthrown that " feudal and chivalrous fyftem" under whofe fhade it firft grew. In religion, learning has fubverted that fuperftition whofe opulent endowments had firft foftered it. Peculiar circumftances foftened the barbarifm of the middle ages to a degree which favoured the admiffion of commerce and the growth of knowledge. Thefe circumftances were connected with the manners of chivalry; but the fentiments peculiar to that inftitution could only be preferved by the fituation which gave them birth. They were therefore enfeebled in the progrefs from ferocity and turbulence, and almoft obliterated by tranquillity and refinement. But the auxiliaries which the manners of chivalry had in rude ages reared, ga-

N 3

thered

thered ſtrength from its weakneſs, and flouriſhed in its decay. Commerce and diffuſed
knowledge have, in fact, ſo compleatly af-
ſumed the aſcendant in poliſhed nations, that
it will be difficult to diſcover any relics of
Gothic manners, but in a fantaſtic exterior,
which has ſurvived the generous illuſions that
made theſe manners ſplendid and ſeductive.
Their *direct* influence has long ceaſed in Europe*, but their *indirect* influence, through
the medium of thoſe cauſes, which would not
perhaps have exiſted, but for the mildneſs
which, chivalry created in the midſt of a barbarous age, ſtill operates with encreaſing vigor.
The manners of the middle age were, in the
moſt ſingular ſenſe, compulſory. Enterpriz-
ing benevolence was produced by general
fierceneſs, gallant courteſy by ferocious rude-

---

* " Thoſe elfin charms that held in magic night
   " Our elder fame, and dimm'd our genuine light,
   " At length diſſolve in TRUTH's meridian ray."

neſs,

nefs, and artificial gentlenefs refifted the tor rent of natural barbarifm. But a lefs incongruous fyftem has fucceeded, in which commerce, which unites men's interefts, and knowledge, which excludes thofe prejudices that tend to embroil them, prefent a broader bafis for the ftability of civilized and beneficent manners.

Mr. Burke, indeed, forbodes the moft fatal confequences to literature from events, which he fuppofes to have given a mortal blow to the fpirit of chivalry. I have ever been protected from fuch apprehenfions by my belief in a very fimple truth, *that diffufed knowledge immortalizes itfelf.* A literature which is confined to a few, may be deftroyed by the maffacre of fcholars and the conflagration of libraries; but the diffufed knowledge of the prefent day could only be annihilated by the extirpation of the civilized part of mankind.

Far

Far from being hoftile to letters, the French Revolution has contributed to ferve their caufe in a manner hitherto unexampled in hiftory. The political and literary progrefs of nations has hitherto been the fame ; the period of their eminence in arts has alfo been the æra of their hiftorical fame ; and no example occurs in which great *political* fplendor has been fubfequent to the *Auguftan age* of a people. Previous to the year 1789, this might have been confidered as a maxim to which hiftory furnifhed no exception. But France, which is deftined to refute every abject and arrogant doctrine that would limit the human powers, prefents a new fcene. There the fhock of a Revolution has infufed the ardor of juvenile literature into a nation tending to decline. New arts are called forth when all feemed to have paffed their zenith. France enjoyed one Auguftan age, foftered by the favor of defpotifm. She feems about to witnefs another, created by the energy of freedom.

In

In the opinion of Mr. Burke, however, fhe
is advancing by rapid ftrides to ignorance and
barbarifm*. " Already," he informs us,
" there appears a poverty of conception, a
" coarfenefs and vulgarity in all the proceed-
" ings of the Affembly, and of all their in-
" ftructors. Their liberty is not liberal. Their
" fcience is prefumptuous ignorance. Their
" humanity is favage and brutal." To ani-
madvert on this modeft and courteous picture belongs not to the prefent fubject; and
impreffions cannot be difputed, more efpecially when their grounds are not affigned.
All that is left is, to declare oppofite impreffions with a confidence authorized by the example. The proceedings of the National
Affembly of France appear to me to contain
models of more fplendid eloquence, and examples of more profound political refearch,
than have been exhibited by any public body

* Burke, p. 118.

in

in modern times. I cannot therefore augur, from thefe proceedings, the downfall of philofophy, or the extinction of eloquence.

Thus various are the afpects which the French Revolution, not only in its influence on literature, but in its general tenor and fpirit, prefents to minds occupied by various opinions. To the eye of Mr. Burke, it exhibits nothing but a fcene of horror. In his mind it infpires no emotion but abhorrence of its leaders, commiferation of their victims, and alarms at the influence of an event which menaces the fubverfion of the policy, the arts, and the manners of the civilized world. Minds who view it through another medium are filled by it with every fentiment of admiration and triumph—of admiration due to fplendid exertions of virtue, and of triumph infpired by widening profpects of happinefs.

Nor

Nor ought it to be denied by the candor of philofophy, that events fo great are never fo *unmixed* as not to prefent a *double* afpect to the acutenefs and exaggeration of contending parties. The fame ardor of paffion which produces patriotic and legiflative heroifm becomes the fource of ferocious retaliation, of vifionary novelties, and precipitate change. The attempt were hopelefs to encreafe the fertility, without favouring the rank luxuriance of the foil. He that on fuch occafions expects unmixed good, ought to recollect, that the œconomy of Nature has invariably determined the equal influence of high paffions in giving birth to virtues and to crimes. The foil of *Attica* was remarked by antiquity as producing at once the moft delicious fruits and the moft virulent poifons. It is thus with the human mind; and to the frequency of convulfions in the ancient commonwealths, they owe thofe examples of fanguinary tumult and virtuous heroifm,

which

which diftinguifh their hiftory from the monotonous tranquillity of modern States. The
paffions of a *nation* cannot be kindled to the
degree which renders it capable of great atchievements, without endangering the commiffion of violences and crimes. The reforming ardor of a *Senate* cannot be inflamed
fufficiently to combat and overcome abufes,
without hazarding the evils which arife from
legiflative temerity. Such are the immutable
laws, which are more properly to be regarded
as libels on our nature than as charges againft
the French Revolution. The impartial voice
of Hiftory ought, doubtlefs, to record the
blemifhes as well as the glories of that great
event, and to contraft the delineation of it
which might have been given by the fpecious
and temperate *Toryifm* of Mr. HUME, with
that which we have received from the repulfive and fanatical invectives of Mr. BURKE,
might ftill be amufing and inftructive. Both
thefe great men would be adverfe to the Revolution ;

volution ; but it would not be difficult to diftinguifh between the undifguifed fury of an
eloquent *advocate* and the well diffembled
partiality of a philofophical JUDGE. Such
would probably be the difference between Mr.
Hume and Mr. Burke, were they to treat on
the French Revolution. The paffions of the
latter would only *feel* the exceffes which had
difhonoured it ; but the philofophy of the former would inftruct him, that the human
feelings, raifed by fuch events above the level
of ordinary fituations, become the fource of
a guilt and a heroifm unknown to the ordinary affairs of nations ; that fuch periods are
only fertile in thofe fublime virtues and fplendid crimes, which fo powerfully agitate and
intereft the heart of man.

SECT.

SECTION IV.

New Conſtitution of France.*

A Diſſertation approaching to complete-
neſs on the new Conſtitution of France
would, in fact, be a vaſt ſyſtem of political
ſcience. It would include a developement of
the principles that regulate every portion of
Government. So immenſe an attempt is little
ſuited to our preſent limits. But ſome remarks
on the prominent features of the French ſyſtem are exacted by the nature of our vindication. They will conſiſt chiefly of a defence of

---

* I cannot help exhorting thoſe who deſire to have accurate notions on the ſubject of this ſection, to peruſe and
ſtudy the delineation of the French Conſtitution, which
with a correctneſs ſo admirable, has been given by Mr.
CHRISTIE.

their

their grand THEORETIC PRINCIPLE, and their moſt *important* PRACTICAL INSTITUTION.

The principle of theory which has actuated the Legiſlators of France has been, that the object of all legitimate Government is the aſſertion and protection of the NATURAL RIGHTS OF MAN. They cannot indeed be abſolved of ſome deviations * from the path preſcribed by this great principle; few indeed compared with thoſe of any other body of whom hiſtory has preſerved any record; but too many for their own glory, and for the happineſs of the human race. This principle, however, is the baſis of their edifice, and if it be falſe, the ſtructure muſt fall to the ground. Againſt this principle, therefore, Mr. Burke has, with great judgment, directed his attack. Appeals to natural right are, ac-

* I particularly allude to their Colonial policy; but I think it candid to ſay, that I ſee in their full force the difficulties of that embarraſſing buſineſs.

cording

cording to him, inconfiftent and prepofterous.
A complete abdication and furrender of all natural right is made by man in entering into
Society, and the only rights which he retains
are CREATED by the compact which holds together the fociety of which he is member.
This doctrine he thus explicitly afferts.—
" The moment," fays he, " you abate any
" thing from the full rights of men each to
" govern himfelf, and fuffer any artificial po-
" fitive limitation on thofe rights, from that
" moment the whole organization of fociety
" becomes a confideration of convenience."
Burke, p. 89. " How can any man claim under
" the conventions of civil fociety rights which
" do not fo much as fuppofe its exiftence—
" Rights which are abfolutely repugnant to
" it?" Ibid. p. 88. To the fame purpofe is
his whole reafoning from p. 86 to p. 92. To
examine this doctrine, therefore, is of fundamental importance. To this effect it is not
neceffary to enter on any elaborate refearch
into

into the metaphyfical principles of politics and ethics. A full difcuffion of the fubject would indeed demand fuch an inveftigation*. The origin of natural rights muft have been illuftrated, and even their exiftence proved againft fome theorifts. But fuch an enquiry would have been inconfiftent with the nature of a publication, of which the object was to enforce conviction on the people. We are befides abfolved from the neceflity of it in a controverfy with Mr. Burke, who himfelf recognizes, in the moft ample form, the exiftence of thofe natural rights.

---

* It might, perhaps, not be difficult to prove, that far from a *furrender*, there is not even a *diminution* of the natural rights of men by their entrance into Society. The exiftence of fome union, with greater or lefs permanence and perfection of public force for public protection (*the effence of Government*) might be demonftrated to be coeval, and co-extended with man. All theories therefore, which fuppofe the *actual exiftence* of any ftate antecedent to the focial, might be convicted of futility and falfehood.

O

Granting

Granting their exiftence, the difcuffion is fhort. The only criterion by which we can eftimate the portion of natural right furrendered by man on entering into fociety is the *object* of the furrender. If more is claimed than that object exacts, it becomes not an *object*, but a *pretext*. Now the *object* for which a man refigns any portion of his natural fovereignty over his own actions is, that he may be protected from the *abufe* of the fame dominion in other men. No greater facrifice is therefore neceffary than is prefcribed by this object, the refignation of *powers* that in their exercife might be injurious to ANOTHER. Nothing, therefore, can be more fallacious than to pretend, that we are precluded in the focial ftate from *any* appeal to natural right*. It re-

* " Trouver une forme d'affociation qui defende & pro-
" tege de toute la force commune la perfonne & les biens
" de chaque affocié, & par laquelle chacun s'uniffant a tous
" n'obeiffe pourtant qu'a lui-même & refte auffi libre qu'au-
" paravant?" Rouffeau du Contrac Social, livre i. chap. vi.

I am

mains in its full integrity and vigor, if we except that *portion* of it which men mutually
facrifice for protection againft each other. They

I am not intimidated from quoting Rouffeau by the
derifion of Mr. Burke. Mr. Hume's report of his literary
fecret feems moft unfaithful. The fenfibility, the pride, the
fervor of his character, are pledges of his fincerity; and had
he even commenced with the fabrication of paradoxes, for
attracting attention, it would betray great ignorance of human nature to fuppofe, that in the ardor of conteft, and the
glory of fuccefs, he muft not have become the dupe of his
own illufions, a convert to his own impofture. It is indeed not
improbable, that when rallied on the eccentricity of his paradoxes, he might, in a moment of gay effufion, have fpoken
of them as a fport of fancy, and an experiment on the credulity of mankind. The Scottifh philofopher, inacceffible
to enthufiafm, and little fufceptible of thofe depreffions and
elevations, thofe agonies and raptures, fo familiar to the warm
and wayward heart of Rouffeau, neither knew the fport into
which he could be relaxed by gaiety, nor the ardor into
which he could be exalted by paffion. Mr. Burke, whofe
temperament is fo different, might have experimentally
known fuch variation, and learnt better to difcriminate between effufion and deliberate opinion.

O 2

do

do not furrender all; that is not exacted by the object they have in view; and whatever Government, under *pretence* of that furrender of natural right which is made for mutual fecurity, affumes more than that object *rigo-rouſly* prefcribes, is an ufurpation fupported by fophiſtry, a defpotifm varniſhed by illufion. It follows from this principle, that the fur-render of right muſt be *equal* in all the mem-bers of fociety, as the object is to all precifely the fame. In effect, fociety, inſtead of de-ſtroying, realizes and fubſtantiates equality. In a ſtate of *nature*, the equality of right is an impotent theory, which inequalities of ſtrength and ſkill every moment violate. It is called into energy and effect only by fociety. As natural equality is not conteſted, and that the fum of right furrendered by every indivi-dual is equal, it cannot be denied that the remnant ſpared by the focial compact muſt be equal alfo. *Civil* inequalities, or, more cor-rectly, civil diſtinction, muſt exiſt in the focial

body,

body, becauſe it muſt poſſeſs organs deſtined
for different functions. But political inequality
is equally inconſiſtent with the principles of
natural right and the object of civil inſtitution*.

Men retain a right to a ſhare in their own
Government, becauſe the exerciſe of the right
by one man is not inconſiſtent with its poſſeſſion by another, which is evidently the only
caſe where the ſurrender of a natural right
can be exacted by ſociety.

This doctrine is not more abſtractly evident than it is practically important. The
ſlighteſt deviation from it legitimates every
tyranny. If the only criterion of Govern-

" But as to the ſhare of power, authority and direc-
" tion which each individual ought to have in the manage-
" ment of a ſtate, that I muſt deny to be among the direct
" original rights of man in civil ſociety." This is evidently
denying the exiſtence of what has been called *political*, in
contradiſtinction to *civil* liberty.

O 3

ments

ments be the fuppofed *convention* which forms them, ALL are equally legitimate, for the only interpreter of the convention is the ufage of the Government, which is thus prepofte-roufly made its own ftandard. Governors muft, indeed, abide by the maxims of the Conftitution they adminifter; but what the Conftitution is, muft be on this fyftem immaterial. The King of France it does not, indeed, permit to put out the eyes of the Princes of the Blood, nor the Sophi of Perfia to have recourfe to *lettres de cachet*. They muft tyrannize by precedent, and opprefs in reverent imitation of the models confecrated by the ufage of defpotic predeceffors. But if they adhere to thefe, there is no remedy for the oppreffed, fince an appeal to the rights of Nature were treafon againft the principles of the focial union. If, indeed, any offence againft *precedent*, in the kind or degree of oppreffion, be committed, this theory may (though moft inconfiftently) permit refiftance. But as long

as the *forms* of any Government are preferved, it poffeffes, in a view of *juftice*, (whatever be its nature) equal claims to obedience.
This inference is irrefiftible, and it is *thus* evident, that the doctrines of Mr. Burke are
doubly refuted by the fallacy of the logic which
fupports them, and the abfurdity of the conclufions to which they lead.

They are alfo virtually contradicted by the
laws of all nations.   Were his opinions true,
the language of laws fhould be *permiffive*, not
reftrictive.   Had men furrendered all their
rights into the hands of the magiftrate, the
object of laws fhould have been to announce
the portion he was pleafed to return them, not
the part of which he is compelled to deprive
them.   The criminal code of all nations con-
fifts of *prohibitions*, and whatever is not prohibited by the law, men every where conceive
themfelves entitled to do with impunity.
They act on the principle which this language

of

of law teaches them, that they retain rights which no power can impair or infringe, which are not the boon of fociety, but the attribute of their nature. The rights of magiftrates and public officers are truly the creatures of Society. They, therefore, are guided, not by what the law does not *prohibit*, but by what it authorizes or enjoins. Were the rights of citizens equally created by focial inftitution, the language of the civil code would be fimilar, and the obedience of fubjects would have the fame limits.

This doctrine, thus falfe in its principles, abfurd in its conclufions, and contradicted by the avowed fenfe of mankind, is even abandoned by Mr. Burke himfelf. He is betrayed into a confeffion directly repugnant to his general principle.—" Whatever each man can " do without trefpaffing on others, he has a " RIGHT to do for himfelf, and he has a " RIGHT to a *fair portion* of ALL that fo " ciety,

" ciety, with all its combinations of fkill and
" force, can do for him." Either this right
is univerfal, or it is not. If it be univerfal, it
cannot be the offspring of convention, for
conventions muft be as various as forms of
government, and there are many of them
which do not recognize this right, nor place
man in this condition of juft equality. All
Governments, for example, which tolerate
flavery neglect this right: for a flave is neither
entitled to the fruits of his own induftry, nor
to any portion of what the combined force
and fkill of fociety produce. If it be not univerfal, it is no right at all, and it can only be
called a *privilege* accorded by fome Governments, and with-held by others. I can difcern no mode of efcaping from this dilemma,
but the avowal that thefe civil claims are the
remnant of thofe *metaphyfic* rights which Mr.
Burke holds in fuch abhorrence, but which it
feems the more natural object of fociety to
protect than deftroy.

But

But it may be urged, that though all appeals to the natural rights of men be not precluded by the focial compact, though the integrity and perfection in their civil ftate may *theoretically* be admitted, yet as men unqueftionably may refrain from the exercife of their rights, if they think their exertion unwife: and as Government is not a fcientific fubtlety, but a *practical* expedient for general good, all recourfe to thefe elaborate abftractions is frivolous and futile, and the grand queftion in Government is not its fource, but its tendency; not a queftion of right, but a confideration of expediency. Political forms, it may be added, are only the *means* of enfuring a certain portion of public felicity. If the *end* be confeffedly obtained, all difcuffion of the theoretical aptitude of the *means* to produce it is nugatory and redundant.

To this I anfwer, *firft*, that fuch reafoning will prove too much, and that, taken in its

proper

proper extent, it impeaches the great fyftem of morals, of which political principles form only a part. All morality is, no doubt, founded on a broad and general expediency—" *Ipfa* " *utilitas jufti prope mater & equi*, may be fafely adopted, without the referve dictated by the timid and inconftant philofophy of the Poet. Juftice is expediency, but it is expediency, fpeaking by general maxims, into which reafon has concentrated the experience of mankind. Every general principle of juftice is demonftrably expedient, and it is this utility alone that confers on it a moral obligation. But it would be fatal to the exiftence of morality, if the utility of every *particular act* were to be the fubject of deliberation in the mind of every moral agent. A general moral maxim is to be obeyed, even if the inutility is evident, becaufe the precedent of deviating more than balances any utility that may exift in the particular deviation. Political firft principles are of this defcription. They are only

moral

moral principles adapted to the civil union of men. When I affert that a man has a right to life, liberty, &c. I only mean to anunciate a MORAL MAXIM founded on *general interest*, which prohibits any attack on thefe poffeffions. In this primary and radical fenfe, all rights, natural as well as civil, arife from expediency. But the moment the moral edifice is reared, its bafis is hid from the eye for ever. The moment thefe maxims, which are founded on an utility that is paramount and perpetual, are embodied and confecrated, they ceafe to yield to partial and fubordinate expediency. It then becomes the perfection of virtue to confider, not whether an action be ufeful, but whether it be right.

The fame neceffity for the fubftitution of general maxims exifts in politics as in morals. Thefe precife and inflexible principles, which yield neither to the feductions of paffion, nor the fuggeftion of intereft, ought to be the

guide

guide of public as well as private morals.—
Acting according to the natural rights of men,
is only another expreſſion for acting according
to thoſe GENERAL MAXIMS of *ſocial morals*
which preſcribe what is *right and fit* in human
intercourſe.   We have proved that the ſocial
compact does not alter theſe maxims, or deſtroy theſe rights, and it inconteſtibly follows, from the ſame principles which guide
all morality, that no expediency can juſtify
their infraction.

The inflexibility of general principles is,
indeed, perhaps more neceſſary in political
morals than in any other claſs of actions.   If
the conſideration of expediency be admitted,
the queſtion recurs, who are to judge of it ?
They are never the *many* whoſe intereſt is at
ſtake :   They cannot judge, and no appeal to
them is hazarded.   They are the *few*, whoſe
intereſt is linked to the perpetuity of oppreſſion and abuſe.   Surely that Judge ought to

be

be bound down by the ſtricteſt rules, who is undeniably intereſted in the deciſion ; and he would ſcarcely be eſteemed a wiſe Legiſlator, who ſhould veſt in the next heir to a lunatic a diſcretionary power to judge of his ſanity or derangement. Far more neceſſary then is the obedience to general principles, and the maintenance of natural rights, in politics than in the morality of common life. The moment that the ſlendereſt infraction of theſe rights is permitted for motives of *convenience*, the bulwark of all upright politics is loſt. If a ſmall convenience will juſtify a little infraction, a greater pretended convenience will expiate a bolder violation. The Rubicon is paſt. Tyrants never ſeek in vain for ſophiſts. Pretences are multiplied without difficulty and without end. Nothing, therefore, but an inflexible adherence to the principles of general right can preſerve the purity, conſiſtency, and ſtability of a free State.

We

We have thus vindicated the firſt theoretical principle of French legiſlation. The doctrine of an abſolute ſurrender of natural rights by civil and ſocial man, has appeared to be deduced from inadequate premiſes; and to conduct to abſurd concluſions, to ſanctify the moſt atrocious deſpotiſm, to outrage the moſt avowed convictions of men, and, finally, to be abandoned, as hopeleſsly untenable by its author. The exiſtence and perfection of theſe rights being proved, the firſt duty of lawgivers and magiſtrates is to aſſert and protect them. Moſt wiſely and auſpiciouſly then did France commence her regenerating labours with a ſolemn declaration of theſe ſacred, inalienable, and impreſcriptible rights—a declaration which muſt be to the citizen the monitor of his duties, as well as the oracle of his rights; by a perpetual recurrence to which the deviations of the magiſtrate are to be checked, the tendency of power to abuſe corrected, and every political propoſition (being

compared

compared with the *end* of fociety) correctly and difpaffionately eftimated. Thefe declarations of the rights of men originated from the juvenile vigor of reafon and freedom in the new world, where the human mind was unincumbered with that vaft mafs of ufage and prejudice, which fo many ages of ignorance had accumulated, to load and deform fociety in Europe. France learned this, among other leffons, from America ; and it is perhaps the only expedient that can be devifed by human wifdom to keep alive the public vigilance againft the ufurpation of partial interefts, by perpetually prefenting the general right and the general intereft to the public eye. Thus far I truft will be found correct the fcientific principle which has been the Polar Star, by the light of which the National Affembly of France has hitherto navigated the veffel of the State, amid fo many tempefts howling deftruction around them on every fide.

There remains a much more extensive and complicated enquiry, the confideration of their political inftitutions. As it is impoffible to examine all, we muft limit our remarks to the moft important. To fpeak then generally of their Conftitution, it is a preliminary remark, that the application of the word DEMOCRACY to it is fallacious and illufive.——— If that word, indeed, be taken in its *etylomogical fenfe*, as the power of the people, it is a Democracy, and fo is all legitimate Government. But if it be taken in its hiftorical fenfe, it is not fo, for it does not refemble thofe Governments which have been called Democracies in ancient or modern times. In the ancient Democracies there was neither reprefentation nor divifion of powers. The rabble legiflated, judged and exercifed every political authority. I do not mean to deny that in Athens, the Democracy of which hiftory has tranfmitted to us the moft monuments, there did exift fome feeble controls.

P

But

But it has been well remarked, that a multi-tude, if it was compofed of NEWTONS, muft be a mob. Their will muft be equally un-wife, unjuft, and irrefiftible. The authority of a corrupt and tumultuous populace has in-deed by the beft writers of antiquity been re-garded rather as an Ochlocracy than a Demo-cracy, as the defpotifm of the rabble, not the dominion of the people. It is a degenerate Democracy. It is a febrile paroxyfm of the focial body, which muft fpeedily terminate in convalefcence or diffolution.

The New Conftitution of France is almoft directly the reverfe of thefe forms. It vefts the legiflative authority in the Reprefentatives of the people, the executive in an hereditary Firft Magiftrate, and the judicial in Judges, periodically elected, unconnected either with the Legiflature or with the executive Magif-trate. To confound fuch a conftitution with the Democracies of antiquity, for the purpofe

of

of quoting hiſtorical and experimental evidence againſt it, is to recur to the moſt paltry
and ſhallow arts of ſophiſtry.———In diſcuſ-
ſing it, on the preſent occaſion, the firſt
queſtion that ariſes regards the mode of conſtituting the Legiſlature, and the firſt diviſion
of this queſtion, which conſiders the right
of ſuffrage, is of primary importance in
Commonwealths. Here I moſt cordially agree
with Mr. Burke * in reprobating the impotent
and prepoſterous qualification by which the
Aſſembly have *disfranchiſed* every citizen who
does not pay a direct contribution equivalent
to the price of three days labour. Nothing
can be more evident than its inefficacy for any
purpoſe but the diſplay of inconſiſtency, and
the violation of juſtice. But theſe remarks
were made at the moment of diſcuſſion in
France, and the plan † was combated in the

* P. 257—8.

† For the hiſtory of this decree, the 27th and 29th days
of October, 1789, ſee the *Procès verbaux* of theſe days.—

 See

Affembly with all the force of reafon and eloquence by the moft confpicuous leaders of the
popular party. M. M. Mirabeau, Target, and
Petion, more particularly diftinguifhed themfelves by their oppofition. But the more timid
and prejudiced members of the democratic
party fhrunk from fo bold an innovation in
political fyftems, as JUSTICE. They fluctu-
ated between their principles and their prejudices, and the ftruggle terminated in an illufive compromife, the conftant refource of feeble and temporizing characters. They were
content that *little* practical evil fhould in fact
be produced.—Their views were not fufficiently enlarged and exalted to perceive, that
the INVIOLABILITY of PRINCIPLES is the
Palladium of virtue and of freedom. The members of this defcription do not, indeed, form
the majority of their party; but Ariftocratic

alfo the *Journal de Paris*, No. 301, & *Les Revolutions
de Paris*, No. 17, p. 73, & *feq.* Thefe authorities amply
corroborate the affertions of the text.

minority,

minority, anxious for whatever might difho-
nor or embarrafs the Affembly, eagerly coalefced with them, and ftained the infant Conftitution with this abfurd ufurpation.

An enlightened and refpectable antagonift
of Mr. Burke has attempted the defence of
this meafure. In a letter to *Earl Stanhope*,
p. 78—9, it is contended, that the fpirit of
this regulation accords exactly with the principles of natural juftice, becaufe even in an
unfocial ftate, the *pauper* has a claim only on
charity, and he who produces nothing has no
right to fhare in the regulation of what is
produced by the induftry of others. But
whatever be the juftice of disfranchifing the
unproductive poor, the argument is, in point
of fact, totally mifapplied. Domeftic fervants
are excluded by the decree of the Affembly,
though they fubfift as evidently on the produce of their own labour as any other clafs of
men in fociety ; and to them therefore the ar-

P 3

gument

gument of our acute and ingenious writer is totally inapplicable*. But it is the confolation of the confiftent friends of freedom, that this abufe muft be fhort-lived. The fpirit of reafon and liberty, which has atchieved fuch mighty victories, cannot long be refifted by this puny foe. The number of primary elec_ tors is at prefent fo great, and the importance of their fingle votes fo proportionally little, that their intereft in refifting the extenfion of the right of fuffrage is infignificantly fmall. Thus much have I fpoken of the ufurpation of the rights of fuffrage with the ardor of anxious affection, and the freedom of liberal admiration. The moment is too ferious for

---

* It has been very juftly remarked, that even on the idea of *taxation*, all men have equal rights of election. For the man who is too poor to pay a direct contribution to the State, ftill pays a tax in the increafed *price* of his food and cloaths. It is befides to be obferved, that life and liberty are more facred than property, and that the right of fuffrage is the only fhield that can guard them.

compliment,

compliment, and I leave untouched to the partizans of defpotifm, their monopoly of blind and fervile applaufe*.

I muft avow, with the fame franknefs, equal difapprobation of the elements of territory and contribution which enter into the proportion of Reprefentatives deputed by the various portions of the kingdom. Territorial or financial reprefentation†, is a monftrous

* " He who freely magnifies what has been nobly done, and fears not to declare as freely what might have been done, better gives you the beft covenant of his fidelity. His higheft praife is not flattery, and his plaineft advice is praife." MILTON's *Areopagitica.*

† Montefquieu, I think, mentions a federative Republic in *Lycia*, where the proportion of Reprefentatives deputed by each State was in a *ratio* compounded of its population and contribution. There might be fome plaufibility in this inftitution among confederated independent States, but it is groffly abfurd in a Commonwealth, which is *totally* ONE. In fuch a ftate, the contribution of all being proportioned to their capacity, it is *relatively* to the contributors EQUAL,

and

relic of ancient prejudice. Land or money cannot be reprefented. Men only *can* be reprefented, and population alone ought to regulate the number of Reprefentatives which any diftrict delegates.

The next confideration that prefents itfelf is, the nature of thofe bodies into which the citizens of France are to be organized for the performance of their political functions.—In this important part of the fubject, Mr. Burke has committed fome fundamental errors. It is more amply, more dexteroufly, and more correctly treated by M. de Calonne, of whofe work this difcuffion forms the moft interefting part.

The Affemblies into which the people of France are divided, are of *four* kinds.—Primary, Municipal, Electoral, and Adminiftrative.

and if it can confer any political claims, they muft derive f.om it equal rights.

To

To the *Municipalities* belong the care of preferving the police, and collecting the revenue within their jurifdiction. An accurate idea of their nature and object may be formed by fuppofing the *country* of England uniformly divided, and governed, like its cities and towns, by magiftracies of popular election.

The Primary Affemblies, the firft elements of the Commonwealth, are formed by all the citizens, who pay a direct contribution, equal to the price of three days labour, which may be averaged at half a Crown Englifh. Their functions are purely electoral. They fend Reprefentatives *directly* to the Affembly of the *Department*, in the proportion of one to every hundred active citizens. This they do not through the medium of the diftrict, as was originally propofed by the Conftitutional Committee, and has been erroneoufly ftated by Mr. Burke. They fend, indeed, Reprefentatives to the Affembly of the diftrict, but it is

the

the object of that Assembly not to depute electors to the department, but to elect the administrators of the district itself.

The Electoral Assemblies of the *Departments*, formed by the immediate delegates of the people in their primary Assemblies, elect the Members of the Legislature, the Judges, the Administrators, and the * Bishop of the Department.

The *Administrators* are every where the organs and instruments of the Executive Power. As the provinces of France, under her ancient Government were ruled by Governors, Intendants, &c. appointed by the Crown, so they are now governed by these administrative bodies, who are chosen by the Electoral Assemblies of the Departments.

* Every Department is an Episcopal See.

Such

Such is the rude outline of that elaborate organization which the French Legiſlature have formed. Details are not neceſſary to my purpoſe ; and I the more chearfully abſtain from them, becauſe I know that they will be ſpeedily laid before the Public by a perſon far more competent to deliver them with preciſion, and illuſtrated with a very correct and ingenious chart of the New Conſtitution of France.

Againſt the arrangement of theſe Aſſemblies, many ſubtle and ſpecious objections are urged, both by Mr. Burke and the exiled Miniſter of France. The firſt and moſt formidable is, " The ſuppoſed tendency of it to " diſmember France into a body of confede- " rated Republics." To this objection there are ſeveral unanſwerable replies. But before I ſtate them, it is neceſſary to make one diſtinction. Theſe ſeveral bodies are, in a certain ſenſe independent, in what regards ſubordinate and interior regulation. But they

are

are not independent in the fenfe which the
objection fuppofes, that of poffeffing a feparate
will from that of the nation, or influencing,
but by their Reprefentatives, the general fyftem of the State. Nay, it may be demonftrated, that the Legiflators of France have
folicitoufly provided more elaborate precautions againft this difmemberment than have
been adopted by any recorded Government.

The firft circumftance which is adverfe to
it is the *minutenefs of the parts* into which the
kingdom is divided. They are too fmall to
poffefs a feparate force. As elements of the
focial order, as particles of a great political
body, they are fomething : but as infulated
States, they would be impotent. Had France
been moulded into great maffes, each of them
might have been ftrong enough to claim a feparate will ; but divided as fhe is, no body of
citizens is confcious of fufficient ftrength to
feel their fentiments of any importance, but

as conftituent parts of the general will. Survey the Adminiftrative, the Primary, and the Electoral Affemblies, and nothing will be more evident than their importance in individuality. The Municipalities, furely, are not likely to arrogate independence. A 48000th part of the kingdom has not energy fufficient for feparate exiftence, nor can a hope arife in the Affembly of fuch a flender community of influencing, in a direct and dictatorial manner, the counfels of a great State. Even the electoral Affemblies of the Departments do not, as we fhall afterwards fhew, poffefs force enough to become independent confederated Republics.

Another circumftance, powerfully hoftile to this difmemberment, is the deftruction of the ancient provincial divifion of the kingdom. In no part of Mr. Burke's work have his arguments been chofen with fuch infelicity of felection as in what regards this fub-

ject.

ject. He has not only erred, but his error is the precise reverse of truth. He reprefents as the harbinger of difcord what is, in fact, the inftrument of union. He miftakes the cement of the edifice for a fource of inftability and a principle of repulfion. France was, under the ancient Government, an union of Provinces, acquired at various times, and on different conditions, differing in conftitution, laws, language, manners, privileges, jurifdiction, and revenue. It had the exterior of a fimple Monarchy, but it was in reality an aggregate of independent States. The Monarch was in one place King of Navarre, in another Duke of Brittany, in a third Count of Provence, in a fourth Dauphin of Vienne. Under thefe various denominations, he poffeffed, at leaft nominally, different degrees of power, and he certainly exercifed it under different forms.—The mafs compofed of thefe heterogeneous and difcordant elements, was held together by the compreffing force of defpotifm.

When

When that compreffion was withdrawn, the provinces muft have refumed their ancient independence, perhaps in a form more abfolute than as members of a federative Republic. Every thing tended to infpire *provincial* and to extinguifh *national* patriotifm. The inhabitants of Bretagne, or Guienne, felt themfelves linked together by ancient habitudes, by congenial prejudices, by fimilar manners, by the relics of their Conftitution, and the common name of their country; but their character as members of the French Empire, could only remind them of long and ignominious fubjection to a tyranny, of which they had only felt the ftrength in exaction, and bleffed the lenity in neglect. Thefe caufes muft have formed the provinces into independent Republics, and the deftruction of their provincial exiftence was indifpenfible to the prevention of this difmemberment. It is impoffible to deny, that men united by no previous habitude, (whatever may be faid of

the

the policy of the union in other refpects) are lefs qualified for that union of will and force, which produces an independent Republic, than provincials on whom every circumftance tended to confer local and partial attraction, and a repulfion to the common center of the national fyftem. Nothing could have been more inevitable than the independence of thofe great provinces, which had never been moulded and organized into one Empire; and we may boldly pronounce, in direct oppofition to Mr. Burke, that the new divifion of the kingdom was the only expedient that could have prevented is difmemberment into a confederacy of fovereign Republics.

The folicitous and elaborate *divifion of powers*, is another expedient of infallible operation, to preferve the unity of the body politic. The *Municipalities* are limited to minute and local adminiftration. The *Primary Affemblies* folely to elections. The *Affemblies*

of

of the Diſtrict to objects of adminiſtration and control of a ſuperior claſs; and the *Aſſemblies of the Departments,* where this may be the moſt apprehended, poſſeſs functions purely electoral. They elect Judges, Legiſlators, Adminiſtrators, and Miniſters of Religion, but they are to exert no authority legiſlative, adminiſtrative, or judicial. In any other capacity but that of executing their electoral functions, in voting an addreſs, an inſtruction, or a cenſure, they are only ſimple citizens*.

---

* Compare theſe remarks with the reaſoning of M. Calonne under the head, " *Que faut-il penſer de l'etabliſſement* " *perpetuel de* 83 *Aſſemblées, compoſées chacune de plus* 600 " *citoyens, chargées de choix des Legiſlateurs Supremes, du* " *choix des Adminiſtrateurs Provinciaux, du choix des Juges,* " *du choix des Principaux Miniſtres du Culte, & ayant en* " *conſéquence le droit de ſe mettre en activité toutes fois &* " *quantes?*" The objection which we are combating is ſtated with great preciſion by M. de Calonne, from p. 358 to p. 372 of his work. The diſcuſſion muſt be maturely weighed by every reader who would fathom the legiſlation of France.

Q   But

But whatever danger might be apprehended from the affumption of powers by thefe formidable Affemblies, the depofitaries of fuch extenfive electoral powers are precluded by another circumftance, which totally difqualifies and unnerves them for any purpofe but that for which they are created by the Conftitution. They are *biennially* renewed, and their fugitive nature makes fyftematic ufurpation hopelefs. What power, indeed, could they poffefs of dictating to the National Affembly*, or what intereft could the members of that Affembly have in obeying the man-

---

* I do not mean that their voice will not be there refpected. That would be to fuppofe the Legiflature as infolently corrupt as that of a neighbouring Government of pretended freedom. I only mean to affert, that they cannot poffefs fuch a power as will enable them to dictate inftructions to their Reprefentatives as authoritatively as Sovereigns do to their Embaffadors; which is the idea of a confederated Republic.

dates

dates of thofe who held as fugitive and precarious a power as their own; not one of whom might, at the next election, have a fuffrage to beftow? The fame probability gives the provincial Adminiftrators that portion of independance which the Conftitution demands. By a ftill ftronger reafon, the Judges, who are elected for fix years, muft feel themfelves independent of conftituents whom *three* elections may fo radically and completely change. Thefe circumftances then, the minutenefs of the divifions, the diffolution of provincial ties, the elaborate diftribution of powers, and the fugitive conftitution of the Electoral Affemblies, feem to form an infuperable barrier againft the affumption of fuch powers by any of the bodies into which France is organized, as would tend to produce the federal form. Thus the firft great argument of Mr. BURKE and MONSIEUR DE CALONNE feems to be refuted in *principles*, if not in the expansion of detail.

The next objection that is to be considered is peculiar to Mr. Burke. The *subordination of elections* has been regarded by the admirers of the French lawgivers as a mafter-piece of legiflative wifdom. It feemed as great an improvement on reprefentative Government, as reprefentation itfelf was on pure Democracy. No extent of territority is too great for a popular Government thus organized ; and as the Primary Affemblies may be divided to any degree of minutenefs, the moft perfect order is reconcileable with the wideft diffufion of political right. Democracies were fuppofed by philofophers to be neceffarily fmall, and therefore feeble ; to demand numerous Affemblies, and to be therefore venal and tumultuous. Yet this great difcovery, which gives force and order in fo high a degree to popular Governments, is condemned and derided

rided by Mr. Burke. An *immediate* connection between the reprefentative and the *primary* conftituent, he confiders as effential to the idea of reprefentation. As the electors in the Primary Affemblies do not immediately elect their lawgivers, he regards their rights of fuffrage as nominal and illufory.*. It will in the firft inftance be remarked, from the ftatement which has already been given, that in ftating *three interpofed elections* between the primary electors and the Legiflature, Mr. Burke has committed a moft important error in point of fact. The original plan of the Conftitutional Committee was indeed agreeable to the ftatement of Mr. Burke. The Primary Affemblies were to elect Deputies to the Diftrict, the Diftrict to the Department,

* P. 270—2. " For what are thefe Primary Electors " complimented, or rather mocked with a choice?—They " can never know any thing of the qualities of him that " is to ferve them, nor has he any obligation to ferve " them "

Q 3

and

and the Department to the National Aſſembly. But this plan was forcibly and ſuccefsfully combated. It was reprefented as tending to introduce a vicious complexity into the Government, and, by making the channel through which the national will paſſes into its public acts ſo circuitous, to enfeeble its energy under pretence of breaking its violence. It was accordingly radically changed. The feries of three elections was ſtill preferved for the choice of provincial Adminiftrators, but the Electoral Aſſemblies in the *Departments*, who are the immediate conftituents of the Legiſlature, are *directly* chofen by the *Primary Aſſemblies*, in the proportion of one elector to every hundred active citizens *.

But

---

* For a charge of ſuch fundamental inaccuracy againſt Mr. Burke, the Public will moſt juftly and naturally expect the higheſt evidence. I do therefore boldly appeal to the *Decret ſur la nouvelle Diviſion du Royaume, Art.* 17.—to the *Price's Verbal* of the Aſſembly for the 22d Dec. 1789. It

this

But to return to the general queftion, which is perhaps not much affected by thefe details. I profefs I fee no reafon why the right of election is not as fufceptible of delegation as any other civil function, why a citizen may not as well delegate the right of choofing law-givers, as that of making laws. Such a gradation of elections, fays Mr. Burke, excludes refponfibility and fubftantial election, fince the primary electors neither can know, nor bring to account the members of the Affembly.

this evidence demanded any collateral aid, the authority of M. *Calonne* (which it is remarkable that Mr. Burke fhould have overlooked) corroborates it moft amply. " On ordonne " que chacune de ces Affemblées *(Primaires)* nommera un " ELECTEUR à raifon de 100 citoyens actifs."—Calonne, p. 300. " Ces cinquantes mille ÉLECTEURS *(des Departe-* " *mens)* élus de deux ans en deux ans parles ASSEM- " BLÉES PRIMAIRES." Id. ibid. The Ex-Minifter, indeed, is rarely to be detected in any departure from the folicitous accuracy of profeffional detail.

This

This argument has (confidering the peculiar fyftem of Mr. Burke) appeared to me to be the moft fingular and inconfiftent that he has urged in his work. Reprefentation itfelf muft be confeffed to be an infringement on the moft perfect liberty, for the beft organized fyftem cannot preclude the poffibility of a variance between the *popular* and the *reprefentative* will. Refponfibility, ftrictly and rigoroufly fpeaking, it can rarely admit, for the fecrets of political fraud are fo impenetrable, and the line which feparates corrupt decifion from erroneous judgment to indifcernibly minute, that the cafes where the Deputies could be made properly refponfible are too few to be named as exceptions. Their *difmiffion* is all the punifhment that can be inflicted, and all that the beft Conftitution can attain is a *high probability* of unifon between the conftituent and his deputy. This feems attained in the arrangements of France. The electors of the *Departments* are fo numerous,

and

and fo popularly elected, that there is the higheft *probability* of their being actuated in their elections, and *re-elections*, by the fentiments of the Primary Affemblies. They have too many points of contact with the general mafs to have an infulated opinion, and too fugitive an exiftence to have a feparate intereft. It is befides to be remarked, that they come immediately from among the people, with all their opinions, and predilections, and enmities, to their elective functions; and it is furely improbable, that, too fhortly united for the acquifition of a corporation fpirit, they fhould have any will or voice but that of their conftituents. This is true of thofe cafes where the merits or demerits of candidates may be fuppofed to have reached the Primary Affemblies. In thofe far more numerous cafes, where they are too obfcure to obtain that notice, but by the polluted medium of a popular canvas, this delegation is ftill more evidently wife. The peafant, or artizan, who

is

is a primary elector, knows intimately men among his equals, or *immediate* superiors, who have information and honesty enough to chuse a good representative. But among this class (the only one which he can know sufficiently to judge) he rarely meets with any who have genius, leisure, and ambition for that situation themselves. Of the candidates to be electors in the *Department*, he may be a disinterested, deliberate, and competent judge. But were " he to be complimented, or rather mocked," with the direct right of electing to the legislative body, he must, in the tumult, venality, and intoxication of an election mob, give his suffrage without any *possible* just knowledge of the situation, character, and conduct of the candidates. So unfortunately false, indeed, seems the opinion of Mr. Burke, that this arrangement in the French Constitution is the only one that substantially, and in good faith, provides for the exercise of deliberate discrimination in the constituent.

The

The *hierarchy* of elections was obtruded on France by neceffity. Had they rejected it, they had only the alternative of tumultuous electoral Affemblies, or a tumultuous Legiflature. If the primary electoral Affemblies were to be fo divided as to avoid tumult, their deputies would be fo numerous as to make the National Affembly a mob. If the number of electoral Affemblies were reduced according to the number of deputies that ought to conftitute the Legiflature, each of them would be numerous enough, on the other hand, **to** be alfo a mob. I cannot perceive that peculiar unftnefs which is hinted at by Mr. Burke* in the right of *perfonal* choice to be delegated. It is in the practice of all States delegated to great officers, who are entrufted with the power of nominating their fubordi-

* " Of all the powers to be delegated by thofe who have " any real means of judging, the moft peculiarly unfit is " .... relates to a perfonal choice." BURKE, p. 271.

nate agents. It is in the moſt ordinary affairs of common life delegated, when our *ultimate* repreſentatives are too remote from us to be within the ſphere of our obſervation.

It is remarkable that M. Calonne, addreſfing his work to a people enlightened by the maſterly diſcuſſions to which theſe ſubjects have given riſe, has not, in all the fervor of his zeal to criminate the new inſtitutions, hazarded this objection. This is not the only inſtance in which the Ex-Miniſter has ſhewn more reſpect to the nation whom he addreſſes, than Mr. Burke has paid to the intellect and information of the Engliſh Public*.

Thus

' Though it may, perhaps, be foreign to the purpoſe, I cannot help thinking one remark on this topic intereſting. It will illuſtrate the difference of opinion between even the Ariſtocratic party in France and the rulers of England.— M. Calonne* rightly ſtates it to be the *unanimous inſtruction*

* Calonne, p. 383.

of

Thus much of the elements that are to generate the Legiflative body. Concerning that body, thus conflituted, various queftions remain. Its *unity* or *divifion* will admit of much difpute, and it will be deemed of the greateft moment by the zealous admirers of the Englifh Conftitution, to determine, whether any femblance of its legiflative organization could have been attained by France, if good, or ought to have been purfued by her, if attainable. Nothing has been afferted with more confidence by Mr. Burke than the facility

of France to her Reprefentatives, to enact the *equal* admiffibility of ALL citizens to public employ!—England adheres to the Teft Act!——The arrangements of M. Neckar for elections to the States General, and the fcheme of M. M. Mounier and Lally Tolendahl for the new Conftitution, included a reprefentation of the people nearly exact. Yet the idea of it is regarded with horror in England!——The higheft *Arijlocrates* of France approach more nearly to the creed of general liberty than the moft popular politicians of England, of which thefe two circumftances are fignal proofs.

with

with which the fragments of the long sub-
verted liberty of France might have been
formed into a Britifh Conftitution *. But of
this

* To place this opinion in a ftronger point of light, I
have collected the principal paffages in which it is announced
or infinuated. " In your OLD STATES you poffeffed that
" variety of parts, corefponding with the various defcrip-
" tions of which your community was happily compofed."
Burke, p. 50. " If diffident of yourfelves, and not clearly
" the almoft obliterated Conftitution of your anceftors, fee-
" ing you had looked to your neighbours in this land, who
" had kept alive the principles and models of the old com-
" mon law of Europe, meliorated and adapted to the prefent
" ftate." Id. p 53. " Have they never heard of a Mo-
" narchy directed by laws, controled and balanced by the
" great hereditary wealth and hereditary dignity of a nation,
" and both again controled by a judicious check from the
" reafon and feeling of the people at large, acting by a fuit-
" able and permanent organ?" Id. p. 184. And in
the fame page he reprefents France as a nation which had
" it in its choice to obtain fuch a Government with eafe,
" *or rather to confirm it when actually poffeffed*."—" I muft
" think fuch a Government well deferved to have its excel-
" lencies

this general pofition he has neither explained
the mode, nor defined the limitations. Nothing is more favourable to the popularity of
a work than thefe lofty generalities, which
are light enough to pafs into vulgar currency,
and to become the maxims of a popular creed.
Touched by definition, they become too fimple and precife for eloquence, too cold and abftract for popularity. But exhibited as they
are by Mr. Burke, they gratify the pride and
indolence of the people, who are thus taught
to fpeak what gains applaufe, without any effort of intellect, and impofes filence, without
any labour of confutation ; what may be acquired without being ftudied, and uttered
without being underftood. Of this nature
are thefe vague and confident affertions, which

" lencies heightened, its faults corrected, and its *capacities*
improved into a Britifh Conftitution." Id. p. 225. The
precife queftion at iffue is, whether the ancient Government
of France poffeffed *capacities* which could have been improved into a Britifh Conftitution.

without

without furnishing any definite idea, afford a
ready jargon for vulgar prejudice, flattering to
national vanity, and sanctioned by a distinguished name. It is neceffary to enquire with
more precifion in what manner France could
have affimilated the remains of her ancient
Conftitution to that of the Englifh Legiflature. Three modes only feem conceivable.
The prefervation of the *three* Orders diftinct.
The union of the Clergy and Nobility in one
upper Chamber, or fome mode of felecting
from thefe two Orders a body like the Houfe
of Lords in England. Unlefs the infinuations
of Mr. Burke point to one or other of thefe
fchemes, I cannot divine their meaning. The
firft mode (the three Orders fitting in feparate
houfes with equal privileges) would neither
have been congenial in fpirit nor fimilar in
form to the Conftitution of England. To
convert the Convocation into an integrant
and co-ordinate Member of our Legiflature,
would give it fome femblance of the ftruc-
ture;

ture; but it would be a faint one. It would
be neceffary to arm our Clergy with an immenfe mafs of property, rendered ftill more
formidable by the concentration of great portions in the hands of a few, to conftitute it in
effect the fame body with the Nobility, by
granting them the monopoly of great bene-
fices, and to beftow on this clerico-military
ariftocracy, in its two fhapes of Priefthood and
Nobility, *two* feparate and independent voices
in Legiflation. This double body, from its
neceffary dependence on the King, muft neceffarily have in both forms become the organ of his voice. The Monarch would thus
poffefs *three* negatives, *one* avowed and difuf-
ed, two latent and in perpetual activity on the
fingle voice which impotent and illufive formality had yielded to the Third Eftate. Such
and much more muft the Parliament of England become before it could in any refpect refemble the divifion of the French Legiflature,
according to thofe ancient Orders which

R

formed

formed the Gothic affemblies of Europe. So monftrous did the arrangement appear, that even under the reign of Defpotifm, the fecond plan was propofed by M. Calonne*—that the Clergy and Nobility fhould form an Upper Houfe, to exercife conjointly with the King and the Commons the Legiflative Authority. It admits, however, of the cleareft proof, that fuch a Conftitution would have been diametrically oppofite in its fpirit and principles to the Englifh Government. This will at once be evident from the different defcription of the body of Nobles in France and England.

* See his Lettre au Roi 9th February, 1789. See alfo Sur d'Etat de France, &c. p. 167. It was alfo, as we are informed by M. Calonne, fuggefted in the *Cahiers* of the Nobility of *Metz* and *Montargis*. It is worthy of incidental remark, that the propofition of fuch radical changes even by the Nobility, is an inconteftible evidence of the general conviction that a revolution or total change in the Government was neceffary. It is therefore an unanfwerable reply to Mr. Burke and M. Calonne.

In

In England they are a small body, united to the mass of the people by innumerable points of contact, receiving from it perpetual new infusions, and returning to it, undistinguished and unprivileged, the majority of their children. In France they formed an immense insulated *cast*, separated from society by every barrier that prejudice or policy could raise, receiving few plebeian accessions, and precluded, by the indelible character of nobility, the equal patrimony of all their children, from the possibility of their most remote descendants being restored to the general mass. The Nobles of England are a *Senate* of 200. The Noblesse of France were a *tribe* of 200,000. Nobility is in England only hereditary, so far as its professed object, the support of a hereditary Senate demands. It is therefore descendible only to one heir. Nobility in France was as widely inheritable as its real purpose, the maintenance of a privi-

leged

leged *caft*, prefcribed. It was therefore neceffarily defcendible to all male children.

There are other points of contraft ftill more
important. The Nobleffe of France were at
once *formidable* from their immenfe body of
property, and *dependent* from the indigence of
their Patrician rabble of *cadets*, whom honour
infpired with fervility, and fervility excluded
from the path to independence. They in fact
poffeffed fo large a portion of the landed property, as to be juftly, and almoft exclufively
confidered as the landed intereft of the kingdom. To this formidable property were added
the revenues of the Church, monopolized by
the Children. The younger branches of thefe
opulent families had in general no patrimony
but their honours and their fword. They
were therefore reduced to feek fortune and
diftinction in military dependence on the
Crown. If they were generous, the habits

of

of military fervice devoted them, from loyalty. If they were prudent, the hope of military promotion devoted them, from intereft, to the King.—How immenfe therefore and irrefiftible would the Royal influence have been in electors, where the majority of the voters were the fervants and creatures of the Crown ? What would be thought in England of a Houfe of Lords, which, while it reprefented or contained the whole landed intereft of the kingdom, fhould neceffarily have a majority of its members feptennially or triennially *nominated* by the King.   Yet it would ftill yield to the French Upper Houfe of M. *Calonne* ; for the monied and commercial interefts of England, which would continue to be reprefented by the Commons, are important and formidable, but in France they are comparatively infignificant.   It would have been a Government where the Ariftocracy could have been ftrong only againft the people, impotent againft the Crown.   The fecond ar-

   rangement

rangement then is equally repugnant to the *theory* of the Britifh Conftitution as the firft. There remains only fome mode of felection of a body from amidft the Nobility and Clergy to form an Upper Houfe, and to this there are infuperable objections. Had the right of thus forming a branch of the Legiflature by a *fingle* act of prerogative been given to the King, it muft have ftrengthened his influence to a degree terrible at any period, but fatal in the moment of political reform. Had any mode of election by the Provinces, or the Legiflature, been adopted, or if they had been vefted with any control on the nomination of the Crown, the new dignity would have been fought with an activity of corruption and intrigue, of which, in fuch a national convulfion, it is impoffible to eftimate the danger. No general principle of felection, fuch as that of *opulence* or *antiquity*, would have remedied the evil, for the excluded and *degraded* Nobles would feel the principle, that nobility is the

equal

equal and inalienable patrimony of all. By
the abolition of nobility, no nobleman was
degraded, for to degrade is to lower from a
rank that continues to exiſt in ſociety. No
man can be *degraded* when the *rank* he poſſeſſed no longer exiſts. But had the rank of nobility remained in the mode of which we have
been ſpeaking, the great body of the Nobles
would indeed, in a proper and *penal* ſenſe,
have been degraded, the new dignity of their
former Peers would have kept alive the memory of what they once poſſeſſed, and provoked them to enterprizes far more fatal than
reſentment of an indignity, that is at leaſt
broken by diviſion, and impartially inflicted
on the greateſt and moſt obſcure.

So evident indeed was the impoſſibility of
what Mr. Burke ſuppoſes attainable with ſuch
eaſe, that no party in the Aſſembly ſuggeſted
the imitation of the Engliſh model, the

R 4

ſyſtem

ſyſtem of his oracles in French politics*. M,
M. Lally and Mounier, approached more near
to the Conſtitution of the American States.
They propoſed a Senate to be choſen for life
by the King, from a certain number of candidates to be offered to his choice by the pro-
vinces†. This Senate was to enjoy an abſolute negative on legiſlative acts, and to form
the great national court for the trial of public
delinquents. In effect, ſuch a body would have
formed a far more vigorous Ariſtocracy than

* " De quelle manière ſera compoſé le Senat ? Sera-t-il
" formé de ce qu'on appelle aujourd'hui la Nobleſſe & le
" Clergé ? Non sans doute. Ce ſeroit perpetuer cette
" ſeparation d'Ordres, cette eſprit de corporation qui eſt le
" plus grand ennemi de l'eſprit Public." *Pièces Juſtificatifs*
de M. Lally Tolendahl, p. 121.

† Après avoir examiné & balancé tous les inconveniens
" de chaque parti peutêtre trouvera t-on que faire nommer
" les Senateurs par le Roi, ſur la preſentation des provinces,
" & ne les faire nommer qu'à vie ſeroit encore le moyen le
" plus propre à concilier tous les interêts. Id. p. 124.

the

the Englifh Peerage. The latter body only preferves its dignity by a wife difufe of its power. *Potentia ad impotentiam abufi* would otherwife be defcriptive of their fate. But the Senate of M. Mounier would be an Ariftocracy moderated and legalized, which, becaufe it *appeared* to have lefs independence, would in fact be emboldened to exert more. Deriving their rights equally with the Lower Houfe from the people, and vefted with a more dignified and extenfive truft, they would neither fhrink from the conflict with the Commons nor the King. The permanence of their authority muft give them a fuperiority over the former; the fpecioufnefs of their caufe over the latter : and it feems proble, that they muft have terminated in fubjugating both. Thofe who fuppofe that a Senate for life might not be infected by the corporation fpirit, may confider the ancient judicatures of France, who were as keenly actuated

actuated by that fpirit, as any body of hereditary Nobles that ever exifted.

But to quit the details of thefe fyftems—a
queftion arifes for our confideration of a more
general and more difficult nature—*Whether a
fimple reprefentative Legiflature, or a Conftitution of mutual controul, be the beft form of Government* ?*—To examine this queftion at
length is inconfiftent with the object and limits of the prefent publication (which already grows infenfibly beyond its intended
fize) but a few general principles may be
hinted, on which the decifion of the queftion
perhaps chiefly depends.

1. It will not be controverted, that the object of a reprefentative Legiflature is to col-

* This queftion, tranflated into familiar language, may
perhaps be thus expreffed,—" *Whether the vigilance of the*
" *mafter, or the fquabbles of the* fervants, *be the beft fecurity for*
" *faithful fervice ?"*

lect

lect the general will.   To accord with this principle, there muſt be the ſame unity in the *repreſentative* as in the *original* WILL.— That will is ONE.   It cannot therefore, without ſolecifm, be *doubly* repreſented.   The ſocial body ſuppoſes a perfect unity, and no man's will can have TWO diſcordant organs. Any *abſolute** negative oppoſed to the national will, deciſively ſpoken by its Repreſentatives, is radically null, as an uſurpation of popular ſovereignty.   Thus far does the abſtract principle of a repreſentative Government condemn the diviſion of the Legiſlature.

2. All bodies poſſeſſed of effectual control have a tendency to that great evil, which all laws have hitherto foſtered, though it be the end of Legiſlation to repreſs, the preponde-

* The *ſuſpenſive veto* veſted in the French King is only an appeal to the people on the conduct of the Repreſentatives. The voice of the people clearly ſpoken, the negative ceaſes.

rance

rance of partial interefts. The fpirit of corporation infallibly feizes every Public body,
and the creation of every new Affembly cre-
ates a new, dextrous, and vigilant enemy to
the general intereft. This alone is a fufficient
objection to a controling Senate. Such a body
would be moft peculiarly acceffible to this contagious fpirit. A reprefentative body itfelf
can only be preferved from it by thofe fre-
quent elections which break combinations,
and infufe into it new portions of popular fentiments. Let us grant that a popular Affembly may fometimes be precipitated into unwife
decifion by the feductions of eloquence, or the
rage of faction. Let us grant that a controling Senate might remedy this evil, but let
us recollect, that it is better the *Public intereft
fhould be occafionally miftaken than fyftematically
oppofed.*

3. It is perhaps fufceptible of proof, that
thefe Governments of balance and control

have

have never exifted but in the vifion of theorifts. The faireft example will be the Conftitution of England. If it can be proved that
the two members of the Legiflature, who are
pretended to control each other, are ruled by
the fame *clafs* of men, the control muft be
granted to be imaginary. That oppofition of
intereft, which is fuppofed to preclude all confpiracy againft the people, can no longer exift.
That this is the ftate of England, the moft
fuperficial obfervation muft evince. The
great proprietors, titled and untitled, poffefs
the whole force of both Houfes of Parliament
that is not immediately dependent on the
Crown. The Peers have a great influence in
the Houfe of Commons. All political parties are formed by a confederacy of the members of both Houfes. The Court party, by
the influence of the Crown, acting equally in
both, fupported by a part of the independent
Ariftocracy. The oppofition by the remain-
der of the Ariftocracy, whether Commoners

or

or Lords.   Here is every fymptom of collu-
fion : No veftige of control.   The only cafe
indeed, where it could arife, is where the intereft of the Peerage is diftinct from that of
the other great proprietors.   But thefe feparate interefts are few and paltry, and have
eftablifhed fo feeble a check, that the hiftory
of England will not afford one undifputed example of this vaunted control.

The rejection of the Peerage Bill of George
the Firft is urged with great triumph by De
Lolme.   There it feems the Commons rejected the bill, purely actuated by their fears,
that the Ariftocracy would acquire a ftrength
from a limitation on the number of Peers, deftructive of that balance of power which forms
the Conftitution.   It is unfortunate that political theorifts do not confult the *hiftory* as well
as the *letter* of legiflative proceedings.   It is a
matter of perfect notoriety, that the rejection
of that bill was occafioned by the feceffion of

Sir

Sir Robert (then Mr.) Walpole from the Cabinet, and the oppofition of him and his party to it was *merely* as a minifterial meafure. The debate was not guided by any general legiflative principles. It was fimply an experiment on the ftrength of two parties contending for power. The readear will no doubt feel a high reverence *for the Conftitutional principles* of that Parliament, when he is informed that to it we owe the *Septennial Act!*

In fact, if fuch a check exifted in much greater force, it would be of little importance to the general queftion. " Through a diver-" fity of members and interefts," if we may believe Mr. Burke, " GENERAL LIBERTY " had as many fecurities as there were fepa-" rate views in the feveral Orders." And if by GENERAL LIBERTY be underftood the power of the collective body of thefe Orders, the pofition is undeniable. But if it means, what it ought to mean, the liberty of mankind,

kind, nothing can be more falfe. The higher clafs in fociety, whatever be their names, of Nobles, Bifhops, Judges, or poffeffors of landed and commercial wealth, have ever been united by a common view, far more powerful than thofe petty repugnancies of intereft to which this variety of defcription may give rife. Whatever may be the little conflicts of ecclefiaftical with fecular, of commercial with landed opulence, they have one common intereft to preferve, the elevated place to which the focial order has raifed them. There never was, or will be, in civilized fociety, but two grand interefts, that of the RICH and that of the POOR. The differences of intereft among the feveral claffes of the rich will be ever too flender to preclude their confpiracy againft mankind. In the mean time the privileges of their feveral ORDERS will be guarded, and Mr. Burke will decide that GENERAL LIBERTY is fecure!—It is thus that a Polifh Palatine harangues in the Diet on the liberty of Poland,

without

without a blush at the recollection of his bondfmen.—It is thus that the Affembly of Jamaica, amidft the flavery and fale of MEN, profanely appeal to the principles of freedom. It is thus that Antiquity, with her pretended political philofophy, cannot boaft one philofopher who queftioned the juftice of fervitude, nor with all her pretended public virtue, one philanthropift who deplored the mifery of flaves.

One circumftance more remains concerning the Legiflature—the exclufion of the King's Minifters from feats in it. This *felf-denying Ordinance* I muft unequivocally difapprove.—I regard all *disfranchifement* as equally unjuft in its principle, deftructive in its example, and impotent for its pretended purpofe. The prefence of Minifters in the Affembly would have been of great utility in a view of bufinefs, and perhaps, by giving publicity to their opinions, favourable on the whole to

S

Public

Pbulic Liberty. To exclude them from the Legiflature, is to devote them to the purpofes of the Crown, by giving them no *intereft* in the Conftitution. The fair and open influence of Minifters was never formidable. It is only that indirect and fecret influence which this exclufion will perhaps enable them to practife with more impunity and fuccefs. It is alfo to be obferved, that it is equivalent to an exclufion of all men of fuperior talent from the Cabinet. The object of liberal ambition will be a feat in the Supreme Affembly; and no man of genius will accept, much lefs purfue, branded and degraded offices, which banifh him from the natural fphere of his powers.

Of the PLAN of JUDICATURE formed by the Affembly, I have not yet prefumed to form a decided opinion. It certainly approaches to an experiment, whether a code of laws can be formed fufficiently fimple and intelligible to fuperfede the neceffity of lawyers

by

by profeſſion*. Of all the attempts of the Aſſembly, the complicated relations of civilized
ſociety ſeem to render this moſt problemati-
cal. They have not, however, concluded
this part of their labours, and the feeblenefs
attributed to the elective judicatures of the
Departments may probably be remedied by the
dignity and force with which they will inveſt
the two high national tribunals *(La Cour de
Caſſation & la Haute Cour Nationale)* which
they are about to organize†.

On the ſubject of the EXECUTIVE MAGI-
STRACY, there is a preliminary remark,

* The ſexennial election of the Judges is ſtrongly and ably
oppoſed by M. Calonne, p. 294, chiefly on the principle,
that the ſtability of judicial offices is the only inducement to
men to devote their lives to legal ſtudy, which alone can
form good magiſtrates.

† I have on this ſubject read with much pleaſure and
inſtruction, the profound and ingenious, though perhaps oc-
caſionally paradoxical remarks of Mr. BENTHAM.

which

which the advocates as well as the enemies of the Revolution have too much neglected. The Affembly have been accufed of violating their own principles by the affumption of executive powers, and their advocates have pleaded guilty to the charge. It has been forgotten that they had a double function to perform. They were not only to erect a new Conftitution, but they were to guard it from deftruction. Hence a neceffary affumption of executive powers in the crifis of a Revolution. Had fuperftitious tendernefs for the principle confined them to theoretical erections, which the breath of power was every day deftroying, they would indeed have merited thofe epithets of vifionaries and enthufiafts with which they have been loaded. To judge, therefore, of the future executive magiftracy of France by its prefent ftate, is abfurd. We muft not, as has been jufty obferved, miftake for the new political edifice what is only the fcaffolding neceffary to its erection.

erection. The powers of the firſt magiſtrate
are not to be eſtimated by the debility to
which the convulſions of the moment have
reduced them, but by the proviſions of the
future Conſtitution.

The portion of power with which the King
of France is inveſted, is certainly as much as
pure theory demands for the executive magiſtrate. An organ to collect the Public will,
and a hand to execute it, are the only neceſſary conſtituents of the ſocial union. The
popular repreſentative forms the firſt; the
executive officer the ſecond. To the point
where this principle would have conducted
them, the French have not ventured to proceed. It has been aſſerted by Mr. Burke,
that the French King has no negative on
laws. This, however, is not true. The minority who oppoſed any ſpecies of negative in
the Crown was only 100, when 800 members were preſent in the Aſſembly. The

King

King poffeffes the power of with-holding his affent to a propofed law for *two* fucceffive Affemblies. If it is propofed by the *third*, his affent, indeed, becomes neceffary. This fpecies of fufpenfive *veto* is with great fpecioufnefs and ingenuity contended by M. Neckar to be more efficient than the obfolete negative of the Englifh Princes *. A mild and limited negative may, he remarked, be exercifed without danger or odium, while a prerogative, like the abfolute *veto*, muft fink into impotence from its invidious magnitude. It is too *great* to be exercifed, and muft, as it has in England, be tacitly abandoned by difufe. Is not that negative really efficient, which is only to yield to the national voice, fpoken after four years deliberation, and in two fucceffive elections of Reprefentatives? What Monarch of a free State, I will be bold

---

* Rapport fait au Roi dans fon Confeil, par le premier Miniftre des Finances, à Verfailles, le 11 Sept. 1789.

to afk, could with decency or impunity oppofe a negative the moft unlimited in law to
the public fentiment, thus explicitly and con-
ftantly expreffed ? The moft abfolute *veto*
muft, if the people perfift, prove eventually
fufpenfive. A fufpenfive *veto* is therefore
equivalent to an abfolute one, and being of
lefs invidious exercife, confers more real power.
" The power of remonftrance *," fays Mr.
Burke, " which was anciently vefted in the
" Parliament of Paris, is now abfurdly en-
" trufted to the executive magiftrate." One
might have fuppofed that this was a power

* The *negative* poffeffed by the King of France is precifely *double* of that which is entrufted to the Affembly.
He may oppofe his will to that of his whole people for *four
years* of the term of two Legiflatures, while the oppofition
of the Affembly to the general voice can only exift for *two
years*, when a new election annihilates them. So inconfi-
derately has this prerogative been reprefented as nominal.
The whole of this argument is in fome meafure *ad hominem*,
for I myfelf am dubious about the utility of any fpecies of
Royal *veto*, abfolute or fufpenfive.

of

of remonſtrance like that of the Parliament of Paris to the *Legiſlature*. It is however, as we have feen, a power of a very different defcription, a power of remonſtrating to the people againſt their Reprefentatives, the only ſhare in legiſlation (whether it be nominally *abſolute*, or nominally *limited*) that a free Government can entruſt to its fupreme ma-giſtrate*.

On the Preragative of WAR and PEACE, Mr. Burke † has ſhortly, and M. Calonne ‡ at great length, arraigned the fyſtem of the Affembly.

In the Conſtitution of France, war is to be declared by a decree of the Legiſlature, on the propofition of the King. He poffeffes ex-clufively the *initiative*. It cannot originate

* Burke, p. 301.
† Burke, p. 295—6.   ‡ Calonne, p. 170—200.

with

with any member of the Legiflature. The firft remark fuggefted by this arrangement is, that the difference between it and the *theory* of the Englifh Conftitution is purely nominal. That *theory* fuppofes an independent Houfe of Commons, a rigorous refponfibility, and an EFFECTIVE power of impeachment. Were thefe in any refpect realized, it is perfectly obvious, that a decifion for war muft in every cafe depend on the deliberation of the Legiflature. No Minifter would hazard hoftilities without the fanction of a body who held a fword fufpended over his head; and, as this theory fuppofes the Houfe of Commons perfectly uninfluenced by the Crown, the ultimate decifion could in no refpect depend on the executive magiftrate, and no power remains to him but the *initiative*. The forms indeed, in the majority of cafes, aim at a femblance of the theory. A Royal meffage announces imminent hoftilties, and a Parliamentary addrefs of promifed fupport,

re-

re-echoes the meſſage. It is this addreſs alone which emboldens and authorizes the Cabinet to proceed in their meaſures. The Royal meſſage correſponds to the French *initiative*; and if the purity of our practice bore any proportion to the ſpeciouſneſs of our theory, the addreſs would be a *decree* of the Legiſlature, adopting the propoſition of the King. No man therefore, who is a ſincere and enlightened admirer of the Engliſh Conſtitution, *as it ought, and is pretended to exiſt*, can conſiſtently reprobate an arrangement, which differs from it only in the moſt frivolous circumſtances. To ſpeak of our practical Government would be an outrage on common ſenſe. There no trace of thoſe diſcordant powers which are ſuppoſed in our theoretical Conſtitution remains. The moſt beautiful ſimplicity prevails. The ſame influence determines the executive and legiſlative power. The ſame Cabinet makes war in the name of the King, and ſanctions it in the

name

name of the Parliament. But France, defti-
tute of the cement which united thefe jarring powers, was reduced to imitate our theory
inftead of our practice. Her Exchequer was
ruined. She could not, therefore, adopt this
admirable fyftem.

Suppofing however, but not granting, that
this formidable prerogative was more abridged
in France than it is by the *theory* of our Government, the expediency of the limitation
remains to be confidered. The chief objections are its tendency to favour the growth of
foreign factions, and to derogate from the
promptitude fo neceffary to military fuccefs.
To both thefe objections there is one general
anfwer. They proceed on the fuppofition of
the frequency of wars. They both fuppofe,
that France will retain part of that political
fyftem which fhe has difclaimed. But if fhe
adheres with good faith to her declarations,
war muft become to her fo rare an occurrence,

that

that the objections become infignificant.—
Foreign Powers have no temptation to purchafe factions in a State which does not in-
terpofe in foreign politics; and a wife nation,
which regards victorious war as not lefs fatally intoxicating to the victors, than widely
deftructive to the vanquifhed, will not furrender their probability of peace from the
dread of defeat, nor purchafe the hope of
victory by provifions for facilitating war.—
France, after having renounced for ever the
idea of conqueft, can, indeed, have no fource
of probable hoftility but her colonies. Colonial poffeffions have been fo unanfwerably demonftrated to be commercially ufelefs, and politically ruinous, that the conviction of philofophers cannot fail of having, in
due time, its effect on the minds of enlightened Europe, and delivering the French Empire from this cumbrous and deftructive appendage.

But

But even were the exploded villainy that has obtained the name of politics to be re-adopted in France, the objections would still be feeble. The firft, which muft be confeffed to have a fpecious and formidable air, feems evidently to be founded on the hiftory of Sweden and Poland, and on fome facts in that of the Dutch Republic. It is a remarkable example of thofe loofe and remote analogies by which fophifts corrupt and abufe hiftory. Peculiar circumftances in the fituation of thefe States difpofed them to be the feat of foreign faction. It did not arife from war being decided by public bodies, for if it had, it muft have exifted in ancient Rome and Carthage—in modern Venice, and Switzerland—in the republican Parliament of England, and in the Congrefs of the United States of America.—Holland too, in her better and more vigorous days, was perfectly exempt from this evil.—No traces of it appear in her hiftory till the age of Charles II.

and

and Louis XIV. when, divided between jealoufy of the commerce of England and dread
of the conquefts of France, fhe threw her-
felf into the arms of the Houfe of Orange,
and forced the partizans of freedom into a
reliance on French fupport. In more recent
periods, domeftic convulfions have more fatally difplayed her debility, and too clearly
evinced, that of that fplendor which fhe
gained from the ignorant indolence of the
world, fhe now only retains the fhadow, by
the indulgence and courtefy of Europe. The
cafe of Sweden is with the utmoft facility
explicable. An indigent and martial people,
whether it be governed by one or many defpots, will ever be fold by its tyrants to the
enterprizes of opulent ambition; and recent
facts have proved, that a change in the Government of Sweden has not changed the
ftipendiary fpirit of its military fyftem. Poland is an example ftill lefs relevant. There
an independent anarchy of defpots naturally

league

League themselves varioufly with foreign Powers. Yet Ruffian force has done more than Ruffian gold; and Poland has fuffered ftill more from feeblenefs than venality. No analogy can be fuppofed to exift between thefe cafes and that of France. I hazard the iffue of the difcuffion on one plain point. All the Powers of Europe could not expend money enough to form and *maintain* a faction in their intereft in France. Let us fuppofe it poffible that the Legiflature of this vaft and opulent kingdom could *once* be corrupted; but let us recollect, that a feries of Legiflatures, collected by the moft extenfively popular election, are to be in fucceffion purchafed, to obtain any permanent afcendant, and it will be evident, that *Potofi* would be unequal to the attempt. If we confider that their deliberations are conducted under the detecting eye of a vigilant and enlightened people, the growth of foreign factions will appear ftill more chimerical. All the States which have been quoted were poor,

therefore

therefore cheaply corrupted ; their Government was an Ariſtocracy, and was therefore only to be *once* bought ; the people were ignorant, and could therefore be ſold by their Governors with impunity. The reverſe of theſe circumſtances will ſave France, as they have ſaved England, from this " worſt of " evils." Their wealth makes the attempt difficult ; their diſcernment makes it hazardous ; their ſhort truſt of power renders the objeĉt worthleſs, and its permanence impoſſible. That ſubjeĉting the deciſion of war to the deliberations of a popular aſſembly will, in a great meaſure, derogate from its energy, and unnerve it for all deſtruĉtive purpoſes, I am not diſpoſed to deny. France muſt, however, when her conſtitution is cemented, be, in a *defenſive* view, invincible ; and if her Government is unfitted for aggreſſion, it is little wonder that the Aſſembly ſhould have made no proviſion for a caſe which their principles do not ſuppoſe.

But

This is the laſt important arrangement re-
ſpecting the executive power which Mr.
Burke has conſidered, and it conducts us to a
ſubject of infinite delicacy and difficulty, which
has afforded no ſmall triumph to the enemies
of the Revolution — the ORGANIZATION
OF THE ARMY. It muſt be confeſſed, that
to conciliate an army of a hundred and fifty
thouſand men, a navy of a hundred ſhips of
the line, and a frontier guarded by a hundred
fortreſſes, with the exiſtence of a free Government, is a tremendous problem. It cannot be denied, that hiſtory affords no example in which ſuch a Public force has not re-
coiled on the State, and become the ready inſtrument of military uſurpation. And if the
State of France were not perfectly unexampled, and to which theſe hiſtorical arguments
are not therefore applicable or pertinent, the
inference would be inevitable. An army,
with the ſentiments and habits which it is
the ſyſtem of modern Europe to inſpire, is not

T

only

only hoſtile to freedom, but incompatible with it. A body of men poſſeſſed of the whole force of a State, and ſyſtematically diveſted of every civic ſentiment, is a monſter that no rational polity can tolerate, and every circum-ſtance clearly ſhews it to be the object of French legiſlation to deſtroy it, not *as a body of armed citizens*—but as an ARMY. This is wiſely and gradually to be effected. Two grand operations conduct to it—arming the people, and *unſoldiering* the army*. The firſt of theſe meaſures, the formation of the muni-cipal army, certainly makes the nation inde-pendent of its military ſervants. An army of four millions can never be coerced by one of a hundred and fifty thouſand; neither can they have a ſeparate ſentiment from the body of the nation, for they are the ſame. Whence the horror of Mr. Burke at thus arming the

* To uſe the language of M. Calonne, " *armant le peu-* " *ple & populariſant l'armée.*"

nation, under the title of a *municipal army*, has arifen, it is even difficult to conjecture. Has it ceafed to be true, that the defence of a free State is only to be committed to its citizens ? Are the long oppofition to a ftanding army in England, its tardy and jealous admiffion, and the perpetual clamor (at length illufively gratified) for a militia, to be exploded, as the grofs and uncourtly fentiments of our unenlightened anceftors ? The Affembly have put arms into the hands of the citizens, and by that means have for ever precluded both their own defpotifm and the ufurpation of the army. " They muft rule," fays Mr. Burke, " by an army." If that be their fyftem, their policy is ftill more wretched than he has reprefented it. For they fyftematically ftrengthen thofe who are to be governed, while they fyftematically enfeeble their engine of Government. They fortify the people, and weaken the army. They reduce themfelves and their army to dependence on

the

the nation, whom alone they ſtrengthen and arm. A *Military Democracy*, if it means a deliberative body of ſoldiers, is the moſt execrable of tyrannies ; but if it be underſtood to denote a popular Government, where every citizen is diſciplined and armed, it muſt then be pronounced to be the only free Government which retains within itſelf the means of preſervation.

The profeſſed ſoldiers, rendered impotent to any dangerous purpoſe by the ſtrength of the municipal army, are by many other circumſtances invited to throw off thoſe abjeĉt and murderous habits which form the perfection of a modern ſoldier. In other States the ſoldiery were in general disfranchiſed. They were too poor to be citizens. But in France a great part may enjoy the full rights of citizens. They are not then likely to ſacrifice their ſuperior to their inferior capacity, nor to elevate their military importance by

committing

committing political fuicide. They feel themfelves fervile as foldiers, they are confcious of being fovereign as citizens. That diffufion of political knowledge among them, which is ridiculed and reprobated by Mr. Burke, is the only remedy that could have fortified them againft the feduction of an afpiring Commander. That alone will teach them, that in lending themfelves to his views, they fubmit themfelves to his yoke ; that to deftroy the liberty of others, they muft facrifice their own. They have, indeed, gigantic ftrength, and they may crufh their fellow citizens, by dragging down the focial edifice, but they muft themfelves be overwhelmed by its fall. THE DESPOTISM OF ARMIES IS THE SLAVERY OF SOLDIERS. An army cannot be ftrong enough to tyrannize, that is not itfelf cemented by the moft abfolute *interior* tyranny. The diffufion of thefe great truths will perpetuate, as they have produced, a Revolution in the character of the French

T 3

foldiery.

foldiery. They will therefore, in the fenfe of defpotic difciplinarians, ceafe to be an army; and while the foldiers affume the fentiments of citizens, and the citizens acquire the difcipline of foldiers, the military character will be diffufed, and the military profeffion annihilated. Military fervices will be the *duty* of all citizens, and the *trade* of none*. To this object their fyftem evidently and inevitably tends. If a feparate body of citizens, as an army, is deemed neceffary, it will probably be formed by rotation. A certain period of military fervice will be exacted from every

* Again I muft encounter the derifion of Mr. Burke, by quoting the ill-fated citizen of Geneva, whofe life was embittered by the cold friendfhip of a Philofopher, and whofe memory is profcribed by the alarmed enthufiafm of an orator. I fhall prefume to recommend to the perufal of every reader his tract entitled, " *Confiderations fur le Gou-* " *vernement de Pologne, &c.*" more efpecially what regards the military fyftem. *Oeuvres de Rouffeau, Geneve,* 1782, tome ii. p. 381—397. It may be proper to remark, that my other citations from Rouffeau are from the fame edition.

citizen,

citizen, and may, as in ancient Republics, be made a neceſſary qualification for the purſuit of civil honors. In the preſent ſtate of France, the national guard is a ſufficient bulwark againſt the enemy, ſhould it relapſe into its ancient habits; and in its future ſtate, no body ſuſceptible of ſuch dangerous habits ſeems likely to exiſt. " *Gallos quoque in bel-* " *lis floruiſſe audivimus,*" may indeed be the ſentiment of our children. The glory of heroiſm, and the ſplendor of conqueſt, have long enough been the patrimony of that great nation. It is time that it ſhould ſeek a new glory, and a new ſplendor, under the ſhade of freedom, in cultivating the arts of peace, and extending the happineſs of mankind.—Happy if the example of that "Manifeſto of Humanity" which has been adopted by the Legiſlators of France into their conſtitutional code, made an adequate impreſſion on ſurrounding nations.

Tunc genus humanum poſitis ſibi conſulat armis
Inque vicem gens omnis amet.——

T 4　　　　　SECT

SECTION V.

Engli/h Admirers vindicated.

IT is thus that Mr. Burke has fpoken of the men and meafures of a foreign nation, where patriotifm could neither excufe his pre-poffeffion nor afperity; where no duty nor feeling ought to preclude him from adopting the feelings of difinterefted pofterity, and af-fuming the difpaffionate tone of a philofopher and a hiftorian. What wonder then that he fhould wanton ftill lefs temperately in all the eloquence and virulence of an advocate againft fellow-citizens, to whom he attributes the flagitious purpofe of ftimulating England to the imitation of fuch enormities. The Revolution and Conftitutional Societies, and Dr. Price, whom he regards as their oracle and

guide,

guide, are the grand objects of his hoftility. For them no contumely is too debafing, no invective is too intemperate, no imputation too foul. Joy at the downfall of defpotifm is the indelible crime, for which no virtue can compenfate, and no punifhment can atone. An inconfiftency however betrays itfelf not unfrequently in literary quarrels. He affects to defpife thofe whom he appears to dread. His anger exalts thofe whom his ridicule would vilify ; and on thofe whom at one mo-ment he derides as too contemptible for re-fentment, he at another confers a criminal eminence, as too audacious for contempt. Their voice is now the importunate chink of the meagre fhrivelled infects of the hour, now the hollow murmur, ominous of convulfions and earthquakes, that are to lay the fabric of fociety in ruins. To provoke againft the doc-trines and perfons of thefe unfortunate Soci-eties this ftorm of execration and derifion, it was not fufficient that the French Revolu-

tion

tion ſhould be traduced, every record of Engliſh policy and law is to be diſtorted.

The Revolution of 1688 is confeſſed to have eſtabliſhed principles by thoſe who lament that it has not reformed inſtitutions. It has ſanctified the theory, if it has not inſured the practice of a free Government. It declared, by a memorable precedent, the right of the people of England to revoke abuſed power, to frame the Government, and beſtow the Crown. There was a time, indeed, when ſome wretched followers of Filmer and Blackwood lifted their heads in oppoſition. But more than half a century had withdrawn them from public contempt, to the amneſty and oblivion which their innoxious ſtupidity had purchaſed.

It was reſerved for the latter end of the eighteenth century to conſtrue theſe innocent and obvious inferences into libels on the Con-

ſtitution

ftitution and the laws. Dr. Price has afferted (I prefume without fear of contradiction) that the Houfe of Hanover owes the Crown of England to the choice of their people, that the Revolution has eftablifhed our right " to " choofe our own Governors, to cafhier them " for mifconduct, and to frame a Govern- " ment for ourfelves." The firft propofition, fays Mr. Burke, is either falfe or nugatory. If it imports that England is an elective Mo- narchy, " * it is an unfounded, dangerous, illegal and unconftitutional pofition." " † If it alludes to the election of his Majefty's an- ceftors to the Throne, it no more legalizes the Government of England than that of other nations, where the founders of dynafties have generally founded their claims on fome fort of election." The firft member of this dilem- ma merits no reply. The people may cer- tainly, as they have done, *chufe* hereditary

* Page 17.   † P. 19.

rather

rather than elective Monarchy. They may *elect* a race inſtead of an individual. Their *right* is in all theſe caſes equally unimpaired. It will be in vain to compare the pretended elections in which a council of Barons, or an army of mercenaries, have impoſed uſurpers on enſlaved and benighted kingdoms, with the ſolemn, deliberate, national *choice* of 1688. It is, indeed, often expedient to ſaction theſe deficient titles by ſubſequent acquieſcence. It is not among the projected innovations of France to revive the claims of any of the poſterity of Paramond and Clovis, nor to arraign the uſurpations of Pepin or Hugh Capet. Public tranquillity thus demands a veil to be drawn over the ſucceſsful crimes through which Kings have ſo often waded to the Throne. But wherefore ſhould we not exult, that the Supreme Magiſtracy of England is free from this blot; that as a *direct* emanation from the ſovereignty of the people, it is as legitimate in its origin as in its adminiſtration. Thus underſtood, the poſition of Dr. Price is

neither

neither falfe nor nugatory. It is not nugatory, for it honourably diftinguifhes the Englifh Monarchy among the Governments of the world ; and if it be falfe, the whole hiftory of our Revolution muft be a legend. The fact was fhortly, that the Prince of Orange was elected King of England, in contempt of the claims, not only of the exiled Monarch and his fon, but of the Princeffes Mary and Anne, the undifputed progeny of James II. The title of William III. was then clearly not *fucceffion* ; and the Houfe of Commons ordered Dr. Burnet's tract to be burnt by the hands of hangman, for maintaining that it was *conqueft.* There remains only *election*, for thefe three claims to Royalty are all that are known among men. It is futile to urge, that the Convention deviated only *flenderly* from the order of fucceffion. The deviation was indeed flight, but it deftroyed the principle, and eftablifhed the right to deviate, the point at iffue. The principle that juftified the eleva-

of

tion of William III. and the preference of the pofterity of Sophia of Hanover to thofe of Henrietta of Orleans, would equally, *in point of right*, have vindicated the election of Chancellor Jefferies or Colonel Kirk. The *choice* was, like every other choice, to be guided by views of policy and prudence, but it was a choice ftill.

From thefe views arofe that repugnance between the conduct and the language of the Revolutionifts, of which Mr. Burke has availed himfelf. Their conduct was manly and fyftematic. Their language was conciliating and equivocal. They kept meafures with prejudice which they deemed neceffary to the order of fociety. They impofed on the groffnefs of the popular underftanding, by a fort of compromife between the Conftitution and the abdicated family. " They drew a " a politic well-wrought veil," to ufe the expreffion of Mr. Burke, over the glorious

fcene

ſcene which they had acted. They affected to preſerve a ſemblance of ſucceſſion, to recur for the objects of their election to the poſterity of Charles and James, that reſpect and loyalty might with leſs violence to public ſentiment attach to the new Sovereign. Had a Jacobite been permitted freedom of ſpeech in the Parliaments of William III. he might thus have arraigned the Act of Settlement—" Is the lan-
" guage of your ſtatutes to be at eternal war
" with truth ?—Not long ago you profaned
" the forms of devotion by a thankſgiving,
" which either means nothing, or inſinuates
" a lie. You thanked Heaven for the preſer-
" vation of a King and Queen on the *Throne*
" *of their anceſtors*; an expreſſion which ei-
" ther was ſingly meant of their deſcent,
" which was frivolous, or inſinuated their
" hereditary right, which was falſe.—With
" the ſame contempt for conſiſtency and
" truth, we are this day called on to ſettle
' the Crown of England on a Princeſs of
" Ger-

" Germany, " becaufe" fhe is the grand-
" daughter of James the Firft. If that be,
" as the phrafeology infinuates, the *true* and
" *fole* reafon of the choice, confiftency de-
" mands that the words after " excellent"
" fhould be omitted, and in their place be
" inferted " Victor Amadeus, Duke of Savoy,
" married to the daughter of the moft excel-
" lent Princefs Henrietta, late Dutchefs of
" Orleans, daughter of our late Sovereign
" Lord Charles I. of glorious memory."—
" Do homage to loyalty in your actions,
" or abjure it in your words—avow the
" grounds of your conduct, and your man-
" linefs will be refpected by thofe who de-
" teft your rebellion." What reply Lord
Somers, or Mr. Burke, could have devifed
to this Philippic, I know not, unlefs they
confeffed that the authors of the Revolution
had one language for novices and another for
adepts. Whether this conduct was the fruit
of caution and confummate wifdom, or of a

narrow,

narrow, arrogant, and daſtardly policy, which regarded the human race as only to be governed by being duped, it is uſeleſs to enquire, and might be preſumptuous to determine. But it certainly was not to be expected, that any controverſy ſhould have ariſen by confounding their *principles* with their *pretexts.* With the latter the poſition of Dr. Price has no connexion ; from the former, it is an infallible inference.

The next doctrine of this obnoxious ſermon that provokes the indignation of Mr. Burke, is, that the Revolution has eſtabliſhed " our right to caſhier our Governors for miſ- " conduct." Here a plain man could have foreſeen ſcarcely any diverſity of opinion. To contend that the depoſition of a King for the abuſe of his powers did not eſtabliſh a principle in favour of the like depoſition, when the like abuſe ſhould again occur, is certainly one of the moſt arduous enterprizes

U

that

that ever the heroism of paradox encountered. He has, however, not neglected the means of retreat. " No Government," he tells us, " could stand a moment, if it could be blown " down with any thing so loose and indefinite " as opinion of *misconduct*." One might suppose, from the dexterous levity with which the word misconduct is introduced, that the partizans of Democracy had maintained the expediency of deposing Kings for every frivolous and venial fault, of revolting against a Monarch for the choice of his titled or untitled valets, for removing his footmen, or his Lords of the Bedchamber. It would have been candid in Mr. Burke not to have dissembled what he must know, that by *misconduct* was meant that precise species of misconduct for which James II. was dethroned—A Conspiracy against the Liberty of his Country.

Nothing can be more weak than to urge the *Constitutional irresponsibility* of Kings or Parliaments.

Parliaments. The law can never suppose them responsible, because their responsibility supposes the dissolution of society, which is the annihilation of law. In the Governments which have hitherto existed, the power of the magistrate is the only article in the social compact. Destroy it, and society is dissolved. A legal provision for the responsibility of Kings would infer, that the authority of laws could co-exist with their destruction. It is because they cannot be legally and constitutionally, that they must be morally and rationally responsible. It is because there are no remedies to be found within the pale of society, that we are to seek them in nature, and throw out parchment chains in the face of our oppressors. No man can deduce a precedent of *law* from the Revolution, for law cannot exist in the dissolution of Government. A precedent of reason and justice only can be established on it; and perhaps the friends of freedom merit the misrepresen-

tation

tation with which they have been oppofed, for trufting their caufe to fuch frail and frivolous auxiliaries, and for feeking in the profligate practices of men what is to be found in the facred rights of Nature. The fyftem of law-yers is indeed widely different. They can only appeal to ufage, precedents, authorities, and ftatutes. They difplay their elaborate frivolity, their perfidious friendfhip, in dif-gracing freedom with the fantaftic honor of a pedigree. A pleader at the Old Bailey, who would attempt to aggravate the guilt of a rob-ber, or a murderer, by proving that King John, or King Alfred, punifhed robbery and mur-der, would only provoke derifion. A man who fhould pretend that the reafon why we had right to property is, becaufe our anceftors enjoyed that right 400 years ago, would be juftly contemned. Yet fo little is plain fenfe heard in the myfterious nonfenfe which is the cloak of political fraud, that the Cokes, the Blackftones, and Burkes, fpeak as if our right

to

to freedom depended on its poffeffion by our anceftors. In the common cafes of morality we would blufh at fuch an abfurdity. No man would juftify murder by its antiquity, or ftigmatize benevolence for being new. The genealogift who fhould emblazon the one as coeval with Cain, or ftigmatize the other as upftart with Howard, would be dif-claimed even by the moft frantic partizan of Ariftocracy. This Gothic transfer of *genea-logy* to truth and juftice is peculiar to politics. The exiftence of robbery in one age makes its vindication in the next ; and the champions of freedom have abandoned the ftrong hold of right for precedent, which, when the moft favorable, is, as might be expected from the ages which furnifh it, feeble, fluctuating, par-tial, and equivocal. It is not becaufe we *have* been free, but becaufe we have a right to be free, that we ought to demand freedom. Juftice and liberty have neither birth nor race, youth nor age. It would be the fame

abfurdity

abfurdity to affert, that we have a right to freedom, becaufe the Englifhmen of Alfred's reign were free, as that three and three are fix, *becaufe* they were fo in the camp of Genghis Khan. Let us hear no more of this ignoble and ignominious pedigree of freedom. Let us hear no more of her Saxon, Danifh, or Norman anceftors. Let the immortal daughter of Reafon, of Juftice, and of God, be no longer confounded with the fpurious abortions that have ufurped her name.

But, fays Mr. Burke, we do not contend that right as created by antiquarian refearch. We are far from contending that poffeffion legitimates tyranny, or that fact ought to be confounded with right. But (to ftrip Mr. Burke's eulogies on Englifh wifdom of their declamatory appendage) the impreffion of antiquity endears and ennobles freedom, and fortifies it by rendering it auguft and venerable in the popular mind. The illufion is ufeful.

uſeful. The expediency of *political impoſture* is the whole force of the argument; a principle odious and ſuſpected to the friends of freedom, as the grand bulwark of ſecular and ſpiritual deſpotiſm in the world. To pronounce that men are only to be governed by deluſion is to libel the human underſtanding, and to conſecrate the frauds that have elevated Deſpots and Muftis, Pontiffs and Sultans, on the ruin of degraded and oppreſſed humanity. But the doctrine is as falſe as it is odious. Primary political truths are few and ſimple. It is eaſy to make them underſtood, and to transfer to Government the ſame enlightened ſelf-intereſt that preſides in the other concerns of life. It may be made to be reſpected, not becauſe it is ancient, or becauſe it is ſacred, not becauſe it has been eſtabliſhed by Barons, or applauded by Prieſts, but becauſe it is uſeful. Men may eaſily be inſtructed to maintain rights which it is their *intereſt* to maintain, and duties which it is

U 4

their

their *interest* to perform. This is the only principle of authority that does not violate justice and insult humanity : it is also the only one which can possess stability. The various fashions of prejudice and factitious sentiment which have been the basis of Governments, are short-lived things. The illusions of chivalry, and the illusions of superstition, which give splendor or sanctity to Government, are in their turn succeeded by new modes of opinion and new systems of manners. Reason alone, and natural sentiment, are the denizens of every nation, and the cotemporaries of every age. A conviction of the utility of Government affords the only stable and honorable security for obedience.

Our ancestors at the Revolution, it is true were far from feeling the full force of these sublime truths; nor was the public mind of Europe, in the seventeenth century, sufficiently enlightened and matured for the grand enterprizes

enterprizes of legiſlation. The ſcience which teaches the rights of man, the eloquence that kindles the ſpirit of freedom, had for ages been buried with the other monuments of the wiſdom and relics of the genius of antiquity. But the revival of letters firſt unlocked only to a few the ſacred fountain. The neceſſary labors of criticiſm and lexicography occupied the earlier ſcholars, and ſome time elapſed before the ſpirit of antiquity was transfuſed into its admirers. The firſt man of that period who united elegant learning to original and maſculine thought was Buchanan*, and,

---

It is not a little remarkable, that Buchanan puts into the mouth of his antagoniſt, MAITLAND, the ſame alarms for the downfall of literature that have been excited in the mind of Mr. Burke by the French Revolution. We can ſmile at ſuch alarms on a retroſpect of the literary hiſtory of Europe for the 17th of 18 centuries; and ſhould our controverſies reach the enlightened ſcholars of a future age, they will probably, with the ſame reaſon, ſmile at the alarms of Mr. Burke.

he

he too feems to have been the firft fcholar
who caught from the ancients the noble flame
of republican enthufiafm. This praife is merited by his neglected, though incomparable
tract, *De Jure Regni*, in which the principles
of popular politics, and the maxims of a free
Government, are delivered with a precifion,
and enforced with an energy, which no former age had equalled, and no fucceeding has
furpaffed. But the fubfequent progrefs of the
human mind was flow. The profound views
of Harrington were derided as the ravings of
a vifionary; and who can wonder, that the
frantic loyalty which depreffed Paradife Loft,
fhould involve in ignominy the eloquent apology of Milton* for the people of England
againft

* " Peffime enim vel naturâ vel legibus comparatum
" foret fi arguta fervitus, libertas muta effet; & haberent
" tyranni qui pro fe dicerent, non haberent qui tyrannos
" debellare poffunt: Miferum effet fi hæc ipfa ratio quo
" utimur Dei munere non multo plura ad homines conver-
" vander,

againſt a feeble and venal pedant. Sidney " by
" ancient learning, to the enlightened love of
" ancient freedom warmed," taught the principles which he had fealed with his blood; and
Locke, whofe praife is lefs that of being bold
and original, than of being temperate, found,
lucid, and methodical, deferves the immortal
honor of having fyftematized and rendered
popular the doctrines of civil and religious liberty. In Ireland, Molyneux, the friend of
Locke, produced the " *Cafe of Ireland*," a production of which it is fufficient praife to fay,
that it was ordered to be burnt by a defpotic

" vandos, liberandos, et *quantum natura fert* INTER SE
" AEQUANDOS quam ad opprimendos et fub UNIUS Imperio
" male perdendos argumenta fuppe ditaret. CAUSAM itaque
" PULCHERRIMAM hac certe fiducia læti aggrediamur; fi-
" linc fraudem, fallaciam, ignorantiam atque barbæriem;
" hinc lucem, veritatem rationem et feculorum omnium
ftudia atque doctrinam nobis cum ftare."

Joannis Miltoni Defenfio Populi Anglicani apud Opera,

tom. 2, p. 258. Ed. Lond. 1738.

Parliament

Parliament; and in Scotland, Andrew Fletcher, the scholar of Algernon Sidney, maintained the cause of his deserted country with the force of ancient eloquence, and the dignity of ancient virtue.

Such is a rapid enumeration of those who had before, or near the Revolution, contributed to the diffusion of political light. But their number was small, their writings were unpopular, their dogmas were proscribed. The habits of reading had only then begun to reach the great body of mankind, whom the arrogance of rank and letters has ignominiously confounded under the denomination of the vulgar. Many causes too contributed to form a powerful Tory interest in England. The remnant of that Gothic sentiment, the extinction of which Mr. Burke so pathetically deplores, which engrafted loyalty on a point of honor in military attachment, formed one part, which may be called the *Toryism of Chivalry*.

Chivalry. Doctrines of a divine right in Kings, which are now too much forgotten even for fuccefsful ridicule, were then fupported and revered.—This may be called the *Toryifm of Superftition.* And a third fpecies arofe from the great transfer of property into an upftart commercial intereft, which drove the ancient gentry of England, for protection againft its inroads, behind the Throne. This may be called the *Toryifm of Landed Arifto-cracy*.* Religious prejudices, outrages on

---

* Principle is refpectable, even it its miftakes, and thefe Tories of the laft century were a party of principle. There were accordingly among them men of the moft elevated and untainted honor. Who will refufe that praife to Clarendon and Southampton, Ormond and Montrofe?—But Toryifm, as a party of principle, cannot now exift in England; for the principles on which we have feen it to be founded, exift no more. The Gothic fentiment is effaced, the fuperftition is exploded, and the landed and commercial interefts are completely intermixed. The Toryifm of the prefent day can only arife from an abject fpirit or a corrupt heart.

natural fentiments, which any artificial fyftem is too feeble to withftand, and the ftream of events which bore them along to extremities which no man could have forefeen, involved the Tories in the Revolution, and made it a truly national act.

But their repugnance to every fhadow of innovation was invincible. Something the Whigs may be fuppofed to have conceded for the fake of conciliation, but few even of their leaders, it is probable, had grand and liberal views. What indeed could have been expected from the delegates of a nation, in which, a few years before, the Univerfity of Oxford, reprefenting the national learning and wifdom, had, in a folemn decree, offered their congratulations to Sir George Mackenzie (infamous for the abufe of brilliancy and accomplifhment to the moft fervile and profligate purpofes) as having confuted the abominable doctrines of Buchanan and Milton,

and

and demonſtrated the divine rights of Kings to
tyrannize and oppreſs mankind !   It muſt be
evident, that a people which could thus, by
the organ of its moſt learned body, proſtrate
its reaſon before ſuch execrable abſurdities,
was too *young* for legiſlation.   Hence the abſurd debates in the Convention about the palliative phraſes of abdicate, deſert, &c. which
were better cut ſhort by the Parliament of
Scotland, when they uſed the correct and
manly expreſſion, that James II. had FOR-
FEITED THE THRONE.   Hence we find the
Revolutioniſts perpetually belying their political conduct by their legal phraſeology.——
Hence their impotent and illuſive reforms.——
Hence their neglect of foreſight   in not pro-

viding

---

* This progreſs of Royal influence from a diſputed ſucceſſion has, in fact, moſt fatally taken place. The Proteſtant
ſucceſſion was the ſuppoſed means of preſerving our liber-
ties, and to that *means* the end has been moſt deplorably ſa-
crificed. The Whigs, the ſincere, though timid and partial

friends

viding bulwarks againſt the natural tendency of a diſputed ſucceſſion to accelerate moſt rapidly the progreſs of Royal influence, by rendering it neceſſary to ſtrengthen ſo much the poſſeſſor of the Crown againſt the pretender to it, and thus partially ſacrificing freedom to the very means of preſerving it.

But to elucidate the queſtion more fully, " let us liſten to the genuine oracles of Re- " volution policy;" not to the equivocal and palliative language of their ſtatutes, but to the unreſtrained effuſion of ſentiment in that me-

friends of freedom, were forced to cling to the Throne as the anchor of liberty. To preſerve it from utter ſhipwreck, they were forced to yield ſomething to its protectors. Hence a national debt, a ſeptennial Parliament, and a ſtanding army. The avowed reaſon of the two laſt was Jacobitiſm. Hence the unnatural Coalition between Whiggiſm and Kings during the reigns of the two firſt Princes of the Houſe of Hanover, which the pupillage of Leiceſter-houſe ſo totally broke.

morable

morable conference between the Lords and Commons, on Tuefday the 5th of February, 1688, which terminated in eftablifhing the prefent Government of England. The Tories, yielding to the torrent in the *perfonal* exclufion of James II. refolved to embarrafs the Whigs, by urging that the declaration of the abdication and vacancy of the Throne, was a change of the Government, *pro hac vice*, into an elective Monarchy. The inference is irrefiftible, and it muft be confeffed, that though the Whigs were the better citizens, the Tories were the more correct logicians. It is in this conference that we fee the Whig leaders compelled to difclofe fo much of thofe principles, which tendernefs for prejudice, and reverence for ufage, had influenced them to diffemble. It is here that we fhall difcover fparks kindled in the collifion of debate fufficient to enlighten the " politic " gloom" in which they had enveloped their meafures.

X

If

If there be any names venerable among the conftitutional lawyers of England, they are thofe of Lord Somers and Mr. Serjeant Maynard. They were both confpicuous managers · for the Commons in this conference, and the language of both will more than fanctify the inferences of Dr. Price, and the creed of the Revolution Society. My Lord Nottingham, who conducted the conference on the part of the Tories, in a manner moft honorable to his dexterity and acutenefs, demanded of the Managers for the Commons, " Whether they " mean the Throne to be fo *vacant* as to null " the fucceffion in the hereditary line, and " fo all the heirs to be cut off? which we " (the Lords) fay, will make the Crown " *elective.*" Maynard, whofe argument always breathed much of the old republican fpirit, replied with force and plainnefs, " It is " not that the Commons do fay the Crown " of England is ALWAYS AND PERPETU- " ALLY ELECTIVE, but it is neceffary there

" be

" be a fupply where there is a defect." It
is impoffible to miftake the import of thefe
words. Nothing can be more evident, than
that by the mode of *denying* that the Crown
WAS ALWAYS AND PERPETUALLY ELEC-
TIVE, he confeffes that it was for the then
exigency *elective*. In purfuance of his argument, he ufes a comparifon ftrongly illuftra-
tive of his belief in dogmas anathematized by
Mr. Burke. " If two of us make a mutual
" agreement to help and defend each other
" from any one that fhould affualt us in a
" journey, and he that is with me turns upon
" me, and breaks my head, he hath un-
" doubtedly *abdicated* my affiftance, and re-
" voked." Sentiments of the Kingly office,
more irreverent and correct, are not to be
found in the moft profane evangelift that dif-
graces the Demoratic canon. It is not unworthy of incidental remark, that there were
then perfons who felt as great horror at novelties, which have fince been univerfally re-

X 2

ceived,

ceived, as Mr. Burke now feels at the " rights
" of men."   The Earl of Clarendon, in his
ſtrictures on the ſpeech of Mr. Somers, ſaid,
" I may ſay thus much in general, that this
" breaking the original contract is a language
" that has not long been uſed in this place;
" nor known in any of our law-books, or
" Public records. It is ſprung up but as taken
" from ſome late authors, and thoſe none of
" the beſt received!"—This language one
might have ſuppoſed to be that of Mr. Burke.
It is not however his; it is that of a Jacobite
Lord of the 17th century !

The Tories continued to perplex and inti-
midate the Whigs with idea of *election.*—
Maynard again replies, " The word *elective* is
" none of the Commons word. The provi-
" ſion muſt be made, and if it be, that will not
" render the kingdom *perpetually* ELECTIVE."
If it were neceſſary to multiply citations to
prove, that the Revolution was to all intents

and

and purpofes an *election*, we might hear Lord Nottingham, whofe diftinction is peculiarly applicable to the cafe before us. " If," fays he, " you do once make it *elective*, I do not " fay you are always *bound* to go to *election*, " but it is enough to make it fo, if by that " precedent there be a breach in the heredi- " tary fucceffion." The reafoning of Sir Robert Howard, another of the Managers for the Commons, is bold and explicit. " My " Lords, you will do well to confider; have " you not yourfelves limited the fucceffion, " and cut off fome that might have a line of " right? Have you not concurred with us in " our vote, that it is inconfiftent with our " religion and our laws to have a Papift to " reign over us? *Muft* we not then come to " an ELECTION, if the next heir be a Papift?" The precife fact which followed.—But what tends the moft ftrongly to illuftrate that contradiction between the *exoteric* and *efoteric* doctrine, the legal language, and the real

X 3

principles,

principles, which forms the bafis of this whole argument, is the avowal of Sir Richard Temple, another of the Managers for the Commons—" We are in as natural a capacity " as any of our predeceffors were to provide " for a remdy in fuch exigencies as this."— Hence it followed infallibly, that their pofterity to all generations *would be in the fame* " *natural capacity*," to provide remedy for exigencies. But let us hear their Statutes. There " the Lords Spiritual and Temporal, " and Commons, do, in the name of all the " people of England, moft humbly *andfaith-* " *fully fubmit themfelves, their heirs and pofte-* " *rity for ever*," &c. Here is the triumph of Mr. Burke—a folemn abdication and renunciation of right to change the Monarch or the Conftitution ! His triumph is increafed by this ftatutory abolition of the rights of men being copied from a fimilar profeffion of eternal allegiance made by the Parliament of Elizabeth !—It is difficult to conceive any thing

more

more prepofterous. In the very act of exercifing a right which their anceftors had abdicated in their name, they abdicate the fame
right in the name of their pofterity. To increafe the ridicule of this legiflative farce,
they impofe an *irrevocable* law on their pofterity, in the precife words of that law irrevocably impofed on them by their anceftors, at
the moment when they are violating it. The
Parliament of Elizabeth fubmit themfelves
and their pofterity for ever. The Convention
of 1688 fpurn the fubmiffion for themfelves,
but re-enact it for their pofterity. And after
fuch a glaring inconfiftency, this language of
ftatutory adulation is ferioufly and triumphant-
ly brought forward as " *the unerring oracles*
" of Revolution policy."

Thus evidently has it appeared, from the
conduct and language of the leaders of the
Revolution, that it was a *depofition* and an
election ; and that all language of a contrary

X 4

tendency,

tendency, which is to be found in their acts, arose from the remnant of their own prejudice, or from conceſſion to the prejudice of others, or from the superficial and presumptuous policy of impoſing auguſt illuſions on mankind. The same ſpirit regulated, the same prejudices impeded their progreſs in every department. " They acted," ſays Mr. Burke, " by their ancient States." They did not—Were the Peers, and the members of a diſſolved Houſe of Commons, with the Lord-Mayor of London, &c. convoked by a ſummons from the Prince of Orange, the Parliament of England ?—No. They were neither lawfully elected nor lawfully aſſembled. But they affected a ſemblance of a Parliament in their convention, and a ſemblance of hereditary right in their election. The ſubſequent act of Parliament is nugatory ; for as that Legiſlature derived its whole exiſtence and authority from the Convention, it could not return more than it had received, and could

not

not therefore *legalize* the acts of the body which created it. If they were not previously legal, the Parliament itself was without *legal* authority, and could, therefore, give no legal sanction. It is therefore without any view to a prior, or allusion to a subsequent Revolution, that Dr. Price, and the Revolution Society of London, think themselves entitled to conclude, that abused power is revocable, and corrupt Governments ought to be reformed. Of the first of these Revolutions, that in 1648, they may, perhaps, entertain different sentiments from Mr. Burke. They will confess that it was debased by the mixture of fanaticism; they may lament that history has so often prostituted her ungenerous suffrage to success, and that the Commonwealth was obscured and overwhelmed by the splendid profligacy of military usurpation. But they cannot arrogate the praise of having been the first to maintain, nor can Mr. Burke support

his

his claim to have been the firſt who reprobated, *ſince that period*, the audacious hereſy of
popular politics. The prototype of Mr. Burke
is not a leſs notorious perſonage than the pre-
deceſſor he has aſſigned to Dr. Price. Hiſtory
has preſerved fewer memorials of Hugh Peters
than of Judge Jeffries. It was the fortune of
that luminary and model of lawyers to ſit in
judgment on one of the fanatical apoſtles of
Democracy. In the preſent ignominious ob-
ſcurity of the ſect in England, it may be neceſſary to mention that the name of this criminal was Algernon Sidney. He had, it is
true, in his time acquired ſome renown : He
was celebrated as the hero, and deplored as
the martyr of freedom. But the learned magiſtrate was above this " epidemical fanati-
" ciſm." He inveighed againſt his peſtilential
dogmas in a ſpirit that deprives Mr. Burke's
invective againſt Dr. Price of all pretenſions
to originality. An unvarniſhed ſtatement will

ſo

fo evince the harmony both of the culprits and the accufers, that remark is fuperfluous—

<table>
<tr><td>

ALGERNON SIDNEY.

(Indictment againft him.)

" And that the aforefaid Algernon Sidney did make, compofe and write, or caufe to be made, compofed and written, a certain falfe, fcandalous and feditious libel, in which is contained the following Englifh words——
" *The Power originally in the*
" *people is delegated to the*
" *Parliament*—He (mean-
" ing the King) is fubject
" to the laws of God, as he
" is a man, and to the people
" that made him a King, in-
" afmuch as he is a King."
—And in another place of the faid libel he fays, " We
" may therefore take away
" Kings without breaking
" any yoke, or that is made
" a yoke, which ought not
" to be one, and the injury
" therefore is making or im-
" pofing, and there can be
" none in breaking it," &c.

</td><td>

DOCTOR PRICE.

His Sermon.

" We have a right to chufe our own Governors, to cafhier them for mifconduct, and to frame a Government for ourfelves."

</td></tr>
</table>

Thus

Thus we see the harmony of the culprits. The one is only a perspicuous and precise abridgment of the other. The harmony of the Judges will not be found less remarkable. Mr. Burke, " when he talks as if he had " made a discovery, only follows a prece- " dent."

<table>
<tr><td>JUDGE JEFFRIES'
Charge to the Jury.</td><td>MR. BURKE.</td></tr>
<tr><td>" The King, it says, is responsible to them, and he is only their trustee. He has misgoverned, and he is to give it up, that they may be all Kings themselves. Gentlemen, I must tell you, I think I ought, more than ordinarily to press this on you, because I know the misfortunes of the late unhappy rebellion ; and the bringing of the late blessed King to the scaffold was first begun by such kind of principles*.</td><td>" The Revolution Society chuses to assert, that a King is no more than the first servant of the Public, created by it, and responsible to it." —" The second claim of the Revolution Society is cashiering the Monarch for misconduct," p. 37. " The Revolution Society, the heroic band of fabricators of Governments, electors of Sovereigns," p. 98. " This sermon is in a strain which has never been heard in this kingdom in any of the pulpits which are tolerated or encouraged in it since 1648."</td></tr>
</table>

* Trial of Algernon Sidney for High Treason. State Trials, vol. iii. page 710, & seq.

Thus

Thus does Mr. Burke chaunt his political fong in exact unifon with the ftrains of the venerable Magiftrate; they indict the fame crimes; they impute the fame motives; they dread the fame confequences.

The Revolution Society felt, from the great event which they profeffedly commemorated, new motives to exult in the emancipation of France. The Revolution of 1688 deferves more the attention of a philofopher from its indirect influence on the progrefs of human opinion, than from its immediate effects on the Government of England. In the firft view, it is perhaps difficult to eftimate the magnitude of its effects. It fanctified, as we have feen, the general principles of freedom. It gave the firft example in civilized modern Europe of a Government which reconciled a femblance of *political*, and a large portion of *civil* liberty with ftability and peace. But above all, Europe owes to it the

ineftimable

ineſtimable bleſſing of an aſylum for freedom
of thought.   Hence England became the pre-
ceptreſs of the world in philoſophy and freedom.   Hence aroſe the ſchool of ſages, who
unſhackled and emancipated the human mind;
from among whom iſſued the Lockes, the
Rouſſeaus, the Turgots, and the Franklins,
the immortal band of preceptors and bene-
factors of mankind.   They ſilently operated
a grand *moral* Revolution, which was in due
time to meliorate the ſocial order.   They had
tyrants to dethrone more formidable than
Kings, and from whom Kings held their
power.   They wreſted the ſceptre from ſuperſtition, and dragged prejudice in triumph.
They deſtroyed the arſenal whence deſpotiſm
had borrowed her thunders and her chains.
Theſe grand enterprizes of philoſophic heroiſm muſt have preceded the reforms of civil
Government.   The Coloſſus of tyranny was
undermined, and a pebble overthrew it.——
From this progreſs of opinion aroſe the American

rican Revolution, and from this, moſt unqueſ-
tionably the delivery of France. Nothing,
therefore, could be more natural, than that
thoſe who, without blind bigotry for the
forms, had a rational reverence for the principles of our anceſtors, ſhall rejoice in a Revolution, where theſe principles, which England had ſo long ſuffered to repoſe in impotent abſtraction, were called forth into energy,
expanded, invigorated, and matured. If, as
we have preſumed to ſuppoſe, the Revolution of 1688 may have had no ſmall ſhare in
accelerating that progreſs of light which has
diſſolved the prejudices that ſupported deſpotiſm, they may be permitted, beſides their
exultation as friends of humanity, to indulge
ſome pride as Engliſhmen.

It muſt be confeſſed that our anceſtors in
1688, confined, in their practical regulations,
their views ſolely to the urgent abuſe. They
puniſhed the uſurper without meliorating the
Government,

Government, and they proscribed usurpations without correcting their source. They were content to clear the turbid stream, instead of purifying the polluted fountain. They merit, however, veneration for their atchievements, and the most ample amnesty for their defects, for the first were their own, and the last are imputable to the age in which they lived.— The true admirers of the Revolution will pardon it for having spared abusive establishments, only because they revere it for having established grand principles. But the case of Mr. Burke is different ; he deifies its defects, and derides its principles; and were Lord Somers to listen to such misplaced eulogy, and tortured inference, he might justly say, " You " deny us the only praise we can claim, and " the only merit you allow us is in the sa- " crifices we were compelled to make to pre- " judice and ignorance. Your glory is our " shame." Reverence for the principles, and pardon to the defects of civil changes, which

arise

arife in ages partially enlightened, are the plain dictates of common-fenfe. Admiration of Magna Charta does not infer any refpect from villainage. Reverence for Roman patriotifm is not incompatible with deteftation of flavery; nor does veneration for the Revolutionifts of 1688 impofe any blindnefs to the grofs, radical, and multiplied abfurdities and corruptions in their political fyftem. The true admirers of Revolution principles cannot venerate inftitutions as fage and effectual protection of freedom, which experience has proved to be nervelefs and illufive. "The " practical claim of impeachment," the vaunted refponfibility of Minifters, is the moft forry juggle of a political empiricifm by which a people were ever attempted to be lulled into fervitude. State profecutions in free ftates have ever either languifhed in impotent and defpifed tedioufnefs, or burft forth in a ftorm of popular indignation, that at once overwhelms its object, without difcrimination

Y   of

of innocence or guilt. Nothing but this irrefiftible fervor can deftroy the barriers within
which powerful and opulent delinquents are
fortified. If this fervor is not with imminent
hazard of equity and humanity gratified in the
moment, it fubfides. The natural influence
of the culprit, and of the accomplices interefted in his impunity, refumes it place. As
thefe trials are neceffarily long, the facts which
produce conviction, and the eloquence which
rouzes indignation, being effaced from the
Public mind by time, by ribaldry and fophiftry, the fhame of a corrupt decifion is ex-
tenuated. Every fource of obloquy or odium
that can be attached to the obnoxious and invidious character of an accufer, is exhaufted
by the profufe corruption of the delinquent.
The tribunal of Public opinion, which alone
preferves the purity of others, is itfelf polluted, and a people wearied, difgufted, irri-
tated, and corrupted, fuffer the culprit to re-
tire

tire in impunity * and fplendor. *Damnatus inani judicio quid enim falvis infamin nummis.* Such has ever been the ftate of things, when the force of the Government has been fufficient to protect the accufed from the firft ebulition of popular impetuofity. The Democracies of antiquity prefented a fpectacle directly the reverfe ; but no hiftory affords any example of a juft medium. State trials will always either be impotent or oppreffive, a perfecution or a farce. Thus vain is the fecurity of impeachment, and equally abfurd, furely, is our confidence in " the control of Parliaments," in their prefent Conftitution, and with their remaining powers. To begin with the laft. They poffefs the *nominal* power of impeachment. Not to mention its difufe in

---

* Part of this defcription is purely *hiftorical.* Heaven forbid that the fequel fhould prove *prophetic.* When this fubject prefents Mr. Burke to mind, I muft fay, TALIS cum fis utinam nofter effes.

the

the cafe of any Minifter for more than feventy years, it is always too late to remedy the evil, and probably always too weak to punifh the criminal. They poffefs a pretended power of with-holding fupplies. But the fituation of fociety has in truth wrefted it from them. The fupplies they muft vote, for the army muft have its pay, and the Public creditors their intereft. A power that cannot be exercifed without provoking mutiny, and proclaiming bankruptcy, the blindeft bigot cannot deny to be purely *nominal.* A practical fubftitute for thefe theoretical powers exifted till our days in the *negative* exercifed by the Houfe of Commons on the choice of the Minifter of the Crown. But the elevation of Mr. Pitt eftablifhed a precedent which extirpated the laft *fhadow* of popular control from the Government of England—

Olim vera fides

Sulla Mario que receptis libertatis obit

Pompeio rebus adempto nunc & ficta perit.

But

But in truth, the force and the privileges of Parliament are almoſt indifferent to the people, for it is not the guardian of their rights, nor the organ of their voice. We are ſaid to be *unequally* repreſented. This is one of thoſe contradictory phraſes that form the political jargon of half-enlightened periods. Unequal freedom is a contradiction in terms. It ought not to be called freedom, but the power of ſome, and the ſlavery of others—the oppreſſion of one portion of mankind by another. The law is the deliberate reaſon of ALL, guiding *their* occaſional will. Repreſentation is an expedient for peacefully, ſyſtematically, and unequivocally collecting this univerſal voice. So thought and ſo ſpoke the Edmund Burke of better times. " To follow, not to " force the Public inclination, to give a di- " rection, a form, a technical dreſs, and a " ſpecific ſanction to the general ſenſe of the " community is the true end of Legiſlature."

Burke's two Letters to Gentlemen in Briſtol.

page

page 52. There fpoke the correfpondent of Franklin*, the Champion of America, the enlightened advocate of humanity and free-dom!—If thefe principles be true, and they are fo true that it feems almoft puerile to re-peat them, who can without indignation hear the Houfe of Commons of England called a popular reprefentative? A more infolent and prepofterous abufe of language is not to be found in the vocabulary of tyrants. The cri-terion that diftinguifhes *laws* from *dictates*, freedom from fervitude, rightful Government from ufurpation, *the law being an expreffion of the general will*, is wanting. This is the grievance which the admirers of the Revo-lution in 1688 defire to remedy according to its *principles*. This is that perennial fource of corruption which has increafed, is increafing, and ought to be diminifhed. If the general

* Mr. Burke has had the honor of being traduced for correfponding, during the American war, with this great man, becaufe he was a *Rebel*.

interest

intereſt is not the object of our Government, it is, it muſt be, becauſe the general will does not govern. We are boldly challenged to produce our proofs; our complaints are aſ-ſerted to be chimerical, and the excellence of our Government is inferred from its beneficial effects. Moſt unfortunately for us, moſt un-fortunately for our country, theſe proofs are too ready, and too numerous. We find them in that " monumental debt," the *bequeſt* of waſteful and profligate wars, which already wrings from the peaſant ſomething of his hard-earned pittance, which already has pu-niſhed the induſtry of the uſeful and upright manufacturer, by robbing him of the aſylum of his houſe, and the judgment of his peers, to which the madneſs of political Quixotiſm adds a million for every farthing that the pomp of Miniſterial empiriciſm pays, and which menaces our children with convulſions and calamities, of which no age has ſeen the pa-rallel. We find them in the black and bloody

Roll

Roll of perfecuting ftatutes that are ftill fuffered to ftain our code; a lift fo execrable,
that were no monument to be preferved of
what England was in the eighteenth century
but her ftatute book, fhe might be deemed
ftill plunged in the deepeft gloom of fuperftitious barbarifm. We find them in the ignominious exclufion of great bodies of our fellow citizens from political trufts, by tefts
which reward falfhood and punifh probity,
which profane the rites of the religion they
pretend to guard, and ufurp the dominion of
the God they profefs to revere. We find them
in the growing corruption of thofe who adminifter the Government; in the venality of a
Houfe of Commons, which has become only a
cumbrous and expenfive chamber for regifter-
ing Minifterial edicts—in the increafe of a Nobility arrived to a degradation, by the profu-
fion and proftitution of honors, which the
moft zealous partizans of Democracy would
have fpared them. We find them, ABOVE

ALL,

ALL, in the rapid progrefs which has been made to filence the great organ of Public opinion, the Prefs, which is the true control on Minifters and Parliaments, who might elfe, with impunity, trample on the impotent formalities that form the pretended bulwark of our freedom. The mutual control, the well-poifed balance of the feveral members of our Legiflature, are the vifions of theoretical, or the pretext of practical politicians. It is a Government, not of check, but of confpiracy—a confpiracy which can only be reprefled by the energy of popular opinion.

Thefe are no vifionary ills, no chimerical apprehenfions. They are the fad and fober reflections of as honeft and enlightened men as any in the kingdom; nor are they allevi-ated by the torpid and liftlefs fecurity into which the people feem to be lulled—*Summum otium forenfe non quiefcentis fed fenefcentis ci-vitatis.* It is in this fatal temper that men become

become fufficiently debafed and embruted to fink into placid and polluted fervitude. It is then that it may moft truly be faid, that the *mind* of a country is flain. The admirers of Revolution principles naturally call on every aggrieved and enlightened citizen to confider the fource of his oppreffion. If penal ftatutes hang over our Catholic brethren*,

* No body of men in any State that pretends to freedom have ever been fo infolently oppreffed as the *Catholic* MAJORITY of Ireland. Their caufe has been lately pleaded by an eloquent Advocate, whofe virtues might have been fuppofed to have influenced my praife, as the partial dictate of friendfhip, had not his genius extorted it as a ftrict tribute to juftice. I perceive that HE retains much of that *admiration* which WE cherifhed in common by his claffical quotation refpecting Mr. Burke—

Soli quippe vacat, ftudiifque adiifque carenti
Humanum lugere genus——— ———

See " The CONSTITUTIONAL INTERESTS of IRELAND with refpect to the POPERY LAWS." P. IV. Dublin, 1791.

if teſt acts outrage our Proteſtant fellow-citizens, if the remains of feudal tyranny are
ſtill ſuffered to exiſt in Scotland, if the preſs
is fettered, if our right to trial by jury is
abridged, if our manufacturers are proſcibed
and hunted down by EXCISE, the reaſon of all
theſe oppreſſions is the ſame. No branch of
the Legiſlature repreſents the people. Men
are oppreſſed, becauſe they have no ſhare in
their own government. Let all theſe claſſes
of oppreſſed citizens melt their local and partial grievances into one great maſs. Let them
ceaſe to be ſuppliants for their rights, or to
ſue for them like mendicants, as a precarious
boon from the arrogant pity of uſurpers. Until
the Legiſlature ſpeaks their voice, it will oppreſs them. Let them unite to procure ſuch
a reform in the repreſentation of the people,
as will make the Houſe of Commons their
repreſentatives. If diſmiſſing all petty views
of obtaining their own particular ends, they
unite for this great object, they muſt ſucceed.

The

'The co-operating efforts of fo many bodies of citizens muft awaken the nation, and its voice will be fpoken in a tone that virtuous Governors will obey, and tyrannical Governors muft dread. It is impoffible to fuppofe the exiftence of fuch infolent profligacy as would affect to defpife the national voice, if it were unequivocally fpoken.

This tranquil and legal reform is the ultimate object of thofe whom Mr. Burke has fo foully branded. In effect this would be amply fufficient. The powers of the King and the Lords have never been formidable in England, but from difcords between the Houfe of Commons and its pretended conftituents. Were that Houfe really to become the vehicle of the popular voice, the privileges of other bodies, in oppofition to the fenfe of the people and their reprefentatives, would be but as duft in the balance. From this radical improvement all fubaltern reform

would

would naturally and peaceably arife. We dream of no more, and in claiming this, inftead of meriting the imputation of being apoftles of fedition, we conceive ourfelves entitled to be confidered as the moft fincere friends of tranquil and ftable Government.—We defire to avert revolution* by reform; fubverfion by correction. We admonifh our Governors to reform, while they retain the force to reform with dignity and fecurity; and we conjure them not to wait the moment, which *will infallibly* arrive, when they fhall be obliged to fupplicate that people, whom they opprefs and defpife, for the flendereft pittance of their prefent powers.

* Let the Governors of all States compare the convulfion which the obftinacy of the Government provoked in France, with the peaceful and dignified reform which its wifdom effected in POLAND. The moment is important, the dilemma inevitable, the alternative awful, the leffon moft inftructive'——

The

The grievances of England do not now, we confefs, juftify a change by violence; but they are in a rapid progrefs to that fatal ftate, in which they will both juftify and produce it. It is becaufe we fincerely love tranquil * freedom, that we earneftly deprecate the moment when virtue and honor fhall compel us to feek her with our fwords. Are not *they* the true friends to authority who defire, that whatever is granted by it " fhould iffue as a " gift of her bounty and beneficence, rather " than as claims recovered againft a ftrug- " gling litigant? Or, at leaft, that if her " beneficence obtained no credit in her con- " ceffions, they fhould appear the falutary " provifions of wifdom and forefight, not as " things wrung with blood by the cruel gripe " of a rigid neceffity†." We defire that the political light which is to break in on England

---

* Manus hæc inimica Tyrannis

    Enfe petit placidam fub libertate quietem.—

    † Burke's Speech at Briftol, page 13.

fhould

ſhould be " through well-contrived and well-
" diſpoſed windows, not through flaws and
" breaches, through the yawning chaſms of
" our ruin*."

Such was the language of Mr. Burke
in caſes nearly parallel to the preſent. But
of thoſe who now preſume to give ſimilar counſels, his alarm and abhorrence are
extreme. They deem the " preſent times,"
favorable " to all exertions in the cauſe of
" liberty." They naturally muſt. Their
hopes in that great cauſe are from the determined and according voices of enlightened
men. The ſhock that deſtroyed the deſpotiſm
of France has widely diſperſed the clouds
that intercepted reaſon from the political and
moral world; and we cannot ſuppoſe, that
England is the only ſpot that has not been
reached by this " flood of light" that has burſt
upon the human race.—We might ſuppoſe

* Burke's Speech at Bristol, p. 15.

too,

too, that Englishmen would be shamed out of their torpor by the great exertions of nations whom we had long deemed buried in hopeless servitude. Thus far we might be pardoned for thinking the present moment peculiarly auspicious to exertions in the cause of freedom.

But nothing *can* be more absurd than to assert, that all who *admire* wish to *imitate* the French Revolution. In ONE view there is room for diversity of opinion among the warmest and wisest friends of freedom, as to the *portion* of Democracy infused into the Government of France. In another, and a more important one, it is to be recollected, that the conduct of nations is to vary with the circumstances in which they are placed.— Blind admirers of Revolutions take them for implicit models. Thus Mr. Burke admires that of 1688 ; but we, who conceive that we pay the purest homage to the authors of that Revolution,

Revolution, not in contending for what they *then* DID, but for what they *now* WOULD DO, can feel no inconfiftency in looking on France, not to model our conduct, but to invigorate the fpirit of freedom. We permit ourfelves to imagine how Lord Somers, in the light and knowledge of the eighteenth century, how the patriots of France, in the tranquillity and opulence of England, would have acted. We are not bound to copy the conduct to which the laft were driven by a bankrupt Exchequer and a diffolved Government, nor to maintain the eftablifhments, which were fpared by the firft in a prejudiced and benighted age. Exact imitation is not neceffary to reverence. We venerate the principles which prefided in both events, and we adapt to political admiration a maxim which has long been received in polite letters, that the only manly and liberal imitation is to fpeak as a great man would have fpoken, had he lived in our times, and been placed in our circumftances.

Z

But

But let us hear the charge of Mr. Burke.
" Is our Monarchy to be annihilated, with
" all the laws, all the tribunals, all the an-
" cient corporations of the kingdom ?   Is
" every land-mark of the kingdom to be done
" away in favour of a geometrical and arith-
" metical Conftitution ?   Is the Houfe of
" Lords to be ufelefs ?   Is Epifcopacy to be
" abolifhed ?"—and, in a word, is France to
be imitated ?   Yes ! if our Governors imitate
her policy, the State muft follow her cataf-
trophe.   Man is every where MAN—imprifoned grievance will at length have vent, and
the form of popular paffion will find a feeble
obftacle in the folemn imbecility of human
inftitutions.   But who are the true friends to
the order of Government, the prorogative of
the Monarch, the fplender of the hierarchy,
and the dignity of the peerage ?   Thofe moft
certainly who inculcate, that to with-hold reform is to ftimulate convulfion ; thofe who
admonifh all to whom honor, and rank, and

dignity,

dignity, and wealth are dear, that they can only in the end preferve them by conceding, while the moment of conceffion remains; thofe who aim at draining away the fountains that feed the torrent, inftead of oppofing puny barriers to its courfe.

"The beginnings of confufion in Eng-
" land are at prefent feeble enough, but with
" you we have feen an infancy ftill more
" feeble growing by moments into a ftrength
" to heap mountains upon mountains, and
" to wage war with Heaven itfelf.———
" Whenever our neighbour's houfe is on fire,
" it cannot be amifs for the engines to play
" a little upon our own." This language, taken in its moft natural fenfe, is exactly what the friends of reform in England would adopt. Every gloomy tint that is added to the horrors of the French Revolution by the tragic pencil of Mr. Burke, is a new argument in fupport of their claims, and thofe only are

the

the real enemies of the Nobility and the Priefthood, and other bodies of men that fuffer in fuch convulfions, who ftimulate them to unequal and defperate conflicts.

Such are the fentiments of thofe who can admire without fervilely copying recent changes, and can venerate the principles without fuperftitioufly defending the corrupt reliques of old Revolutions.

" Grand fwelling fentiments of liberty," fays Mr. Burke, " I am fure I do not defpife. " Old as I am, I ftill read the fine raptures of " Lucan and Corneille with pleafure." Long may that virtuous and venerable age enjoy fuch pleafures. But why fhould he be indignant that " the glowing fentiment and the " lofty fpeculation fhould have paffed from " the fchools and the clofet to the Senate," and no longer ferving " to point a moral or " adorn a tale," fhould be brought home to

the

the bufinefs and the bofoms of men. The
fublime genius whom Mr. Burke admires, and
who fung the obfequies of Roman freedom,
has one fentiment, which the friends of liberty
in England, if they are like him condemned
to look abroad for a free government, muft
adopt——

——Redituraque nunquam
LIBERTAS ultra Tigrim Rhenumque receffit
Et *toties* nobis JUGULO quæfita negatur!——

SECTION

SECTION VI.

Speculations on the probable Confequences of the French Revolution in Europe.

THERE is perhaps only *one* opinion about the French Revolution in which its friends and its enemies agree. They both conceive that its influence will not be confined to France; they both predict that it will produce important changes in the general ftate of Europe. This is the theme of the exultation of its admirers, this is the fource of the alarms of its detractors. It were indeed difficult to fuppofe that a Revolution fo unparalelled fhould take place in the moft renowned of the European nations, without fpreading its influence throughout the Chriftian Commonwealth ;

connected

connected as it is by the multiplied relations
of politics, by the common interest of commerce, by the wide intercourse of curiosity and
of literature, by similar arts, and by congenial
manners. The channels by which the prevailing
sentiments of France may enter into the other
nations of Europe, are so obvious and so numerous, that it were unnecessary and tedious,
to detail them, but I may remark, as among
the most conspicuous, a central situation, a
predominating language, an authority almost
legislative in the ceremonial of the private intercourse of life. These and many other causes
must facilitate the diffusion of French politics
among the neighbouring nations, but it will
be justly remarked, that their effect must in a
great measure depend on the *stability* of the
REVOLUTION. The suppression of an *honour-*
able result would strengthen all the governments of Europe; the view of a splendid *re-*
volution would be the signal of insurrection to

their

their fubjects. Any reafonings on the influence of the French Revolution may therefore
be fuppofed to be premature until its permanence be afcertained. Of that permanence
my conviction is firm, but I am fenfible that
in the field of political prediction, where ve-
teran fagacity* has fo often been deceived; it
becomes me to harbour with diftruft, and to
propofe with diffidence a conviction influenced
by partial enthufiafm, and perhaps produced
by the inexperienced ardor of youth. The
moment at which I write is peculiarly critical
(Auguft 25th, 1791.) The invafion of FRANCE
is now fpoken of as immediate by the exiles
and their partizans; and the confederacy of

---

* Witnefs the memorable example of HARRINGTON,
who publifhed a demonftration of the impoffibility of re-
eftablifhing monarchy in England *fix months* before the re-
floration of CHARLES II. Religious prophecies have ufually the ineftimable *convenience* of relating to a diftant fu-
turity.

despot,

defpots* is announced with new confidence; but notwithftanding thefe threats, I retain my doubts whether the jarring interefts of the European courts will permit this alliance to have much energy or cordiality; and whether the cautious prudence of defpots will fend their military flaves to a fchool of freedom in France; but if there be doubts about the likelihood of the enterprize being undertaken, there can be few about the probability of its event. Hiftory celebrates many conquefts of obfcure tribes, whofe valor was animated by enthufiafm, but fhe records no example where

---

* The malignant hoftility difplayed againft French freedom by a perfidious Prince, who occupies and difhonors the throne of GUSTAVUS VASA, cannot excite our wonder, though it may provoke our indignation. The *Poifoner* of French defpotifm could not rejoice in its deftruction, nor could a monarch, whofe boafted talents have hitherto been confined to perjury and ufurpation, fail to be wounded by the eftablifhment of freedom; for freedom demands genius, not intrigue; wifdom, not cunning.

foreign

foreign force has subjugated a powerful and gallant people, governed by the most imperious passion * that can sway the human breast. Whatever wonders fanaticism has performed, may be again effected by a passion as

* May I be permitted to state how the ancestors of a nation now stigmatized for servility, felt this powerful sentiment. The Scottish nobles, contending for their liberty under ROBERT BRUCE, thus spoke to the Pope, " *Non pugna-* " *mus propter divitias honores, aut dignitates sed propter* LI- " BERTATEM *tantummodo quam* nemo bonus *nisi simul cum* " *vita amittit!*" Nor was this sentiment confined to the *Magnates,* for the same letter declares the assent of the Commons: " TOTAQUE COMMUNITAS REGNI SCO- " TIÆ." Reflecting on the various fortunes of my country, I cannot exclude from my mind the comparison between its present reputation and our ancient character —"*terrarum et literarum extremos*"—nor can I forget the honorable reproach against the Scottish name in the character of BUCHANAN by THUANUS, who remarks of that illustrious scholar " *Libertate* GENTI INNATA *in regium fastigium* " *animos.*" This melancholy retrospect is however relieved by the hope that a gallant and enlightened people will not be slow in renewing the *æra* of such reproaches.

ardent,

ardent, though not so transitory, because it is
sanctioned by virtue and reason. To animate
patriotism, to silence tumult, to banish divi-
sion, would be the only effects of an invasion
in the present state of France. A people abandoned to its own inconstancy, have often
courted the yoke which they had thrown off;
but to oppose foreign hostility to the enthusiasm of a *nation*, can only have the effect
of adding to it ardor, and constancy, and
force. These and similar views must offer
themselves to the European cabinets, but
perhaps they perceive themselves to be placed
in so peculiar a situation, that exertion and inactivity are equally perilous. If they fail in
the attempt to crush the infant liberty of
France, the ineffectual effort *will recoil* on
their own Governments, and hasten their destruction. If they tamely suffer a school * of

freedom

* The most important materials for the philosophy of
history are collected from remarks on the adaptation of the

situations

freedom to be founded in the *centre* of Europe, they muſt force the hoſts of diſciples that are to iſſue from it for the ſubverſion of their deſpotiſm.

They cannot be blind to a ſpecies of danger which the hiſtory of Europe reveals to them in legible characters. They ſee, indeed, that the negociations, the wars, and the revolutions of vulgar policy, paſs away without leaving behind them any veſtige of their tran-

ſituations and ſentiments of diſtant periods, and it may be curious as well as inſtructive, to preſent to the Reader the topics by which the CALONNES of CHARLES I. were inſtructed, to awaken the jealouſy and ſolicit the aid of the European Courts. " A dangerous combination of his Ma-" jeſty's ſubjects have laid a deſign to diſſolve the Monarchy " and frame of Government—becoming a dangerous *prece-* " dent to all the MONARCHIES of Chriſtendom, if attended " with ſucceſs in their deſign."

King Charles I's Inſtructions to his Miniſter in Den-mark, in LUDLOW'S MEMOIRS, *vol. iii. p.* 257.

ſitory

ſitory and ignominious operation. But they muſt remark, that beſides this *monotonous vil-lainy*, there are caſes in which Europe, actuated by a *common* paſſion, has appeared as *one* nation. When a ſociety of nations are ſo cloſely united as to reſemble the union of the provinces of a State, the propagation of ſentiment is indeed inevitable, and the European annals already afford ſufficient evidence of its effect. The religious paſſion animated and guided the ſpirit of chivalry—Hence aroſe the *Cruſades*. " A nerve was touched of exquiſite " feeling, and the ſenſation vibrated to the " heart of Europe*." In the ſame manner the Reformation gave riſe to religious wars, the duration of which exceeded a century and a half. Both examples prove the exiſtence of that *ſympathy*, by the means of which a great paſſion, taking its riſe in any conſiderable State of Europe, muſt circulate through the whole

* Gibbon.

Chriſtian Commonwealth. Illuſion is, however, tranſient, and truth is immortal. The epidemical fanaticiſm of former times was ſhort-lived, for it could only flouriſh in the eclipſe of reaſon. But the virtuous enthuſiaſm of liberty, though it be like that fanaticiſm contagious, it is not like it tranſitory.

But beſides the facility with which we have ſeen a common paſſion to be diffuſed in Europe, there are other circumſtances which entitle us to expect, that the example of France will have a mighty influence on the ſubjects of deſpotic Governments. *The Gothic Governments of Europe have lived their time.* Man, and for ever! is the ſage exclamation of Mr. HUME. Limits are no leſs rigorouſly preſcribed by Nature to the age of Governments than to that of individuals. Whether it be owing to our fickleneſs or our wiſdom, to the inflexibility or the imperfection of our inſtitutions, or to the combined operation of theſe

various

various caufes, certain it is, that the wide furvey of hiftory difcovers with as much clear-nefs, the growth, the decay, and the diffo-lution of Governments, as the narrow view of perfonal experience can remark the pro-grefs and the death of individual man. The heroic Governments of Greece yielded to a body of legiflative republics. They were in their turn fwallowed up by the conquefts of Rome. That great empire itfelf, under the fame forms, paffed through various modes of Government. The firft ufurpers concealed it under a republican difguife ; their fucceffors threw off the mafk, and avowed a military defpotifm. The empire expired in the often-tatious feeblenefs of an Afiatic monarchy *.

* See this progrefs ftated by the concife philofophy of Montefquieu, and illuftrated by the copious eloquence of Gibbon. The republican and ... defcents from *Auguftus* to *Severus*. The military defpotifm from *Severus* to *Dio-*... The *Afiatic Sovereignty* from *Diocletian* to the final extinction of the Roman name.

It

It was overthrown by favages, whofe rude inftitutions and barbarous manners have, until
our days, influenced Europe with a permanence refufed to wifer and milder laws. But,
unlefs hiftorical analogy be altogether delufive,
the *deceafe* of the *Gothic* Governments cannot
be diftant. Their maturity is long paft, and
fymptoms of their decrepitude are rapidly accumulating. Whether they are to be fucceeded by more beneficial or more injurious
Governments may be doubted, but that they
are about to perifh, we are authorized to fuppofe, from the ufual age to which the Governments recorded in hiftory have arrived.

There are alfo other prefumptions furnifhed
by hiftorical analogy, which favour the fuppofition that *legiflative Governments* are about
to fucceed the rude ufurpations of Gothic
Europe. The commonwealths which in the
fixth and feventh centuries before the Chriftian æra were erected on the ruins of the *be-*

roic monarchies of Greece, are perhaps the only genuine example of Governments truly *legiſlative* recorded in hiſtory. A cloſe inſpection will, perhaps, diſcover ſome coincidence between the circumſtance which formed theſe Governments and thoſe which now influence the ſtate of Europe. The Phenician and Egyptian colonies were not like our colonies in America, numerous enough to ſubdue or extirpate the native ſavages of Greece. They were, however, ſufficiently numerous to inſtruct and civilize them. From that alone could their power be derived. To that therefore were their efforts directed. Imparting the arts and the knowledge of poliſhed nations to rude tribes, they attracted, by avowed ſuperiority of knowledge, a ſubmiſſion neceſſary to the effect of their legiſlation ; a ſubmiſſion which impoſtors acquire from ſuperſtition, and conquerors derive from force. An age of legiſlation ſuppoſes a great inequality of knowledge between the legiſlators and thoſe who

A a

receive

receive their inftitutions. The Afiatic Colonifts, who firft fcattered the feeds of refinement, poffeffed this fuperiority over the *Pelafgic hordes*, and the legiflators who in fubfequent periods organized the Grecian commonwealths, acquired from their travels in
the polifhed States of the Eaft, that reputation
of fuperior knowledge, which enabled them
to dictate laws to their fellow-citizens. Let
us then compare Egypt and Phenicia with
the enlightened part of Europe, feparated as
widely from the general mafs by the *moral*
difference of inftruction, as thefe countries are
from Greece by the *phyfical* obftacles which
impeded a rude navigation. We muft difcern,
that when philofophers become legiflators,
they are colonifts from an enlightened country reforming the inflitutions of rude tribes.
The prefent moment indeed refembles with
wonderful exactnefs the legiflative age of
Greece. The multitude have attained fufficient knowledge to value the fuperiority of

enlightened

enlightened men, and they retain a fufficient confcioufnefs of ignorance to preclude rebellion againft their dictates. This is the precife ftate in which the human mind is equally by difcernment and deference prepared for legiflation. This is the prefent condition of Europe. Philofophers have long remained a diftinct nation in the midft of an unenlightened multitude. It is only now that the conquefts of the prefs are enlarging the dominion of reafon, as the veffels of *Cadmus* and *Cecrops* fpread the arts and the wifdom of the Eaft among the Pelafgic barbarians*.

* The fubject of this argument merits a more ample illuftration. Profound and ingenious philofophers have even queftioned the exiftence of Grecian Legiflation. No competent judge will refufe thefe *epithets* to PROFESSOR MILLAR. But this important fubject, and more efpecially the fimilarity between the legiflative age of Greece and the prefent condition of Europe, I referve for a more undifturbed leifure ; for a reflection and refearch which may enable me to reafon with more force, and entitle me to decide with more confidence.

A a 2

Thefe

Thefe general caufes, the *unity* of the European Commonwealth, the *decrepitude* on which its *fortuitous* governments are verging, and the fimilarity between our age and the only recorded period when the afcendant of philofophy dictated laws, entitle us to hope that freedom and reafon will be rapidly propagated from their fource in France. But there are not wanting fymptoms of their probable progrefs, which juftify the fpeculation. The firft fymptoms which indicate the approach of a contagious difeafe are the precautions adopted againft it. The firft marks of the probable progrefs of French principles are the alarms betrayed by defpots. The *Courts* of Europe feem to look on France, and to exclaim in their defpair—

Hinc Populum late Regem belloque fuperbum
Venturum excidio Libyæ——

The Courts of Europe have in various modes paid the homage of their fears to the

French

French Revolution. The King of Spain already seems to tremble for his throne, though it be erected on so firm a basis of general ignorance and triumphant priestcraft. By the expulsion of foreigners, and by subjecting the entrance of travellers to such multiplied restraints, he seeks the preservation of his despotism in a vain attempt to convert his kingdom into a *Bastile*, and to banish his subjects from the European Commonwealth. The Chinese Government has indeed thus maintained its permanency, but it is insulated by *nature* more effectually than by *policy*. Let the Court of Madrid recall her Ambassadors, shut up her ports, abandon her commerce, sever every tie that unites her to Europe; the effect of such shallow policy must be that of all ineffectual rigors (and all rigors short of extirpation are here ineffectual) to awaken reflection, to stimulate enquiry, to aggravate discontent, and to provoke convulsion.——*There are no longer Pyrenees*, said Louis XIV.

on

on the acceffion of his grandfon to the Spa-
nifh throne.   *There are no longer Pyrenees,*
exclaim the alarmed ftatefmen of *Aranjuez,*
to protect our defpotifm from being confumed
by the Sun of Liberty.

The alarms of the Pope for the little remnant of his authority naturally increafe with
the probability of the diffufion of French principles.   Even the mild and temperate Ariftocracies of Switzerland feem to apprehend the
arrival of that period, when men will not be
content to owe the benefits of Government to
the fortuitous character of their Governors,
but to the intrinfic excellence of its conftitution. Even the unfuccefsful ftruggle of *Liege,*
and the *Theocratic* infurrection of *Brabant,*
have left behind them traces of a patriotic
party, whom a more favorable moment may
call into more fuccefsful action.   The defpotic
Court of the Hague are betraying alarms that
the Dutch Republic may yet revive, The

Stadt-

Stadtholderian Government, fupported only by the terror of foreign arms, naturally dreads the deftruction of a Government odious and intolerable to an immenfe majority of the people.

Every where then are thofe alarms difcernible, which are the moft evident fymptoms of the approaching downfall of the European defpotifms. But the impreffion produced by the French Revolution in England, in an enlightened country, which had long boafted of its freedom, merits more particular remark. Before the publication of Mr. Burke, the public were not recovered from that aftonifhment into which they are plunged by unexampled events, and the general opinion could not have been collected with precifion. But that performance divided the nation into marked parties. It produced a controverfy, which may be regarded as the trial of the French Revolution before the enlightened and

A a 4

independent

independent tribunal of the Englifh public.—
What its decifion * has been, I fhall not prefume to decide ; for it does not become an
advocate to announce the decifion of the
Judge. But this I may be permitted to remark, that the conduct of our enemies has
not refembled the ufual triumph of thofe who
have been victorious in the war of reafon.
Inftead of the triumphant calmnefs that is

* Thofe who doubt the fervice done by Mr. Burke to
his caufe may be pleafed with this paffage of Milton.—
" Magnam a regibus iniiffe te gratiam omnes principes et
terrarum Dominos demeruiffe Defenfione hâc regiâ te fortè
putes Salmafi ; cum illi fi bona fua remque fuam ex veri-
tate potius quam ex adulationibus tuifvellent æftimare neminem te pejus, odiffe, neminem a fe longius abigere, atque
arcere debeant. Dum enim regiam poteftatem in immen-
fum extollas admones eâdem operâ omnes fere populos fer-
vitutis fuæ nec opinatæ ; eoque vehementius impellis ut
veternum illum *quo fe effe liberos inaniter fomniabant* repentè
excutiant."

Milton, *Def. Pop. Anglic. apud opera, tom. ii. p.* 266.
Ed. Lond. 1738.

ever

ever infpired by confcious fuperiority, they
have betrayed the bitternefs of defeat, and the
ferocity of refentment, which is peculiar to
the black revenge of detected impofture.
Prieftcraft and Toryifm were fupported only
by literary advocates of the moft miferable defcription*. But they were abundantly fupported by auxiliaries of another kind.   Of the
two great claffes of enemies to political reform—the INTERESTED and the PREJUDICED
—the activity of the firft ufually fupplies
what may be wanting in the talents of the
laft†.   Judges forgot the dignity of their

---

* *A* DOCTOR COOPER, or *a* DOCTOR TATHAM, cannot be fo infatuated as to dream, that even their academical
titles can procure them the perufal, not to mention the refutation of men of fenfe. The infolence of the latter pedant
had, indeed, nearly obtained him the honor of a caftigation,
which would have made him for ever fick of political controverfy !

† Both are admirably delineated by HELVETIUS.

" Entre ceux-ci il en eft qui, naturellement portés au
" vrai, ne font ennemis des verités nouvelles, que parce
" qu'ils

function, Priefts the mildnefs of their religion; the Bench, which fhould have fpoken
with the ferene temper of juftice; the Pulpit,
whence only fhould have iffued the healing
founds of charity, were proftituted to party
purpofes, and polluted with invective againft
freedom. The churches refounded with language at which *Laud* would have fhuddered,
and *Sacheverell* would have blufhed; the moft

"qu'ils font pareffeux, et qu'ils voudroient fe fouftraire a
" la fatigue d'attention neceffaire pour les examiner.

" Il en eft d'autres qu'animent des motifs dangereux &
" ceux-ci font plus a craindre: ce font des hommes dont
" l'efprit eft depourvu de talents & l'ame de vertus: incapa-
" bles de vues elévées et neuves, ces derniers croient que leur
" confideration tient au refpect imbecille ou feint qu'ils
" affichent pour toutes les opinions & les erreurs recues:
" furieux contre tout homme qui veut en ebranler l'Empire,
" ils ARMENT *contre lui les paffions & les prejugés* mémes
" qu'ils MEPRISENT & ne ceffent d'effaroucher les foibles
" efprits par le mot de *nouveauté!*"

The laft paffage muft be explained by fome WARWICK-
SHIRE COMMENTATOR!

profane

profane comparifons between the duty to the Divinity and to Kings, were unblufhingly pronounced ; flattery to Minifters was mixed with the folemnities of religion, by the fervants, and in the temple of God. Thefe profligate proceedings were not limited to a fingle fpot. They were general over England. In many churches the French Revolution was *exprefly named!* In a majority it was the conftant theme of invective for many weeks before its intended celebration. Yet thefe are the peaceful paftors, who fo fincerely and meekly deprecate political fermons* !

* Thefe are no vague accufations. A fermon was preached in a parifh church in *Middlefex* on the anniverfary of the reftoration of CHARLES II. in which ETERNAL PUNISHMENT *was denounced* againft POLITICAL DISAFFECTION ! Perfons for whofe difcernment and veracity I can be refponfible. were among the indignant auditors of this infernal homily.

Nor

Nor was this fufficient. The groffnefs of the popular mind, on which political invective made but a faint impreffion, was to be roufed into action by religious fanaticifm, the moft intractable and domineering of all deftructive paffions. A clamor which had for half a century lain dormant was revived. *The* Church *was in danger!* The fpirit of perfecution againft an unpopular fect was artfully excited, and the friends of freedom, whom it might be odious and dangerous profeffedly to attack, were to be overwhelmed as Diffenters. That the majority of the advocates for the French Revolution were not fo, was, indeed, fufficiently known to their enemies. They were well known to be philofophers and friends of humanity, who were fuperior to the creed of any fect, and indifferent to the *dogmas* of any popular faith. But it fuited the purpofe of their profligate adverfaries to confound them with Diffenters, and to animate againft them

the

the fury of prejudices which they themfelves defpifed.

The diffufion of thefe invectives produced thofe obvious and inevitable effects, which it may require fomething more than candor to fuppofe not forefeen and defired. A *banditti*, who had been previoufly ftimulated, as they have fince been excufed and panegyrized by incendiary libellifts, wreaked their vengeance on a PHILOSOPHER, illuftrious by his talents and his writings, venerable for the fpotlefs purity of his life, and amiable for the unoffending fimplicity of his manners. The exceffes of this mob of *churchmen and loyalifts* are to be poorly expiated by the few mifguided victims who are facrificed to the vengeance of the law.

We are, however, only concerned in thefe facts, as they are *evidence* from our enemies of

the

the probable progreſs of freedom. The probability of that progreſs they all conſpire to
prove. The briefs of the Pope, and the
pamphlets of Mr. BURKE*, the edicts of the

* The only thing that I recollect to have the air of argument in the *two laſt* pamphlets of Mr. Burke is, the reaſoning againſt the right of a majority to change a Government. Whatever be the plauſibility or dexterity of this
reaſoning, its *originality* will be beſt eſtimated by the following paſſage of a PROFANE PHILOSOPHER!

" The controverſies that ariſe concerning the RIGHTS
" of the PEOPLE proceed from the equivocation of the
" word. The word PEOPLE has *two* ſignifications. In one
" ſenſe it ſignifieth a number of men diſtinguiſhed only by
" the place of their habituation, as the people of England,
" or the people of France, which is no more than the mul-
" titude of thoſe particular perſons inhabiting theſe regions,
" without conſideration of any covenants or contracts be-
" tween them. In another ſenſe it ſignifieth a perſon civil,
" either one man or one council, in the will whereof is
" included and involved the will of every individual. Such
" as do not diſtinguiſh between theſe two ſenſes do uſually
" attribute ſuch rights to a *diſſolved* MULTITUDE as belong
" only to the PEOPLE virtually contained in the body of the
" Commonwealth or Sovereignty."
See HOBBES' *Tripos*, p. 170, et ſeq. edit. 12mo. Lond. 1684.

Spanish Court, and the mandates of the Spanish inquisition, the Birmingham rioters, and the Oxford graduates, equally render to Liberty the involuntary homage of their alarm.

F I N I S.